Bogus Bills

Return to Cyprus

Cyberworld Publishing

www.cyberworldpublishing.com

This book is copyright © Gina Drew 2011
First published by Cyberworld Publishing in 2011.
Cover design by S Bush © 2011
Cover Photo - The Treasury at Petra © Marta Mirecka | Dreamstime.com
All rights reserved.
E Book ISBN 978-1-921879-40-1
Print ISBN 978-1-921879-41-8

All characters in this book are the product of the author's imagination and no resemblance to real people, or implication of events occurring in actual places, is intended.

Published by
Cyberworld Publishing
Jindalee St
Toronto, NSW
Australia, 2283

Koniotis Mysteries Series

Each book in this series stands alone, but they are also all connected in various ways and form the different parts of one story.

Laughter's Echo

Salted Away

Mouflon Brigade

Amathus Armageddon

Bogus Bills

Homewrecker

Bogus Bills

Return to Cyprus

Koniotis Mysteries Book Five

Gina Drew

Caitlyn's map of sites in Cyprus

Karpas Pen.
Rizokarpaso
Kantara Cast.
Kyrenia
Ardhana
Bellapais
Boğaz
Pendaktylos
Buffavento Pass
yeli Cast.
A R I A
Salamis
Engom
NICOSIA
lonittisa
FAMAGUSTA
Varosha
Dherina
Dhekelia
Paralimni
Protaras
Ayia
Napa
Lefkara
LARNACA
irokitia
Zygi

Primary Characters

Bill Burch—Head of the American Archaeological Institute in Cyprus

Stuart Claymore—Head of the UNICIS computer lab division

Roulla Dahir—Mysterious Omodhos resident

Lala Hatan—Turkish Cypriot vice president of the Federated State of Cyprus (FSC)

Gladys "Billie" Holiday—Archeology worker

Ingrid Bittmann Isaksen—Former UN undersecretary general; now head of the international management and environmental consultancy and research and development firm, RayGo

Chrystalla Ioannou—Greek Cypriot president of the Federated State of Cyprus (FSC)

Wilhelm Jacobs—Secret Service officer assigned to the U.S. embassy in Cyprus

Ahmad Jallud—Cypriot chief of police

Ujay Khahalbi—Iranian general

Caitlyn Spencer Koniotis—American archaeologist in Cyprus and professor at Colombia University; wife of Takis Koniotis

Takis Koniotis—UN undersecretary general for security affairs

Ellen Larkin—Director of the UN International Crime Investigations Service (UNICIS)

Uri Lukenov—Manager of the Cassa Carioca club in Famagusta

Demetris Mattas—Publisher of the Cypriot newspaper *Semerini*; husband of Cypriot interior minister Maria Solonos Mattas

Ginger Nives-Smyth Baldwin Remington Hamilton Patterson—Perpetual Widow

Andre Piccard—General Manager, Piccard holdings, Cyprus division

Maria Solonos Mattas—Cypriot interior minister

Sergey Stepanov—Russian mafia figure in Cyprus

William Stevens—Officer at the Australian high commission to Cyprus

Christiana Tzavella—RayGo records system official

Dr. Andriko Visiliou—Chief of the Cypriot Archaeology Department

Prologue

Flight MEA 262 from Larnaca landed in Beirut several hours late that Saturday after nearly no time in the air, and very few of the disgruntled passengers on the aircraft realized how lucky they were to have survived the flight at all.

The airplane had been buffeted by the air waves from the explosion of the fuel truck on the Larnaca tarmac and all had heard the explosion. But the pilot of the MEA 262, with the cockpit crew being the only ones on board who could see the flames below, had quickly assured his passengers over the sound system that everything was fine—that they had just hit an air pocket at the same time one of the fighter planes from the airstrip at the nearby British sovereign base at Akotiri had broken the sound barrier. If he had suspicions about why the fuel vehicle had burst into flames, he was keeping these suspicions to himself. As it was, he held his breath for nearly the entire thirty-minute, sixty nautical-mile trip from Cyprus to Lebanon. Not in his wildest dreams would he have guessed that this mishap had been the result of a failed rocket attack to prevent his own plane, carrying Russian agents on a mission, from landing in Beirut.

The five Russian agents from Cyprus merged again outside the Beirut terminal immediately after having cleared customs and were met and swept away in two automobiles to the Russian embassy. After a short, but intense briefing at the embassy, the five and a guide descended via three separate routes on the copper and souvenir shop near the Beirut corniche that was supposedly owned by Anwar Jabril.

The street was deathly quiet. No one was about and the coffee shop across from the souvenir shop was closed, its tables turned with tops toward the establishment's windows in an apparent effort to keep the table tops dry in anticipation of a late-evening rain. The street was entirely too quiet. But this section of the city was not frequented by the guide from Moscow's embassy in Beirut and the men from Cyprus had never been to Beirut before—so their suspicions were not aroused.

A small alleyway, hardly large enough for a grown man to pass through, ran down the eastern side of Jabril's shop. Four of the Russians disappeared down this alleyway, being careful that they could not be seen from the shop's interior, and they fanned out in two different approaches to the back of the shop. The two Russians who had approached the shop from the west stopped just short of the front of the souvenir shop and hugged the wall, almost within reach of the shop's glass front door. Two of the men who had entered the alley continued down the side of the building, turned to the left, and crouched beside the shop's rear door. The other two Russians deftly climbed up the side of the building and swung around to the balcony that ran across the front of the shop on the floor above.

At a prearranged signal from the mission leader on his handheld radio, the Russians stormed the building from three different directions. Those who crashed through the front jumped in opposite directions and hit the deck as they entered. If the noise from the breaking glass of the panels slid across the front of the shop at night had not been enough to surprise and alert the Hizballah terrorists in the back of the building, the sound of two bodies skidding through copperware, on one side, and pottery, on the other, would have done the trick. The entry of the rear-guard team, splintering through the flimsy wooden back door, and the crash through the glass window above into a storeroom filled with porcelain dishes only added to the noise, a noise that was designed to immobilize the terrorists for the brief moment it would require to obtain the upper hand in the attack.

But the Hizballah terrorists weren't immobilized, and the Hizballah terrorists didn't seem particularly surprised. There was no evidence anyone was there at all. But there, there in the light of a flickering candle, back through two doorways and near the back of the building, the mission leader, who had been one of the pair who had come through the front door, could see something or someone. He lifted his assault rifle and started to squeeze the trigger. But in his night-vision targeting scope he obtained enough of a sense of familiarity with the target to stay his hand. He checked his firing but did not lower his rifle.

The figure was moving ever so slightly in the bonds that kept it pinned tightly to a chair. The mission leader circled cautiously around the room, motioning both the man on his right and his other comrades who were appearing from other areas of the building to remain where they were.

Yes, as he moved a bit closer, he became sure they had, indeed, found Irina Lukenov. The figure had a blanket thrown over its head, but the clothes he could see on the figure matched the description the searchers had been given of what the Lukenov woman had been wearing when she first disappeared. He reached over and lifted up the edge of the blanket, but just as he was at the point of a positive identification, he tripped the wire and the explosives under the woman's chair carried her, the Russians, and millions of bits and pieces of the best souvenirs Lebanon had to offer up into the sky over Beirut.

— From *Mouflon Brigade*

Chapter One

The presses were whirring almost too loudly for General Ujay Khahalbi to be heard by the sour-faced dignitaries from Syria and Lebanon's Al-Baqa' Valley. Outside of the Iranian Central Bank's thick walls, the early-evening traffic on Tehran's Shohada Street added yet another layer of deafening noise. It had been a long day of negotiations, and each of the representatives had grown irritable. The noise was only adding to the heavy tension in the air. The Hizballah representative's right eye began to twitch in time with the thumping of the press.

With a sigh and sensing his guests were at the breaking point, Khahalbi started to lean over toward the computer board to stop the presses, a costly move that would put his crew behind the production curve for the evening and that would ruin a length of precious paper. It couldn't be helped, though. Two of the delegates—in some respects the two most important ones—would have to leave within the next two hours to make their carefully constructed connections to Beirut and then on to the Mediterranean island of Cyprus, and it would be better to sacrifice some of the paper than to lose the interest and goodwill of these two. The paper was even more worthless if the distribution system broke down.

But just as Khahalbi's fingers were lowered to the computer's keyboard to type in a command, his movement was arrested when, with his peripheral vision, he caught sight of one of the visitors scooping up paper from the bin next to one of the presses and, with a sweeping gesture, showering his companion—the most important dignitary in the room—with hundred-dollar bills in U.S. currency. Khahalbi's expression froze and quickly turned to ice as he sensed both the Syrian and the Hizballah operatives reach for their holsters.

For the briefest second the dignitary stood in shocked silence, and then the sound of hoarse, but lusty laughter wafted over the noise from both the presses and the traffic outside, the bin of another press was invaded, and the visitor's amused expression was obliterated by a ream of floating euro banknotes.

In that instant, all tension drained from the room, and a highly relieved Khahalbi ushered a tittering group toward the private lounge and its generous bar, while the press workers raced along behind them, gathering up the drifting banknotes.

* * * *

The exhilaration of homecoming swept over Dr. Caitlyn Spencer Koniotis as the luxurious hydrofoil sea transporter *Daphne* jetted into Larnaca Harbor and negotiated a neat turn, its hydrofoils folded, and it settled on the water to glide past the town's seafront to the cruise line sea terminal to the west of the old city. Caitlyn involuntarily held her breath as her eyes searched the southern coast of the Mediterranean island of Cyprus for points of connection with her Cypriot past.

Not that she was a Cypriot. She was an American archaeologist, who had first arrived in Cyprus nearly two decades earlier on a Fulbright short-term grant, who had met her Adonis here, and who had adopted the island as her own for several years. She had never given up her U.S. citizenship nor her American persona, but she didn't denigrate the importance and pull of her Cypriot life either. Cyprus had given her her highly respected and lucrative career, her beloved husband, and her twin sons, who now both were very successfully pursuing very different preprofessional degree interests at very different, but excellent, preparatory schools back in the United States.

And, also very important, Cyprus had given her itself. It was a fascinating island, steeped in archaeological treasures, history, international politics, and natural beauty. It now also seemed to be regaining a centrality in world economic and political affairs that it had not fully enjoyed since Roman times. As the *Daphne* slowly paraded past the Larnaca seafront, with its wide promenade, traditional-style, ochre-colored and green-shuttered hotel facades, swaying palm trees, and sailboat and luxury craft marina, Caitlyn enjoyed her first sense of homecoming. She had not been back to Cyprus in years—this despite it being the land of her husband's people. She had, however, remained actively engaged in the archaeological exploration and unveiling of the island, even more so in the few short years since the island's still-uneasy political settlement. What most made her think of this as home, however was that the residence she loved above all of the others she had known, the one that had always represented home to her, was here—as well as the memories.

She had always had a vivid imagination, and she had some form of second sight that sent her visioning back into the past in some sort of dream state. And these dream states had intensified and focused when she had been living in Cyprus. They had helped her find a few archeological sites but they also had provided insights into a personal connection she had with the past here—something that found a bit of explanation when her mother told her that her family indeed had Cypriot connections.

Caitlyn was heartened to see that the town center of Larnaca—one of the longest-inhabited cities on earth and reputed to have been founded by Noah's grandson—appeared on the surface to be much as she remembered it to have been. In fact, it seemed much cleaner and more quaint then she remembered it. But was it now too quaint, too plastic, too homogenized as a "representative" Cypriot seaside town? As she looked closer, Caitlyn could see that there had even been attempts to develop the illusion of a traditional Greek harbor village, even though the hills didn't come down to the sea at Larnaca as they did in the most memorable Greek island harbor settings.

But Larnaca never had been a typical Greek harbor town. In her period of Cyprus residency, it had exuded more of the feel of a western European Mediterranean seaside town, complete with corniche promenade. In that, it reminded her of Nice in France. Whereas in remembered days, the Larnaca seafront reflected a happy hodgepodge of architectural styles and generations, Caitlyn could now see, upon closer inspection, that the traditional British colonial style of façade—ochre paint, stone facings, green shutters, and red tile roofs now predominated the promenade. Also, enveloping earthen and rock arms had been built beside the marina at the eastern end of the waterfront—where the commercial port had once been— and at the Turkish fort at the western end to provide the illusion of a natural harbor.

And, was it her imagination, or was the stony beach that separated the sea from the promenade narrower now than in times remembered? Or was it just that the open-air café tables were descending closer to the water's edge?

And then, looking up from the seafront toward the bluish-cast Troodos foothills in the interior's distance, Caitlyn received the real shock of the change in Larnaca. Starting just behind the waterfront's village façade rose graduated banks of medium- and high-rise buildings. Caitlyn had not noticed them at first, because they uniformly faced the sea with mirrored glass fronts, but now that she could see them, she immediately realized that the lazy little town of Larnaca, with its crazy-quilt streets and eclectic architecture that had naturally developed from a millennium of varied fortunes, was lost to her forever. Larnaca had turned into a bustling metropolis, with only its seafront—and even that had been over-prettified—providing a hint of the town she had once known, notable in her days of residency primarily because it had then provided the gateway from the air to the island. That too had changed. The island's international airport no longer was here.

Caitlyn sighed wistfully and started to form thoughts of regret for the "real" Larnaca. But her sigh changed to an ironic audible chuckle.

"Who can say what the 'real' Larnaca is like?" Caitlyn chided herself. "After some ten centuries of constant change and adjustment to reality and the fortunes that have come their way, who can begrudge the Larnacans their current definition of themselves and their choices for facing life?"

As she chuckled, Caitlyn became aware that she was being watched. She involuntarily touched her hand to her cheek and looked at her fingers, discovering a dark smudge. She now saw that the handrail in front of her was lightly smeared with grease. Self-consciously she reached into her purse and pulled out a compact, which snapped open at a touch, and brought its mirror up to her face. Sure enough, her cheek was slightly smudged, although probably as a result of putting her hand to her face after grasping the greasy handrail rather than because of an earlier happenstance. Caitlyn dabbed at the stain on her cheek.

She still, half way into her fourth decade, used only a minimum of makeup, and she still was a stunningly beautiful woman. A natural honey-blonde, miraculously—and naturally—without a trace of gray, Caitlyn had been blessed with the classic, high-cheek-boned facial structure that typified the most successful runway models, coupled with the ability to lightly tan without wrinkling, and a figure and carriage that was trim and graceful rather than skeletal and that moved with an authority that belied any sense of weakness or insipid delicacy.

The easy, assured control of her movements resulted from nearly twenty years of work at the top of the very demanding, highly competitive archaeological profession. The ability to tan with minimum damage from the sun's rays, which became more lethal with each passing year of attack on the earth's ozone layer, was probably the greatest gift Mother Nature had given a woman who spent much of her time digging into hot, dusty hillsides in search of history's secrets.

But if this had been the gods' greatest natural gift to Caitlyn, the second greatest must have been either her keen sense of humor or her ability to make her friends and colleagues comfortable in her presence, both attributes that served to curb the natural envy that professional rivals and casual acquaintances would normally project toward one of Caitlyn's beauty and professional standing. More than one closely argued disagreement at a world-class archaeologists' seminar or major dig had been neutralized by the mischievous twinkle in her brown eyes and the easy, lilting laughter on her lips.

None of this seemed to go to Caitlyn's head, which only added to the power of her personality. Not giving herself a second look after she's wiped away the blemish on her cheek, Caitlyn touched a button on her compact and the lid snapped shut. The feeling that she was being watched, however, persisted, and, as she returned the compact to her purse, Caitlyn turned a cautious gaze along the deck toward the prow of the ship where white foam was rising like one of the skyscrapers in the background of the town. The hydrofoil was now cutting smartly through the blue Mediterranean as it cleared the steel pier that supported Larnaca's huge water desalinization and tidal electricity generation unit and pointed its nose at the passenger ship terminal that had replaced what had been Cyprus' seaside international airport before the island's recent political settlement.

Although she was trying to be natural and unobtrusive in her survey of the other passengers lining the rail, a habit that resulted from many years as the wife of a well-known international criminologist who had often suffered surveillance and sometimes worse from the world's criminal underclass, Caitlyn was nearly nonplussed by what she saw. There, not more than three people farther down the rail and giving her a frank and open visual assessment, was a face from her past.

Or, at least she thought it was someone she had known in the past—and here in Cyprus. She quickly averted her eyes, but she was unable to keep herself from taking another guarded glance. He was still looking at her, a half smile—or a very frank and open appraisal—on a face that was handsome in a northeastern European out-door sportsman fashion but that reflected some long-suffered tragedy or chronic disease.

Their eyes met briefly—and it was there, in his eyes, that she had obtained the sense of a veil of perpetual pain. He retreated from her penetrating, assessing gaze, and Caitlyn expanded her attention to take in the entire figure. No, this could not be someone she had known in Cyprus a decade and a half earlier. He appeared to be barely in his thirties—well-proportioned and ruggedly handsome, but big boned and broad featured in that Slavic way that could too easily turn to a beer belly and coarse visage in later years. He couldn't have been anyone she had known before as an adult, Caitlyn reasoned to herself. And yet, there was still a familiarity about him, and she was convinced that he had registered the same reaction when he had first seen her.

A ship's whistle blew just as Caitlyn's elbow was jostled and she turned to her right to respond to her traveling companion and old friend, Dr. Andriko Visiliou, the chief of the Cypriot Archaeology Department. Dr. Visiliou was waving enthusiastically at the sea terminal that was looming grandly ahead of the *Daphne*. On the other side of her colleague stood an amused Demetris Mattas, the publisher of the Cypriot newspaper *Semerini* and also an old friend of Caitlyn's, who had accompanied Caitlyn and Andriko on their lecture tour to cover for his newspaper their trip around the famous archaeological sites of the Mediterranean.

Bill Burch, the head of the American Archaeological Institute in Cyprus, filled out the lecture tour foursome, but he had not yet appeared on deck.

Visiliou had accidentally jogged her arm, but, aside from wanting to share a moment of joyful homecoming from three weeks of archaeological lectures in the region and wanting

Caitlyn to notice Mrs. Visiliou—and her accompanying entourage of children, children's spouses, and grandchildren who could now be seen on the terminal's observation deck—Visiliou was not making any special claims on Caitlyn's attention, but, rather, was proudly gesturing to his large family and lecturing an amused Mattas on the glories of fatherhood.

Caitlyn turned her gaze back toward the prow of the ship, but the young man who had claimed her interest had vanished. She only had a split second to ascertain this, however, as her field of vision was invaded by the second and third shocks of her afternoon. Bellying up to the rail very close to Caitlyn was a tall, statuesque-to-the-point-of-intimidation woman Caitlyn had not seen since the Amazon had given up her quest for the UN secretary general position nearly a decade previously. She had left her lower UN post and had moved to the eastern Mediterranean to head up a successful international management and environmental consultancy and research and development firm. This firm had, since that time, skyrocketed both itself and Cyprus to the forefront of international corporations on the strength of what was known as the RayGo process, a formula for storing solar heat for conversion to power generation.

Caitlyn Koniotis and her husband, Takis, had first met Ingrid Bittmann Isaksen when the latter had been the United Nations coordinator for a politically divided Cyprus, the division of which had been monitored and supervised by a special UN peacekeeping force for nearly thirty-five years. Then Ingrid had moved on to the UN Secretariat in New York and Takis Koniotis had moved to the United Nations to form a central headquarters office of the UN International Criminal Investigations Service that he had earlier established in Cyprus. The Koniotises had occasionally come into contact with Bittmann. This, however, had been more a result of professional necessity and because they were personal friends of her now-deceased husband, Eric Isaksen, who had been a special UN negotiator and who had sponsored Takis's move to the UN, rather than because either had any warm feeling for Ingrid.

Caitlyn and Ingrid had been social friends when they both lived in Cyprus, but since then a tension had built between them constructed mostly on Ingrid's jealousies. She was jealous of Takis because he was received in the halls of the UN much more readily than she was, and she was jealous of Caitlyn because Caitlyn and Ingrid's husband, Eric, had enjoyed a special relationship that Ingrid felt put her at a disadvantage.

And here Ingrid was, on the same vessel that had carried Caitlyn around the Mediterranean, bigger than life—bigger and more commanding, in fact, than Caitlyn had ever seen her before—puffing her distinctive Lebanese cigarette in Caitlyn's face, her arm possessively entwined in that of a dark-haired, pale-complexioned, sensitive-looking man who must have been nearly a third of Ingrid's sixty plus years.

Ingrid was giving Caitlyn that wide-mouthed, half smile, half sneer expression of self-absorbed superiority that Caitlyn had grown to know so well during years of UN Headquarters cocktail parties. Having struck her pose, Ingrid grandly swept her cigarette out of her ruby-red lips and laughed her signature full-throated laugh that had the result of enveloping Caitlyn in a cloud of acrid tobacco smoke.

The effect of the unexpected, high-drama entrance was that Caitlyn stood, speechless before the former UN undersecretary for political affairs, which was, of course, the effect Isaksen was trying to achieve. However, it was not Ingrid who had caused the shock. Here, thought Caitlyn, who was fighting an involuntary tightening sensation in her throat, is yet another too-young face from the past. But Caitlyn was not looking into Ingrid's face. She was looking beyond her to the quiet young man enveloped within Ingrid's obviously highly possessive clutches. Here was a youthful version of a past memory, but in this case Caitlyn had no trouble naming the source. Without a doubt this must be a Piccard, a member of that both enduring and sinister French shipping empire family that had touched Caitlyn's life in Cyprus at several points—from Eleni Piccard, Caitlyn's first mentor and benefactor on the island, from whom Caitlyn had inherited her Cypriot home; to the French ambassador and arms and drugs smuggler, Jacques Piccard, who had both wooed and tried to murder Caitlyn; to

Eleni's supposedly long-lost husband, Guy, whose terrorist activities had directly challenged and threatened the Koniotis family.

Ingrid was rambling at Caitlyn, and the latter fought to pull herself up from the shock of brushing once more against the Piccard family. She shook her head and tried to focus back on Ingrid. There was no reason the sight of a Piccard should shock her so, she chided herself. After all, the Piccard family must be large, and she knew it was still a dominant economic force in the Mediterranean. She also was fully cognizant that she had chosen to travel on a Piccard line vessel for her Cyprus-sponsored lecture tour.

"Excuse, me, Ingrid," Caitlyn managed. "What were you saying to me? I'm just so surprised—and happy—to see you here on board the *Daphne*. I had no idea you were traveling with us. I hadn't seen you on deck before."

"I've only been aboard since last night," Ingrid was trumpeting for all on deck to hear. "We embarked at Beirut. I am *trying* to point out that you have dropped your purse and the contents are spreading toward the Cypriot shore." Ingrid managed a superior smile, obviously delighted to be pointing out Caitlyn's clumsiness to all of those at the ship rail.

"Oh!" Caitlyn exclaimed. And, sure enough, she could see that when Andriko had jostled her arm, she must have dropped her purse. Caitlyn, Andriko, Demetris, Ingrid, and the man-who-must-be-a-Piccard all dropped to their knees simultaneously and grabbed at scattering personal effects. Bill Burch had appeared on deck, and he and a few other passengers were aiding in the hunt as well. Ingrid was snorting and laughing like a boar in full flight. Caitlyn saw the Piccard look-alike-scuttling after her wallet, which had skidded from Ingrid's grasp and down the deck toward the prow.

And then, there he was, the man of the Slavic features Caitlyn had seen earlier, leaning down toward Caitlyn's wallet. The two young men reached the leather case at the same moment, and their hands touched. They looked at each other, and Caitlyn caught a glance of electricity and familiarity between the two that she could not fathom but that was to recur and gnaw at her mind for several days to come.

And then all were on their feet again, stuffing their found treasures into Caitlyn's purse and sharing the mirth of the moment—everyone, of course, except for the two young men. The first man, whom Caitlyn had sensed she had known before had once again vanished, and Isaksen's companion was turned toward the prow of the ship, as if he too was wistfully searching for an elusive familiar landmark.

The vessel touched the dock, and Ingrid, young prisoner in tow, was disappearing in a cloud of smoke, throwing behind her an open invitation to visit her in her seventeenth-floor penthouse high above Ayia Napa Beach near the southeast corner of the island. As Visiliou, Mattas, and Burch also hurried off to see to their luggage, Caitlyn turned and asked a deck steward to summon a porter to her stateroom to transport her luggage to the shore.

The Sudanese porter reached her cabin at the same time she did. Caitlyn couldn't quite adjust to the Sudanese and Ethiopian immigrants who had flooded into the Mediterranean region and who seemed to have gravitated to all of the bottom-level service occupations throughout the Middle East and Europe. In the process they had pushed out the Filipinos, Bangladeshis, and Sri Lankans who had been moving into these positions the last time Caitlyn lived in Cyprus and who had, in turn, pushed out a generation of Turks and Armenians. Many of these nationalities—and more—now roamed the world nationless and doomed to poverty and servitude, Caitlyn reflected with concern. They had been displaced from their traditional homelands in much the same as the East Europeans and Armenians of her own youth had been—by poverty and overcrowding at home.

When she reached her cabin, Caitlyn tossed the last of her unpacked dresses into the open suitcase. The porter patiently stood nearby, his eyes surveying the room for forgotten possessions.

Caitlyn found her own eyes wandering in concert with his, and the inspection turned her attention to the door of the cabin, where she saw the mystery, Slavic-featured man of earlier moments walking by. Caitlyn was drawn to the doorway, but he was nowhere to be seen by the time she got out onto the deck. The only person there now was Bill Burch, who gave her a friendly wave. When she returned to the room, she found the porter standing in the center of the cabin with her open purse in his hand. He looked at her guiltily and stammered that he had found the purse open on the floor beside the bed.

"Yes, of course," Caitlyn responded instantly. "I've had trouble hanging onto that bag and keeping it closed this afternoon."

And when she had taken the purse, she saw that the clasp was loose, which must be why it kept opening. She marched over to the suitcase and snapped it shut.

The sea terminal was in pandemonium when Caitlyn disembarked from the *Daphne*, not the least as a result of the gaggle of Visiliou family members who had shown up to welcome her colleague home. Demetris Mattas and Bill Burch trundled off with the expedition's baggage to arrange monorail tickets into Nicosia, while Caitlyn went to the money exchange to change some of her U.S. dollars into euro banknotes, now the standard currency throughout much of Europe. She then joined Andriko, who was trying to gather up his children and his children's children so that they could all monorail back to the capital together. This proved to be more of a challenge than the organization of his lecture tour had been.

Andriko's failure to see the two burly Turks bearing down on Caitlyn from different directions was wholly the result of the all-too-familiar wail of his youngest granddaughter, which he heard wafting from the direction of a vending machine several yards away. Similarly, Demetris Mattas and Bill Burch were too busy guessing just how many monorail tickets the group would need to notice that Caitlyn had been accosted and was being herded toward a deserted corner of the passenger terminal.

Nothing had escaped Ingrid Isaksen's piercing glance, however. She opened her broad mouth to roar her approval as she saw Caitlyn being hustled away, but her laugh turned into a rasping cough. She flipped her cigarette out of her mouth and obliterated it on the terminal's tiled floor—much as she would like to personally obliterate both Caitlyn and her husband.

As Caitlyn and captors turned a dimly lit corner, Ingrid summoned the Sudanese porter who was returning from having taken Caitlyn's luggage out onto the monorail platform, whispered something into his ear, and pressed some euro banknotes into his hand. Then she turned and guided her companion toward the terminal's marina, where her yacht awaited to deliver them to the Ayia Napa pier.

But Ingrid was not the only one to observe the unceremonious exit of the famous American archaeologist. Two other sets of eyes—one contemplative and the other flashing in satisfaction—had seen the entire scene unfold below them from separate positions at the *Daphne*'s main-deck rails.

Chapter Two

As always, everything was hazy and the events—always the same events—proceeded in painful slow motion. The most horrible aspect was that he always knew what would happen next; there was nothing he ever could do to keep it from happening again and again. The expressions on their faces were unforgettable. The surprise registered when the vessel he was in unexpectedly rounded the point and bore down on theirs. The immobilizing shock when he and his comrades lifted their machine guns and strafed the other vessel. The two ships were no more than a few yards apart. He could see the palpable fear change to distress and obliteration in the hail of gunfire. He was laughing hysterically. His magazine was empty, yet he still clicked away on the trigger. His father laid a hand on his arm, took the gun, and replaced it with another weapon. As he pumped the bullets out of this replacement weapon across the deck of the adjacent ship, the other vessel caught fire and the heat of the explosion knocked him on his back. There he remained, still firing into the air, as the sky turned blood red.

Uri Lukenov sat up, fully awake in his sweat-drenched bed. His hands were trembling. In fact, he was trembling all over. At first he didn't know where he was. All he knew was that he had been struck by the dream once more. But it had not just been a recurring nightmare, one that had plagued him for most of his life. It had happened. It had really happened, and nothing he did henceforth in life could erase that. He had not had the dream for months, but now that he was here, back in Cyprus, he knew that he would continue to suffer from the dream and from the guilt and revulsion that it produced.

He had known as soon as he had seen the American woman, Caitlyn Koniotis, on the ship earlier today that the nightmare would be back and that it would not release its hold on him as long as he stayed on the island. But he would have to tough it out. Two women who haunted his dreams—one saved and the other one not, or so he had thought. He had heard that she—the other one—had returned here—that other demon that would not let him rest. He must find her and find out why she had done what she had done. It seemed he had been searching for her for years—for longer, as a matter of fact, than he had been burdened with the nightmare stemming from that day. That day when his father, then the chief Russian spy at Moscow's embassy in Cyprus, had gathered his goons together and wiped out the band of Hizballah fighters that had come to Cyprus and kidnapped his mother.

Uri had insisted that he be included in the attack party that day. He had insisted on the basis of the right of a son to avenge the violent murder of his mother. And his father had permitted him to come along—indeed had welcomed the presence of his eleven-year-old son, judging that this would both give him some solace for the untimely loss of his mother and transform him into a man in the harsh real-world terms of his father's profession.

But it had all been wrong, so terribly wrong. There was nothing Uri could do about his part in the deaths of the Hizballah fighters. But maybe, if he found what he came here looking for and got some sort of understandable explanation, he could reorder his life and the debilitating nightmares would go away.

If only he could find what he was looking for here.

"But where is 'here'?" he spoke out into the darkness.

He rolled over and switched on the bedside lamp and looked around the room. Ah, yes. "Here" was his new fourth-floor apartment in the Ingrid Beach Tower near the Mediterranean shoreline between the Ayia Napa and Nissei Beach resort complexes. He opened the drawer in the night stand and pulled out and unwrapped a stick of nicotine gum. Only the hopelessly addicted, the very rich, or the very important could afford tobacco enough to fill his needs these days. Only people like that bitch Ingrid Bittmann Isaksen, who he had, with the help of that strange, compelling young man, maneuvered into hiring him, because of his Russian connections, to come to Cyprus to manage the Cassa Carioca nightclub. It was the same club that Uri had known was once located in the hills above the southern port city of Limassol and that had always reflected the underseam of excess in Cyprus. It had been acquired by the RayGo Corporation and had been reopened recently in the nearby regenerated metropolis of Famagusta—and still reflected the underseam of excess in Cyprus.

Isaksen had hired him in Beirut, where he had originally been searching for relief from his nightmares. He had arranged through that young acquaintance of his to "accidentally" meet Ingrid, and she had hired him on the spot, assuming that his Russian connections included those of the mafia variety. But she had made it clear to him, as he had been forewarned, that the services he would be expected to render could include those that were far more personal than using his intelligence and his family's underworld connections to increase the profits of the Cassa Carioca.

He had figured he could keep one step ahead of the old bag and could find what he was looking for and depart before the CEO of RayGo tired of the French youth. But, if not, that was no big deal. Life in the underside of the Russian Republic had required him to do a lot of things he had found distasteful.

And the search was far too important for personal revulsion against his new boss to get in the way.

Uri pulled himself out of bed, went out on the balcony, and felt his nerves relax. The nicotine gum took effect as he gazed out upon the quiet Mediterranean. He wasn't sleepy anymore and, if he had been willing to admit it to himself, he did not want to risk a second visitation by his nightmare tonight. The sea looked so peaceful and it beckoned irresistibly to him.

Sometime later, on the top floor of the same tower block, Andre Piccard, general manager of the Cyprus division of the Piccard shipping line, export houses, and resort hotel complexes, quietly extracted himself from underneath the bulky Ingrid and padded to the balcony at the seaward end of the large room. Ingrid, slack-mouthed but satisfied for now in her slumber, snorted and rolled onto her side.

"All this power for all these years," Andre thought bitterly to himself as he plastered himself to the balcony rail—as far from his sleeping partner as he could get, "and the Piccards still have to prostitute themselves to stay in business." RayGo didn't actually own the Piccard holdings—one of the few major holdings in Cyprus to have, at least thus far, escaped the wildly successful conglomerate's grasp. But it jolly well controlled the Piccard's Cyprus business by controlling all services in the region. He had been told he had to keep RayGo happy and supportive, and the corporation's CEO had made quite clear how that was to be accomplished.

Andre turned a dejected eye on the sea and the complex's marina many floors below. The full moon reflected dazzling light off slack sails, the foam of the tidal waves, and the occasional quartz stone on the beach. As he watched, he saw movement in the moonlight. A figure was ambling down the beach toward the sea. It stopped and struggled with clothes briefly and then entered the surf, arms stretched out full length, welcoming the engulfing tide.

Andre had a sudden urge for freedom himself.

Quietly and carefully he sought from the foot of the bed the shirt and trousers that Ingrid had ripped off him earlier in the evening in one of her attacks of urgency, pulled them on, and left the room with a mere click of the closing pocket door.

Although the figure in the sea had provided the impetus for his own night-time journey to the beach, Andre had not come to the sea in search for companionship. Thus, he was a little disappointed when he reached the terrace leading to the sand to discover that the other late-night bather's clothes were still on the beach. Upon seeing the garments, Andre veered off at an angle. As luck would have it, however, the other bather was walking back out of the sea in the very direction in which Andre was headed. They saw each other at the same moment. The other bather smiled and waved. Andre grinned in sudden recognition and quickened his movement across the sand, pulling at buttons as he headed for the water.

* * * *

A sense of unease had settled in even before the minister's car pulled up to the door of Takis Koniotis's hilltop villa in the Makedonitissa suburb to the west of Nicosia and deposited Takis at the doorstep, where he and Maria Mattas said their good-byes. Caitlyn was supposed to have arrived at the house ahead of him from her two-week lecture tour of the countries bordering the Mediterranean, but there were no lights burning either inside or outside the house.

He hadn't seen Caitlyn for the full two weeks, and he became irritable when his wife was away from him for any length of time. Caitlyn may have cured him of the traditional Greek husband's expectation to be waited on hand and foot, but she had not cured him of his desire to be with her every waking movement. Nearly twenty years of marriage hadn't made a single dent in his love for and dependence on his wife.

Having bundled the twins off to their respective prep schools, for the first time in many years Takis and Caitlyn had time completely to themselves. Caitlyn already had this Cyprus-sponsored lecture tour scheduled, so they had decided to meet in Cyprus at the end of her trip to reacquaint themselves with the island and the home they had left there when Takis had been transferred to UN headquarters in New York.

Takis had originally feared that his career move would challenge their marriage, as he had already once refused a move to New York because Caitlyn had fallen in love with this Makedonitissa villa she had inherited from Eleni Piccard. Takis, who at that time had been the innovative and highly celebrated head of a special international investigations unit of the Cypriot national police, had been asked to open such a unit for the United Nations by UN security chief Eric Isaksen. In consultation with Caitlyn, he had answered that he would only do so if the unit headquarters was established here in Cyprus, and, to his surprise, Isaksen had agreed. Within a couple of years, however, both Takis and Caitlyn had realized that Takis's part in the formation of the United Nations International Criminal Investigation Service—UNICIS—and his ability to obtain the cooperation of the region's security authorities had been so successful that it was inevitable that he would be asked to move to a more central administrative point.

Luckily, at about the same time Takis was offered the job of undersecretary general for security affairs at UN headquarters in New York City's Turtle Bay, Caitlyn received an offer of a professorship in archaeology at New York's Colombia University. By that time both Takis and Caitlyn had also come to believe that they would prefer their sons to have an American education. And so the family closed the Makedonitissa residence, leaving its care to Takis's aunt, Irene, and moved to New York.

This was the first time since that move that Caitlyn and Takis had returned to Cyprus at the same time.

Workaholic that he was, Takis couldn't just take a vacation, he couldn't just be cruising around in Caitlyn's entourage for the two weeks. He always was able to merge in some international police work while he was gone from New York. Thus, Irene had prepared the house for a visit, Takis had arrived by air yesterday, and Caitlyn had been due to arrive by ship today. To take advantage of the extra day alone in Cyprus, Takis had arranged with his old colleague, Maria Solonos Mattas, for a visit to the current location of the UNICIS headquarters complex in the town of Morphou in the farming sector to the west of Nicosia.

Maria, who had followed Takis as the chief of the Cypriot international investigations unit and who was married to *Semerini* publisher Demetris Mattas, was now the Cypriot interior minister. She and Takis had shared a terrific day, followed by dinner in the still-picturesque Kyrenia harbor village on the island's north coast and topped off by promises to return soon with their respective spouses in tow. It was thus well past midnight when Takis reached the Makedonitissa house, and Caitlyn should have arrived hours previously.

The light above the entry door lit up as Takis approached, and he had a sudden feeling of relief, believing that Caitlyn must have turned it on. But then he remembered that the light was triggered by a motion sensor—that Irene had modernized the house in ways like this since last they were here. So much had happened in Cyprus since they last were here. Takis had almost been reluctant to come back. He didn't want anything to change. But change it had.

As he struggled to find the right key, there was a piercing scream behind him. He instinctively crouched as he turned and reached for his holster gun, only to be greeted by the sight and sound of a supersonic passenger jet skimming across his line of vision uncomfortably close and seemingly at the same level as the house. Another one of those changes Takis didn't welcome.

"Damn that airport!" Takis exclaimed in disgust. That was the first negative result that he had associated with the recent long-awaited settlement of the island's division. Divided since 1974 between the Greek Cypriots in the bottom two-thirds and the Turkish Cypriots in the upper third, separated by a UN peacekeeping force-patrolled buffer zone. Prior to the settlement and the frenzied building boom that immediately followed it, the Makedonitissa Valley had been a quiet suburb of luxury homes abutting the UN buffer zone. However, the former Nicosia International Airport had been trapped in that self-same buffer zone, immediately adjacent to the western rim of that valley, for the twenty-five years of the island's division, and the international airport had been relocated to Larnaca. When peace struck in Cyprus and the international airport reopened in Nicosia, the Makedonitissa Valley—and most particularly the western valley ridge upon which the once-remote and quiet Koniotis villa was perched—fell completely within the close approach pattern for the ever-larger and ever-noisier commercial and military air planes landing in Nicosia.

Takis knew Caitlyn would be devastated when she found out just how noisy their neighborhood had become. But, right at this moment, Takis would be pleased to see his wife in any stage of anger or disappointment. He entered the house, and the lounge lights came on, because they also had been set for movement. Takis frowned. This was also the security setting. He had the sinking feeling that no one had been in the house since he had left that morning.

He called Caitlyn's name but felt even more alone when there was no answer. He took the stairs in the glass block tower at the run. At forty-eight, Takis was still trim and in fine fighting shape. In his line of work he couldn't afford to let himself go to fat as happened to too many Greek men in later life. Greek men enjoyed their brandy and tobacco far too much to be vain. Thus, what so often started out as perfection personified in physique and face for Greek men was ruined by Greek habits before forty. This had not happened in Takis's case. He was still the handsome man Caitlyn had married, and the graying at his temples only seemed to enhance his appeal.

Caitlyn wasn't in the bedroom, and the bed had not been slept in. It was then that he noticed the pulsing red light on the telephone. He walked over to the phone and picked it up and dialed the voice mail number.

The worried voice of Demetris Mattas arrested Takis's attention. "Takis or Maria, I'm putting this general call to you both at home, at the office, and your cell phones. As soon as you receive this, you need to come down to the Larnaca port authority. It's about Cait . . ." The message stopped there. Takis was out the door and on his way to the monorail station for the fifteen-minute zip to the Larnaca sea terminal port authority.

* * * *

Ingrid Isaksen rolled over and reached for Andre. Finding he was not there, she turned the bedside light on and sought the young man elsewhere in the apartment. She was only mildly curious where he had gone. She wasn't really in the mood again and, although he was a pleasant diversion, he really was too young and too unenthusiastic, highbrow, and "delicate" for her. If it did not give her a little extra thrill to have control over the heir to the snotty Piccard empire, she probably wouldn't even bother with him. No, the dangerous-looking Uri Lukenov looked more her style.

For one brief moment, Ingrid contemplated descending to the fourth floor to start putting the Russian through his paces, but then she spied her overflowing desk in the study and opted to do paperwork until she was sleepy enough to return to bed.

Paperwork. She detested paperwork. But she realized that paperwork went with the territory of being the CEO of the world's most important corporation, and she fully appreciated that in a worldwide corporation in which businesses revolved within businesses—not all of which were completely legitimate—and in which the success formula upon which the whole house of cards was based rested on a lie and a theft, a good deal of the paperwork could only be accomplished by the CEO. And some of that was for her eyes only and must be secreted here rather than in her corporate offices.

Not that RayGo was built on *her* lie or *her* theft.

That had happened more than a year before she had agreed to take on what was then just a nice, cushy regional consultancy firm. But once she had seen the formulas and realized their import, she had had no scruples about helping cover up their origin and taking full advantage of their opportunities.

As Ingrid brushed aside the dummy papers that were on her desk and opened the panel behind the desk with a coded keypad lock, she once more savored the irony that had brought her corporation its phenomenal success. They had started out as consultants in the Mideast region on environmental issues under the name of the Middle East Investment and Accounting Company—MEIAC. During this market entry phase, they were busy using glib and handsome Cypriots who had acquired highly specialized foreign doctorates that had practically no use in their own country and who learned the knack of delivering pious and largely meaningless advice for large sums to governments that were far more interested in being able to point to their environmental efforts than to actually do anything to improve their environment.

Even before the time Ingrid had come on board as CEO, the consultancy teams were involved in far more interesting and lucrative—if highly illegal—activities under the cover of their consultancies.

And not long before she had been recruited to give the company an international identity they had stumbled on the innovation formulas that almost—but not quite—forced them back wholly into their legal cover activities. Someone in Cyprus discovered the key to efficiently storing indefinitely solar energy for conversion to electricity. That someone made the mistake of sharing that information with a shady diplomat who already was involved in some of the MEIAC's extracurricular activities, and, as a result, the inventor died, supposedly by natural causes, and the RayGo Corporation was born.

The small handful of entrepreneurs who had formed MEIAC and who had fallen heirs to the solar power generation formula realized they needed to enlist as their CEO someone of world-class stature who thought globally. Enter the flashy then UN undersecretary general for political affairs, Ingrid Bittmann Isaksen, stymied in her quest for higher position in the UN and already herself up to at least her knees in extracurricular Mideast activities.

As RayGo's fortunes rose, the ancient western coast harbor town of Famagusta, and specifically its formerly deserted resort sector of Varosha, were rejuvenated as the company's center of power. Within the same time frame, the RayGo-dominated Varosha, the southern coast town of Larnaca, and the Lebanese city of Beirut rose in concert as a new three-pointed hub for international economic activity.

In her early years as CEO, Ingrid Isaksen redirected RayGo's activities to successfully introducing stored solar power generation to the transport, electrical, and heating sectors of the earth's sun belt, and RayGo shot up the international corporation charts to the top of the bill. But Ingrid was more smitten and attracted to the darker, more dangerous side of the corporation's activities, and, in recent years, RayGo had expanded its activities to the point that, even sitting at the top of the world's value chart, its legal activities had merely become the tip of the iceberg of its involvement in world politics and trade.

And at the top of the heap was Ingrid Bittmann Isaksen. This was even better than being the UN secretary general. Her only regret was that few people knew what she had accomplished. Supreme egotist that she was, however, this was not really good enough for her. So, she was keeping a detailed diary of all of her activities. If her associates knew she was doing so, of course, she would be eliminated. But this was all part of the game, a game that she found fascinating. And she didn't mind one bit going down in history as the world's greatest criminal. After all, she was a feminist, and even superlative international crime should be claimed by a woman.

She drew out her diary and recorded the activities that had occasioned her presence on the *Daphne* and ended with the ironic twist that had been provided at the expense of Takis Koniotis's wife, Caitlyn. She was laughing so freely while writing this entry that she almost missed the opening click of the apartment's front door. She was, in fact, probably only alerted in time because of the sensory alarm that was connected between all entries and the panel at the back of the secret compartment above her desk. She barely had time to return the papers and close the compartment when a wet Andre Piccard entered the room.

Andre began to stammer an explanation for his absence. Unfortunately for Andre, however, Ingrid wasn't particularly interested in where he had gone. She was more interested in what he was going to do for the next half hour. In his absence, she had had time to reawaken her appetite for handsome young Frenchmen.

Chapter Three

Ginger sat bolt upright. The sobbing from the house next to her own had stopped abruptly. This should have come as a relief, as the multilingual wailing—none of the languages of which a highly educated Ginger could fathom—had started near midnight and had not been reduced to dry, heaving sobs until nearly 2:00 AM. This wasn't the first night the village neighborhood had thusly been entertained, and the other, mainly Cypriot, villagers who lived nearby were beginning to grumble.

The small village of Omodhos in the southern coastal foothills of the Troodos Mountains was one of the few spots remaining in Cyprus where one could enjoy peace and quiet— and, indeed, Ginger herself had moved here more than six years ago from Lefkara, a larger village in the eastern foothills of the Troodos, for this very reason. When the tourist industry in Cyprus collapsed in the late 1990s as a result of overdevelopment and overpricing in relationship to other developing tourist destinations in the Mediterranean, the economies of villages such as Lefkara collapsed. Omodhos itself, which was one of the original mountain villages to be refurbished in an imagined facsimile of quaintness to attract the tourists, replacing the cobbles of its village square and the adjacent streets with paving stones and closing the central village area off to vehicular traffic, then welcoming the makeover of its old courtyard houses by British and German retirees, had shared in suffering this depression.

When such towns as Lefkara grabbed at the modernization euros that had come in the wake of the island's unification and the economic enrichment of the rising RayGo Corporation, however, Omodhos had opted not to abandon its previous choice to provide an homogenized picture of Cyprus' past. Thus, although the wealth of Cyprus' burgeoning development had passed it by, it had also escaped most of the disadvantages associated with fast-paced modernization.

Ginger Nives-Smyth Baldwin Remington Hamilton Patterson had made her move from Lefkara to Omodhos specifically in search of what the latter village still had to offer. She had already suffered enough tragedy in her seventy-six years not to want to ride the wave of Cyprus' rise to economic significance in the world. And, although she liked the mysterious, reclusive woman who had appeared in the next courtyard earlier in the year in spite of the woman's prickly insistence to keep to herself, Ginger was growing just as tired of these nocturnal scenes of melancholy as the rest of the residents were.

Ginger turned on her bedside lamp and instinctively reached for her glasses and her mirror. British, of the stiff-upper-lip aristocratic background variety, the five-times contender in the marriage sweepstakes had lost her vanity slightly over fifteen years earlier, albeit not without a valiant struggle. But old habits died hard. All in all, if Ginger had really cared any more, she would have been relatively pleased by the visage that appeared in her mirror. Always a slender, but strongly muscled woman—she had once been a fashion model, Ginger's fair complexion and high cheekbones were serving her well. In fact, she looked even prettier now that she had permitted her hair to go gray and had stopped trying to stave off the ravishes of time with battle paint.

Perhaps more than the physical appearances, however, Ginger had improved with age and become more beautiful with the passing years because of a change in temperament and attitude. Once self-centered, man hungry, strident, snide, and grasping, she had experienced a sudden change in outlook over fifteen years previously when she had believed she had lost her fourth husband—who she had belittled and betrayed but had suddenly come to find she actually deeply loved and respected.

She had led a tragic life, however. Her first couple of marriages had been short-lived youthful flings of lust. Her third marriage, to a military attaché, had ended in his suicide when he had mistakenly thought she was a Russian spy. She had, indeed, been involved with a highly successful Russian intelligence operation against NATO headquarters in Brussels, but it had been as a dupe rather than as an intentional participant. Her fourth, explosive marriage, to a British infantry major who had retired to Cyprus and become an outspoken crime journalist for the *Cyprus Mail*, had turned out to be the love of her life, but she had, unfortunately, discovered that fact almost too late in life. They only were able to enjoy two years of shared bliss following the false alarm in which Ginger had thought he had been murdered when he, in fact, was murdered, leaving her an empty shell emotionally.

Some years later, Ginger wed for a final time. She married a friend, a scientist who headed the computer lab at the UNICIS crime-fighting organization Takis Koniotis founded and who had recently lost his own companion under tragic circumstance. Neither came to this late marriage with undue expectations. Both had known it was an arrangement of mutual comfort and support, but it had been a solid partnership nonetheless. And Ginger had grieved no less for John Patterson than she had for Willie Hamilton when Patterson suffered a fatal heart attack while visiting Beirut.

He died during a meeting he was attending there with some representatives of the MEIAC consultancy firm.

Ginger still, after all these years, had not had the courage to go through the papers her husband gave to her in a locked box and that were now resting in the secret compartment she had had constructed in the wall of this house she'd had restored and moved to after John's death.

Ginger put the mirror down—she had been sitting there with it in her hand, but she had not actually bothered to look at herself in the glass—and turned to switch off the light. Her movement was arrested, however, as she heard noises again from across the stone wall—a strange grunting noise.

All right, that was enough. Ginger could respect another's privacy as well as the next person, but she had been the only person Roulla Dahir had been even marginally civil to in the four months since the obviously foreign woman mysteriously appeared in the village, and it was high time Ginger tried to find out what was wrong and to alleviate it—if for no other reason than to allow everyone near the Omodhos square to sleep undisturbed once more.

Ginger rose, wrapped herself in a crocheted shawl, and walked out into her courtyard. The moon was full and the sky clear. The lights from her windows caused the magenta-colored bracts of a copious bougainvillea vine to sparkle, and the pleasant scent of a white jasmine vine flooded the courtyard. Although she was in a hurry, Ginger couldn't help but linger in her gateway long enough to drink in the night and to once again rejoice in her life, solitary as it was, in the Cyprus hills.

Another, new sound dispelled her momentary trance, however, and she hurried out into the narrow street. It had been a hollow sound. It had sounded like wood banging on stone.

Whereas Ginger's four-room house had a single story and surrounded a small courtyard on three sides, Roulla's abode had two floors—with basically only one room per floor—and the front entryway opened directly from the street into the ground floor room. Ginger rapped on the door, which opened on its own under the strong force of her fist. Still, she hesitated to enter.

"Roulla. Roulla, it's me, Ginger Hamilton. Are you all right?"

Silence.

She tried again. "Roulla, I heard you crying. Is there anything I can do? Can I come in?"

But then Ginger's blood froze in her veins. Her queries had not really been met with silence. There was another noise coming from deep in the room—not a loud noise, but a frightening noise, one that Ginger could not quite have been able to describe, but a noise that she would not want to have to recall.

She pushed her way into the room.

"Oh, Roulla, honey. No, you don't want to do this," Ginger chided the other woman in a clucking voice, as she righted the chair and stepped up on it to support and raise the other woman's body, while her long, strong fingers sought to loosen the knot in the rope that had been tied to the ceiling beam.

An observer would have thought that Ginger was taking her grim discovery unusually calmly, but Ginger wasn't calm enough just then to notice and marvel at the piles of euro and U.S. banknotes that drifted around the legs of the now upright chair.

* * * *

Omodhos was not the only Troodos mountain village to be plagued with the distress of the tormented. Across Mount Olympus, the highest peak on Cyprus—indeed, the name the Greeks reserved for the highest peak on all of their islands, and a short way down its northern face, at the head of the Solea Valley, the secret head of the Piccard family fortunes also sat, distraught with life and unable to sleep.

From the balcony of the apartment that crowned the towering Old Mill Inn and Restaurant in the mountain resort village of Kakopetria, the recluse watched the car of his caretaker drive out of the car park below and then sat down on a wooden bench, trying to forget the pain, and looked down the valley onto the flickering lights of approaching civilization on the floor of the central plain that descended down to the Morphou Bay in the west.

The Solea Valley, which descended from Mount Olympus to the sea and which, during the early centuries had provided the most direct access from the central plain of Cyprus to the copper-rich Troodos Mountains and in later centuries had been home to the only river of the island that ran into the plain year round, was rich in history. It had been inhabited almost as long as the history of man by such civilizations as the Phoenicians, Greeks, and Romans, a fact that had been proved over several excavation and discovery seasons by Dr. Caitlyn Spencer Koniotis and Dr. Andriko Visiliou. But in time the valley had lost its blessing from the gods, what had been the glories of previous civilizations were abandoned and covered by the ravages of time, and even its river had been reduced to a trickle by the robbing of its water for irrigation. The island's civilizations developed elsewhere. Even in the latest, phenomenal growth period afforded by the political reunification of the island and the worldwide success of the Cyprus-based RayGo Corporation, the Solea Valley had been bypassed.

RayGo, with its close connections with the resurgent city of Beirut on the Lebanese coast, had caused the new growth on the island to concentrate in a triangle that stretched along the island's southeast coast, from the ancient, formally Turkish Cypriot–occupied port of Famagusta, to the even more ancient seaside city of Larnaca and angled back to the capital city of Nicosia positioned near the island's center.

However, not everyone thought the health resort villages of the Solea Valley to have been unlucky in not having been graced by the results of the RayGo success formula. One of these was the occupant in the apartment atop the former multistoried stone grain warehouse perched against the slope above Kakopetria. Although he was glad the area had escaped the recent rush to civilization, he felt as used and as discarded as the valley itself. The richness of the man's immediate surroundings—the luxury hotel and restaurant that had resulted from the devoted work of a Piccard by marriage, Eleni Piccard—contrasted starkly with the mere husk of a human being who hunched on the balcony of the apartment Eleni had created as an escape from her many business responsibilities on the plain and the coast and as a tribute to the husband and son she had lost during the 1974 Turkish invasion of Cyprus.

Not that old in actual years, the sufferer had been tortured by ill health throughout his life. The various ailments were now beginning to combine to close down systems, and the current force behind the Piccard fortunes had come here to die—without knowing why, of all places, this was to be the chosen last resting place.

This apartment had never been home. Even Cyprus seemed terribly remote considering the intervening years of his treatment and convalescing in France and at the family's castle in Switzerland. But, looking down the valley in the gathering light of the early morning hours and seeing the church towers of Kakopetria and of Galata, the next village down the valley, begin to emerge, the thought formed that perhaps this wasn't such a bad choice for the culmination of the final journey after all.

There was a brief, hopeful thought that perhaps this did not need to be the end. Perhaps the miracle cure was just around the corner. Even this valley itself was beginning to reblossom. The combination of the reforestation campaign of the past thirty years and of the massive project that had permitted desalinized water to be pumped back into the water table and up to the top of the mountains had increased the moisture content dramatically. Already the valley's hillsides had jumped back to life, its rivers now reached the sea at Morphou Bay, which had brought the small fish of the Mediterranean back to the island's shores, and its orchards were expanding. Even the silk and leather-tooling industries were reviving in the valley thanks to the bequest and organization the philanthropist Eleni Piccard had set up for her home village before she died, brutally murdered by a former lover here in her own retreat.

But, no. The revival of Solea Valley was not to be shared by the controller of the Piccards' destiny. It had grown too late for hope for such miracles. But there were measures to take and the Piccard fortunes to ensure before that final rest.

The tragic figure trudged back into the apartment's lounge and shut the balcony doors. The beauty of the view down the valley from the balcony was not comforting tonight. The view screamed out that all was right with the world. But the tortured man knew that everything was definitely not right with his own world.

* * * *

Caitlyn had never felt so powerless and humiliated—and, yes, downright scared—as she had when the two hefty Turks, identifying themselves as policemen, accosted her and dragged her off to the customs police shed at the Larnaca sea terminal.

At first she had been completely confused. Why were they asking all these questions about who she was and where she had been? Why wouldn't they tell her what was wrong? And why hadn't Andriko or Demetris come looking for her and straightened all of this out? Surely when they had seen her luggage standing by the terminal entry they must have known she was still in the vicinity. And all of this must only be a misunderstanding.

The two were quite belligerent and threatening at first. When they found out she was Mrs. Takis Koniotis, however, they quite suddenly became very polite. At first she used her own, professional name, but she probably should have had the presence of mind to mention Takis from the beginning. Takis was a legend among the police in Cyprus—still—and these men probably hadn't heard about her at all, even though her name was the one of note and respect in the Koniotis family in the island's cultural circles. The citing of her husband's name, however, had not stopped the questions from coming her way or encouraged the policemen to tell her what had precipitated her arrest.

Unfortunately, Caitlyn had lost her passport during one of the recent mishaps with her purse, so she could not prove her nationality and wasn't fully sure that she had convinced her interrogators of her claimed relationship to Takis. At this point, two other men had appeared—men whom the customs officers seemed to know well and to trust, and Caitlyn's incarceration improved dramatically. The younger of the two introduced himself as Wilhelm—Will for short—Jacobs, a Secret Service officer assigned to the U.S. embassy in Nicosia. Although he had never met Caitlyn personally, he had attended one of her lectures at Colombia University as he was preparing to come out to Cyprus, a historical perspective on ancient artifact smuggling in the Mediterranean basin, and he readily verified both her identity and citizenship to the customs authorities. He also asserted that, as a U.S. embassy official himself, he was quite concerned that Mrs. Koniotis be treated well. At nearly this same time, the results of the fingerprint scan the authorities had run on Caitlyn were computed back, and her identity had been fully and satisfactorily settled at last.

As soon as she had gotten the chance, Caitlyn pointed out that she had been traveling with friends, who, for some inexplicable reason, had left the terminal without her and that she needed to contact them—as well as her husband, who must be very worried that she hadn't reached Nicosia as scheduled. A slightly embarrassed-looking Jacobs promised to help, and the police got busy trying to reach one of her three traveling companions on a cell phone. Both Jacobs and the man who had entered the customs shed with him already had a pretty good idea why Caitlyn's companions had left her, but for different reasons, neither was interested in revealing their knowledge.

The second gentlemen turned out to be William Stevens of the Australian high commission and, although Stevens didn't further identify his function, Caitlyn quickly gathered from his familiarity with both the customs police and Jacobs that he had some sort of police liaison role. In contrast to Jacobs's solicitous approach to Caitlyn's dilemma, Stevens was almost surly, and Caitlyn got the impression that he had come into the customs shed more to find out what was happening and to savor her predicament than to help her.

This feeling proved to be borne out when Jacobs was able to find out why Caitlyn had been apprehended.

"Did you exchange some large-denomination U.S. dollars when you arrived here, Mrs. Koniotis?"

"Yes, why? I didn't have any euros after I'd given gratuities on the ship."

"The dollars you used at the money exchange were counterfeit."

"Counterfeit? I don't understand."

"We are experiencing a lot of this, Mrs. Koniotis—and by well-known Cypriots and well-to-do foreigners visiting Cyprus as well—you're the first American to be involved, though, I think."

Having told her that, Jacobs went on to give some background. Because of sophisticated advances in currency counterfeiting, the U.S. and European banknotes had been redesigned. Now, in an apparent effort to undermine the Western economies, some other country or force had gotten its hands on the special paper used for the U.S. currency—and not just this currency but the cloth-infused paper used for the European Community's euro banknotes as well—and was forging very convincing notes.

Jacobs explained that these notes were flooding into the Mediterranean area and that agents of the countries concerned with the problem, including he himself and Stevens, were working hard to try to trace down the source of the counterfeits.

"Where did you obtain the U.S. banknotes you exchanged in the sea terminal, Mrs. Koniotis?"

"Why, in New York. That's where I started out on this lecture tour I'm on. I live most of the year there and work at Colombia University. I'm sure I accumulated the notes over time. I didn't go to the bank especially to withdraw the money at one time."

"That's perplexing," Jacobs answered. "The counterfeits aren't known to have reached America as yet. May I examine any other U.S. notes you have with you?"

"I'm sorry, I exchanged all I had at the money exchange here."

Jacobs was gently guiding Caitlyn through a description of where she had been and what money transactions she had had since leaving New York two weeks previously, when Stevens finally became exasperated. Grabbing Caitlyn's purse, he rummaged around inside, apparently looking for more banknotes, not accepting her statement that she had no more U.S. notes. Jacobs's complexion turned red, and the customs policemen looked a bit embarrassed, but Stevens was not apologetic.

"Look, Mrs. Koniotis. This isn't a tea party. This counterfeiting is very serious business. It is spreading so far, so fast, and so thickly that we know some very important people are behind it—probably even people no one would suspect. So, let's hear where you really got those notes."

"I have told you what I know about those notes," Caitlyn answered coolly. "I assure you that I fully appreciate the gravity of the issue, but this is all as much a surprise to me as it is to you."

"I am not easily surprised," retorted Stevens, sticking his chin out.

Jacobs intervened, and Stevens left soon after, declaring that he doubted Caitlyn had heard the last from him as yet.

Caitlyn was still pretty collected at that point. And although she became quite exhausted over the succeeding hours of waiting for someone to retrieve her, her assurances weren't actually rocked until both Takis and her old friend, Maria Mattas—having learned of the problem from her husband, Demetris—arrived almost simultaneously to rescue her. In the face of the presence of both the UN's highest-level police official and the Cypriot interior minister, the Customs officials still asked her not to leave the island again without checking with them first. If her new friend, Will Jacobs, who had stayed with her at the police office for several disturbing hours, had not given her a reassuring smile at this point, she felt she might have been reduced to tears of frustration.

Her confusion returned, however, when they left the customs police office and she saw her luggage being maneuvered off the *Daphne*—for the second time. She knew that the baggage had been taken off the ship earlier, but she was unable to convince either Takis or Maria of this. And the porter who had originally transported it was now nowhere to be found. No wonder, she thought, that neither Andriko nor Demetris had come looking for her. They must have thought she had gone on to Nicosia without them because neither she nor her baggage were at the terminal entrance when they had reached it. There were entirely too many twists to this little affair for her brush with the law to have been coincidental or accidental, she thought. Someone was toying with her. But who? And why?

* * * *

Sometime later, as the dawn was breaking over the city's skyscrapers, one of Caitlyn's interrogators reached the safety of his home, where he withdrew Caitlyn's passport from his pocket. He could not have returned it to her at the customs shed without raising questions on how he had obtained it. He didn't want the passport. He would get it back to her. He didn't want it found in his possession. The question was how he would do it. Hopefully in a way that would benefit him and his colleagues.

＊ ＊ ＊ ＊

When Takis and Caitlyn entered the Makedonitissa villa, the phone was ringing. Caitlyn gave Takis a look that indicated she couldn't face any further discussions this night and headed for the staircase. When Takis answered, he heard that the caller was Ellen Larkin, an old friend who had been a Canadian diplomat and who had, at Takis's request, joined UNICIS as its operations chief and had risen to the directorship following the tragic death of her predecessor.

Ellen sounded very concerned and got right to the point. "What's happening with Caitlyn, Takis?" she queried.

"What do you mean?" Takis responded a bit testily, and then grimaced and went on. "I'm sorry, Ellen, the protectiveness is reflexive. What I mean is how did you find out so quickly?"

"Her fingerprints came across for checking for possible criminal connections," Ellen said with concern.

"It was all just a mistake, Ellen. She was apprehended when she arrived here at the Larnaca sea terminal for exchanging counterfeit money. It just took me a long time to get to her because Maria and I had been visiting you in Morphou and Maria's cell phone is out of order."

"Passing counterfeit notes? That's serious business, Takis. By 'mistake' do you mean it wasn't Caitlyn who had them in her possession?"

"No, I'm afraid she apparently had them all right. But she must have picked them up somewhere. She was too exhausted for me to ask her about it while we were railing back from Larnaca. Luckily, Will Jacobs was there, however, and helped her out."

"Will Jacobs." Ellen repeated. "Hmm, wonder what he was doing there."

"Beats me, but I'm glad he showed up."

"Takis," Ellen said thoughtfully. "You don't suppose Caitlyn was being set up, do you?"

"The thought hadn't even entered my mind. What makes you ask?"

"Well," Ellen responded. "While we were reporting in our findings on Caitlyn's fingerprints, we noticed that someone else was trying to access the data but wouldn't identify themselves when we queried."

"Were you able to trace the request?" asked Koniotis, suddenly alert.

"Only as far Lebanon. Our guess was it came from Beirut. But why would anyone in Beirut be checking in Caitlyn's file, Takis?"

"I don't know," Takis said grimly. "That's the last place her ship stopped before she landed in Larnaca, but I don't know why anyone would be trying to access her police file. I don't know what this means, but I'll talk to her about it tomorrow. She's too tired now for a discussion."

"Meanwhile, Takis, I suggest you not tell her precisely why I called. Just tell her I called to welcome her back and am looking forward to seeing her at the lecture and the president's dinner tomorrow night."

"Will do," Takis answered. "Maybe you and I will have a few minutes then to discuss these developments again. Now that you mention it, it is a little strange that Jacobs just happened to be around at the Larnaca sea terminal when Caitlyn was picked up for passing counterfeit notes."

After Takis turned off the lights downstairs, he started up the stairs, deep in contemplation. Without notice, the silence of the early hours of dawn was ripped apart by a high whining noise, which exploded out into a large boom. Caitlyn came rushing out onto the upper landing.

"What in the hell is that noise?" she yelled over the sonic boom.

"Progress. Our own little gift from the political settlement," he answered dully. And then when she didn't seem to comprehend, he added, as he herded his wife back into the bedroom: "It's air transporters taking off. The international airport has reopened. Try to ignore it; it won't hurt us and it won't go away. We'll discuss it tomorrow—or, rather, later today. Later. We'll discuss a lot of things later."

Chapter Four

Ginger Patterson was sitting so that she could see out of the window at the rear of the building. The house was near the edge of the village, so she could clearly see the hillside rising from the slope, reaching for Mount Olympus. Beyond the houses, the neat rows of staked grape vines climbed up toward the upper road. From the other side of the road, an olive grove continued on up the slope. The dusty-green leaves of its squat trees swaying ever so slightly in the breeze that came up from the sea that could be seen from the distance at the other, southern edge of the village. The wall outside the window was covered with a full-blooming bougainvillea with mixed magenta and white bracts that had encroached into the room around the window frame when Ginger had opened the shutters.

The morning sun glinted off the windshield of an automobile that was carefully climbing the pebbled road on its way to the former British colonial-period summer hill station of Platres, and, as Ginger watched, it overtook an even older means of conveyance on the island, a mule, which was moved to the side of the road by an old woman in black as the automobile passed. The rays of the sun that deflected off the automobile reached Ginger's eyes and momentarily blinding her. This also served to bring Ginger back into the present. Reluctantly.

She looked down at the sleeping woman, and her thoughts reached out, unspoken, to the other. "I know that the tragedies and unfairness of life can push you to the brink of despair. But you'll find the longer you live in a place as beautiful as Cyprus is, the less willing you will be to separate from this life. You've just arrived among us. You must give Cyprus some time."

The woman stirred, and Ginger looked around the room to ensure that everything was back in place before Roulla awoke.

Ginger had reached the woman the previous night before much harm had been done. Not much more physical damage than a slight rope burn. The woman was so thin and frail that her weight was not nearly sufficient to have caused her neck to snap when she kicked the chair away. There also had been few tears. Those had all been spent during several previous hours. Roulla had built up her strength to take her own life with the help of a bottle of Scotch, and she was more groggy than winded when Ginger untied the knot and helped the woman back to the floor. Ginger shuffled the woman over to a nearby daybed and rocked her in her arms until Roulla drifted off into sleep.

When the woman was sleeping deeply, Ginger stood, finished off the last couple of inches in the Scotch bottle herself, and began to pick up and sort the banknotes that literally covered the floor. There was a large number of both European and U.S. notes—and they included many notes in large denominations, as well.

At least the mystery was solved of the woman's ability to so easily and quietly insert herself into what was actually a fashionable and pricey restored district, Ginger had mused as she gathered the notes together and stacked them on a small table in the shadows. There were other mysteries here, though, Ginger had thought with a frown. Mysteries that were literally driving the woman of indeterminate background over the edge.

"Roulla Dahir," Ginger had muttered to herself. "Sounds Middle Eastern—but she doesn't look Middle Eastern, and the heavy accent she uses to communicate in English sounds more Slavic in origin than Arabic."

Then Ginger sighed and sat down in the only comfortably overstuffed chair in the room. She had looked hopefully at the Scotch bottle, but it was still as empty as it had been when she had drained it a few moments earlier to steady her nerves. She momentarily regretted her deceased husband, Willie, wasn't alive and living here; he would have other bottles of Scotch secreted away that wouldn't be all that hard to find.

She then sat and stared at the sleeping woman for several minutes. She didn't like mysteries—especially mysteries that brought her out to interrupt attempts at suicide in the night. She began looking intently about the room. Then she began to pick objects up from the table tops and examine them. This effort had been rewarded only with a few family photographs—one was of a man who obviously, in contrast to Roulla, was of Middle Eastern origin. There were one or two others of Roulla and the same man. Another mystery solved—at least partially. Roulla had married someone from the Middle East; she was not necessarily Mid Eastern herself—hence the mismatch on her surname. And then there were a couple of group photos—all of very serious-looking people. But none of any children. Roulla's marriage had been childless? Could that be one of the reasons for her despair. Had her only loved one died and now life was too lonely for her to bear?

More inspections of surfaces, but nothing more of interest—certainly nothing to rival the stacks of banknotes that kept whispering to Ginger from the shadows.

After having opened the first drawer, there seemed to be no more boundaries to observe, so Ginger had moved on to pretty much take apart the lower floor in search of clues. Nothing much was to be found. The best she could come up with was a framed picture of an older couple, the woman closely resembling Roulla. Therefore, probably her parents. Heavy clothes and snowy backdrop. Another clue that Roulla probably wasn't herself from the Middle East.

Ginger had almost failed to notice the disturbing aspect of some of the other photographs she found in a drawer. Group photos, including several of the people she had seen in the framed photographs on the top of the bureau. But in these, they were all carrying arms and looking quite militant. Rifles, machine guns, and belts around their waists and across their chests with grenades and bullets.

Ginger had then checked on the other woman and headed for the stairs. The upper room was smaller than the single room on the ground floor. The rear portion of the house was a grape-vine-draped, trellis-covered balcony. What was under roof was furnished as a bedroom. More framed pictures covered the bedside table. One, in particular, had caught Ginger's eye. Roulla again—a much younger and happier-looking Roulla—but this time with a European-featured man and two small children. And there, in the back of a drawer another photograph of an even younger and happier-looking woman with yet a different young man.

Ginger had barely had time to glance at any of these older photographs, however, before she had heard Roulla stirring and muttering to herself in the room below. The older woman then slipped back down the stairs. Roulla was still sleeping, but she had turned over on the divan. Ginger quickly straightened up the room and then returned to the somewhat younger woman's side.

Roulla awakened only once in the last hour of darkness. She looked up into Ginger's face, first in fright and then in embarrassment, and finally, when Ginger maintained an expression of acceptance and comfort, with a rueful smile.

"It's all right. You needn't talk about it or explain," Ginger spoke first.

"No, please," Roulla whispered.

"Do you want me to leave now?"

"No, not just yet. Not, of course, unless you need to be somewhere."

Needed to be somewhere, Ginger thought, with a melancholy of her own. It had been many years since she had "needed" to be anywhere. Ginger patted the other woman's hand and remained at the side of the bed.

The other woman drifted back into sleep, but only for a couple of moments. Upon waking this time, and almost as if she remembered for the first time the hour and the circumstance, Roulla sat up and spoke in a louder tone and in a rush. "Oh, I'm sorry. I've kept you awake, haven't I? Of course you must leave. You must be exhausted. I've been such a nuisance."

"No, no, it's all right. I have nothing better to do and at my time of life I have neither pressing engagements nor the need for sleep."

"But, I've been so horrid. I normally don't drink like this and forget myself. I'm so sorry that I've been such a nuisance to bring you over here like this."

The younger woman had started searching the room with her eyes, her gaze moving from corner to corner, from empty bottle to village wooden chair and stopping at the wooden beam in the ceiling above. Ginger had not been able to gauge the other's expression. Had it been fear, despair, disgust, confusion, or recognition? She also couldn't be sure at this point just how much of the events of the previous night the other woman could remember. Ginger had been sure, however, that Roulla's inspection of the room took in the stacks of banknotes on the table in the shadows.

Neither spoke then of the banknotes or about any other aspect of the evening. Ginger put her arms around the younger woman and lowered her back to the daybed. And, stroking loose strands of hair out of Roulla's face, Ginger suggested that she try to sleep some more.

"But aren't you tired, as well?" Roulla whispered in a clearly exhausted voice. "I mustn't keep you here. You may go back home. I'm fine now—just too much to drink."

"Yes, I am a bit tired," Ginger answered. "But I would like to sit here and rest a few minutes, unless, of course, you would rather I leave."

"No, no, please stay if you wish," Roulla barely managed before she drifted off again.

After a while, Ginger moved over to the window, drawn by the light of the dawn. This was her favorite time of the Cypriot day—when the white and ocher stuccoed walls began to glow in the warming morning light and when the sounds of renewed life started once again to drift through the village. Most of her friends said they preferred the evening light on the Cypriot village scenes—and that had once been her favorite as well. But now, in her waning days of life and with reflection upon all of the pain she had seen and experienced, the twilight frightened her and made her melancholy. It was the return of the morning light and of the village activity that gave her strength and courage now.

Ginger was only half conscious and was drifting into sleep when the light glinting off the automobile's windshield brought her back into the present. It was with a nagging thought that she looked back at Roulla to see that she was all right. Something had surfaced in her mind as she had been drifting off. She had seen something significant in her search of Roulla's small village house, something besides the large number of high-denomination banknotes. Something about the photographs—something she should have recognized. The thought of the photographs of the people with the guns and ammunition suddenly made her shudder and she rose, retrieved her shawl from near the entryway where it had dropped when she had sprung forward to save Roulla from choking, and wrapped it around her shoulders. As she was walking back to the window, she thought that what she'd seen in the photographs hit her, and she shuddered again. It was not the cold that had made her tremble.

Both Roulla and the man who presumably had been her husband had been in the photograph of the armed group—and they had been as fully weighted down with guns and grenades as had been the rest. It was hard to think of a small, old woman such as Roulla as a revolutionary—but, if she had been, that was even further reason for her avoidance of other people these past couple of months.

Ginger moved toward the bureau to open the drawer and recheck the photograph, but she first instinctively looked down at Roulla, only to find that the woman was awake and staring back at her. Her gaze was steady and searching, but it revealed nothing of Roulla's own thoughts.

"Oh, good. You are awake," Ginger stammered out. "I could use some coffee and a bit of breakfast. But I'd really rather not eat alone this morning. If you don't mind, I'll go over to my house and bring something back for us to eat here."

Roulla didn't answer directly, but she sat up on the edge of the daybed. The fingers of one hand went up to the bruise on her neck and she first looked slightly surprised and then nodded in a slight smile that was otherwise unrevealing toward Ginger.

Taking that as an assent, Ginger backed out of the house. When she returned with a breakfast tray, Roulla had washed and changed and was laying a cloth on an old pine table. Ginger noticed that both the empty Scotch bottle and the stacks of money had disappeared.

Ginger tried to engage Roulla in conversation while they ate, but she didn't have much success.

"Your name is Middle Eastern?"

"Yes, it's Lebanese. I'm from an area south of Beirut."

"Is it a desert area?"

"No, no. It is a beautiful valley. Much like this, but even greener. The Al-Baqa' still has beautiful stands of cedar trees."

"But you don't really look like a Lebanese, and you speak English with a much different accent," Ginger probed.

"No, I wasn't originally Lebanese. But that was so long ago that I tend to forget." And then, after a while, when Ginger didn't take up the conversation. "That was a beautiful mountain valley too. I originally came from the Caucasus Mountains. But I lost that country. Thankfully, I gained another one." Prolonged silence.

"And do you have a family?" Ginger ventured at length, and she turned toward the bureau where she had seen the framed photograph of Roulla and a man, presumably her

Lebanese husband. But the photograph was gone, and Ginger quickly looked back at Roulla in slight embarrassment.

The younger woman had apparently not noticed the arrested gesture.

"No, I no longer have a family."

"And is that why you cry at night?" Ginger asked gently?

The other woman looked at her sharply.

"I'm sorry, I don't mean to intrude," Ginger quickly interjected into the tense atmosphere. "But I have lost family—more than one family, I'm afraid—and I am all alone now. I just thought that if you had recently suffered the same loss and were suddenly alone in the world, you should know that you really aren't alone."

Roulla seemed to soften a bit and quietly muttered the question "More than one family?" And then she shivered and was silent once more. Ginger reached over and patted her hand. But the younger woman did not reopen the conversation, and Ginger left soon thereafter. As she was leaving the house, however, Roulla called quietly to her.

"Thank you. And . . . please come again."

Ginger turned with a smile. "I'm British, and we have tea in the late afternoon. I love to sit in my courtyard and have tea as the sun goes down, but I hate to set everything up just for myself. Would you like to join me this evening?"

A bit of silence, punctuated by the sound of the breeze off of the sea and of the early morning activity in the nearby town square. But Roulla did answer before Ginger turned away to return to her own home. "Yes, Thank you, yes. I think I would enjoy that very much. We always had afternoon tea in my family, as well . . . when I was a child."

Ginger was humming happily to herself when she returned to her house. She was even humming when she drew water into the dish pan, added soap, and began to wash up the breakfast dishes. However, she abruptly stopped humming as she stared out her window and saw the automobile from earlier in the morning making its way back down the upper road from the direction of Platres.

The nagging thought that had entered her subconscious earlier and had disturbed her was not that Roulla had photographs of an armed band. It wasn't even that she had seen Roulla in these photographs. Somewhere among the photographs—the other photographs—she had seen someone familiar. Not just someone who looked like someone she had known, but someone she had, in fact, either known personally or whose visage had made a profound effect on her at one time or another. In either case, the vibrations Ginger was getting from this were evil vibrations. Whatever was involved, it was something she had tried to forget, something that made her heart race and threatened her.

"My God," Ginger thought as she left the sink and sank into a chair. "How can this be? And, more important, why is this mystery having such a profound effect on me? Could Roulla's appearance be something other than a coincidence? Am I in some sort of danger? Think, Ginger, think. What have you seen?"

Outside, in the village square, Omodhos once more burst into life, its simple villagers returning to the same activities that had given them purpose and pleasure for hundreds of years, before the advent of the European retirees with their fantasy reconstructions of the central village houses, even before those that preceded them in long procession—the British colonialists, the Ottoman Turks, the Venetians, the Genoese, the Lusignans, Richard the Lionhearted and his crusaders, the Byzantines, the Romans, the Greeks, the Persians, the Assyrians, the Egyptians, the . . . .

Chapter Five

"What was that you said, honey? I can't hear you over those blasted jets." Takis Koniotis turned his morning copy of the *Cyprus Mail* toward the southwest as if it would provide a barrier between him and the plane that was now settling down on the nearby Nicosia International Airport runway.

"I said," Caitlyn Spencer Koniotis enunciated loudly and clearly, "that I couldn't even think because of those blasted jets."

Both gave a dry little laugh and lifted their coffee cups. They had chosen—but apparently not too wisely—to enjoy their first breakfast together in many long years at their Makedonitissa hilltop home on the villa's rear terrace. They had once enjoyed the peace and quiet of the Cypriot countryside here, in their sparsely housed suburb that had abutted the UN buffer zone to the west of the capital city. But that serenity had been destroyed when the division of the island had ended and the bustle of life had reached their hilltop. They had also particularly enjoyed breakfasting on this terrace and enjoying the vistas toward the east and north, which included a view down into the up-scale Makedonitissa Valley and on up the valley's plush eastern slope to the higher-rise buildings of downtown Nicosia in the middle distance.

In the far—but not really *very* far—distance, from the east, wrapping around on the north, and continuing on around the edge of their own residence to the west rose the imposing Kyrenia Mountain range. These mountains were not particularly high in relation to the Troodos Mountains to the west and south of Nicosia, but they were closer to Nicosia, they were more rugged than the Troodos, and three of their peaks were capped with crusader castles.

Unfortunately, as Takis and Caitlyn had known but only this morning had seen for themselves, this favorite vista was no longer available from the Koniotises's rear terrace. Although their house was on a hilltop, it fronted on the west—still with beautiful sunset views of the Messaoria Plain descending to the Morphou Bay between the tail of the Kyrenia Range to the north and the distant Troodos Range to the south but now dominated by the arrival and departure of large airplanes. It thus had a line of building lots at its rear that fronted above the Makedonitissa Valley.

After they had moved into the house, which had been the second one to be built on the hilltop, the Koniotises's had tried, in vain, to acquire the lot behind their own villa in order to preserve their view over the city. But now a house had been built on both that lot and the plot of ground adjoining it toward the north, and the only view that had been left from the Koniotis terrace was of the tops of the highest Kyrenia peaks.

"You know, we're lucky in a way," volunteered Takis in an attempt to look on the bright side. "There really isn't as much air traffic as there would have been if the solar energy storage problem hadn't been solved and the petrol crisis wasn't deepening. This situation has been a boost for sea and land travel. Of course, RayGo will probably manage to equip air transport with solar energy storage soon and then we can expect more traffic into this airport."

"Thin consolation that, I'm afraid," Caitlyn answered in a disappointed tone. "I suppose it's true that you can never go back or stop the clock at a favored time."

Takis put his paper down and took Caitlyn's hand into his. "Would you really have wanted to stop the clock in the middle of the last decade or the one before that, Caitlyn? Was that time so much better than what we have seen and done since then?"

Caitlyn had to will herself not to drift off into one of her channeling visions back into the past. If only she could tell Takis. Indeed, there had been many periods in the slower-paced past on Cyprus where living had been better. She somehow knew that she had lived in some of these times in an earlier incarnation. But of course she couldn't speak to Takis—or anyone else now living—about this. The only one Caitlyn thought could have understood what she felt and the visions of the past that she had was Eleni Piccard. And now Eleni Piccard was part of that beyond-the-veil past.

"No, of course not. I guess losing most of what we loved about this house I inherited from Eleni Piccard is worth the life that you, I, and the boys have had since then. But we *were* happy here, Takis. You, I, and the boys. And now the boys are slipping away from us, and this house has lost its charm for me. I'd always had that to fall back on in all of our travels and moves and amid our separate, busy professional lives. I've always felt there was a slice of peace and quiet that was ours to come back to."

"We could always lease out this house and return to the Acropolis house my parents left me, you know. It's much closer to the Nicosia downtown area, but it's much quieter and more peaceful there then it is here just now."

"Yes, I suppose that's a possibility," Caitlyn answered moodily. "But I'm not sure it's the answer. Let's think about it; I would like to keep a retreat here in Cyprus, but I would want it to seem like a retreat. I'm afraid that Nicosia as a whole has become too busy and congested to qualify as a retreat."

Then she stood and began clearing the breakfast dishes onto a tray. "I guess I'd better check over my notes for the lecture tonight."

"No, wait, honey. Sit back down for a few minutes. We still have to talk about yesterday."

"You no longer are a policeman here, Takis, and I am not ready for a third degree." Caitlyn had reddened and stiffened, but she sat down as requested.

"Don't be so defensive, Caitlyn," her husband said soothingly. "I know you haven't done anything wrong, but I can never stop being a policeman, and the UN is no less concerned about this insidious counterfeiting operation than are the individual countries involved. If this is some sort of intentional move to undermine the world's major economies, it is succeeding all too well. All I need you to do is to tell me about each money transaction you made since you left New York and started your Mediterranean tour and who was present. I know you explained this all to the authorities last night, but I wasn't there."

And so Caitlyn explained how she flew out of New York and met up with Andriko Visiliou, Bill Burch, and Demetris Mattas in Rome for their lecture tour at ancient archaeological sites around the edge of Mediterranean that had taken in Italy, France, Spain, Algeria, the exciting new sites in Libya that were being uncovered now that the despotic rule of the deranged and isolationist colonel had come to an end, Egypt, Greece, and, last, Lebanon, where Beirut, the former Paris of the Middle East, had risen majestically from the ashes of decades of civil war and regional use as a political shuttlecock. And attached to the description of her activities at each ancient site was the best recollection she could give of her monetary transactions. Luckily, Caitlyn was organized in her thoughts, and, doubly luckily, she was not a "shopper."

". . . and so," Caitlyn was winding down, "I admit there was some mild surprise at the back of my mind that I still had so many U.S. banknotes when we reached Larnaca, but it didn't really register in my mind. I mean, all travelers anticipate that our money could be stolen or that we could have spent more than we thought we had, but who worries much about finding more money in their wallets than they thought they had?"

"Well, let me see what you have with you now."

"It's all in euro notes now, and, besides, they kept all that I had last night and exchanged everything for good notes from the bank exchange."

"Still, let me make sure that we're operating from a safe basis now."

Caitlyn returned with her purse, which opened and scattered its contents on the patio table.

"Damn. That clasp keeps opening," Caitlyn voiced in exasperation. "I'm going to have to use a different purse until I can get this one fixed."

"Did this happen to you during the trip?" Takis asked sharply.

"Yes, out on deck just as we were docking at the Larnaca sea terminal—and then, again, in my cabin as the porter was collecting my trunk. And he did take my trunk off the *Daphne* and out into the terminal, Takis." Caitlyn was still smarting from the skepticism that had met her claim the previous evening that her luggage had come off the ship twice.

"And who was in the vicinity at these times?" Takis chose to keep pursuing his point rather than be sidetracked by another issue.

"Well, only the porter in my cabin. But, when the purse opened out on deck, I'm afraid its contents scattered everywhere, and everyone who was nearby helped to pick things up. Let's see, there were Andriko, Demetris, and Bill Burch, of course. And then there was Ingrid Bittmann. And several other men. And, now that I think if it, two of those men . . ."

"Ingrid Bittmann?" Takis interjected. "Ingrid Bittmann Isaksen?"

"The very same. That was the first time I had seen her on the trip. She indicated she had embarked in Beirut the evening before. But, I was saying, Takis, two of the men at the ship's rail yesterday were faces that seemed very familiar to me. The young man who was with Ingrid was very definitely a Piccard. He looked just like Eleni. And then there was another man, a bit older but still under thirty, who was standing further down the rail. I couldn't figure out who he reminded me of, but he looked familiar too—and he seemed to recognize me as well when I caught him looking at me."

"And you think this was when your passport was lost?"

"It must have been. I had it when we went into Beirut for the lecture the previous day."

Takis was looking at the banknotes from Caitlyn's purse. "They all look fine to me. Let me go get my wallet and compare them with what I have."

He entered the house and went up to the master bedroom, but, instead of going straight to his bureau, he picked up the telephone, dialed the number of UNICIS headquarters. He managed to connect to Ellen and, after initial pleasantries, asked if the UNICIS computers could tap into the Piccard Shipping Lines databanks.

"Certainly," Ellen responded. "What are we looking for?"

"I need a complete passenger list for the *Daphne*'s last cruise around the Mediterranean—including where the passengers embarked and disembarked."

Ellen agreed to send the information to him within the next hour.

Takis returned to the terrace and compared the banknotes. All seemed to be fine. And, as he handed Caitlyn's money back to her, she suddenly sat up and burst forth. "Of course, that's why he was there when I was being questioned. Now I remember. One of the other men who was helping to pick up my things on the deck was that American diplomat, Will Whatshisname. Will Jacobs. I hadn't known him before he came into the customs shed to help me with the Cypriot police, and the tension of the moment blocked the memory of having seen him earlier on deck. Now, I wonder what *he* was doing on the *Daphne.*"

"As do I," Takis thought grimly to himself. "I'm even more interested now than ever to see that passenger list."

* * * *

Uri Lukenov had taken an early-morning tram to the RayGo headquarters building in the newly constructed urban area in the southern part of Famagusta. He wanted to set the search rolling before Ingrid Isaksen showed up at the office.

Once known as Varosha, the southern sector of Famagusta had, for two and half decades, been a deserted no-man's land abutting the UN controlled buffer zone but just inside the Turkish-occupied area. Varosha had been the island's first resort hotel coast, and it still provided the best beaches to be had on the island. All of the important, mid-rise hotels had started here. But, in the Turkish invasion of 1974, the mainland Turkish troops had gotten carried away as they chewed up Cypriot territory and had taken more ground to the south of the primarily Turkish-Cypriot populated ancient port of Famagusta than they had anticipated before they were stopped. When the lines were drawn, Varosha's resort area had wound up isolated between the two belligerents, the Turkish troops to the north and the mainland Greek-commanded Greek Cypriot national guard to the south.

For twenty-five years no one lived in Varosha's tower blocks. No one drove down its weed-infested streets. No one cared for its gardens. And no one, except adventuresome Turkish soldiers, swam off its lovely beaches.

Similarly, even though it continued to function as the main port of the internationally embargoed Turkish Cypriot pseudo state, Famagusta, to the north, also slept and waited for an improvement in its fortunes. After the reunification of the island, the RayGo corporation chose the Famagusta area primarily because of its strategic location vis-à-vis the Levant, where Beirut was reemerging once again as a major economic center for the region. Larnaca, on the island's southern coast, had also benefited in growth at this time, but what had once been Cyprus' major port, Limassol, located even further to the west, had picked this time to decline. Having overdeveloped its tourist sector construction without having maintained the development of its tourist amenities, its economy went into more serious recession than that of the rest of the island. The nail in the coffin of Limassol's dominance in shipping was a devastating earthquake that destroyed both its commercial port and the large marina that had just opened off its central seafront promenade.

Going for a combination of location and cheap land, the phenomenally growing RayGo Corporation latched onto the recently reopened Varosha area. Buying land, acquiring cheap leases, and cornering the market on construction companies, RayGo led the reconstruction of the island's southeast coast. While being careful to preserve what was left of the walled town of Famagusta, all of the old, decaying buildings in Varosha were pulled down and a RayGo-dominated city plan was developed and initiated. Now Varosha was an urban commercial center, dominated by glass-faced skyscrapers that backed a rim of "quaint" Cypriot-village-style seaside resort hotels. All of the best building and hotel locations, of course, were owned and occupied by RayGo.

The bedroom community for this planned city center, which, much like its predecessor, was virtually deserted at night and during the weekends, stretched out to the southeast. It had incorporated the former border-crossing village of Dherina and the weekend flats and villas of Paralimni and Protaras, and it had reached as far as the former monastery town, turned beach resort, of Ayia Napa, once famous as the location for Cyprus' first topless beach.

Just as a solar-powered monorail system now connected Famagusta with the central capital of Nicosia and thence on to Larnaca and Limassol and with the slowly growing western town of Morphou, a solar-powered tram system between the Varosha area of Famagusta and Ayia Napa transported all of the workers whose jobs had spun off from RayGo's international success from home to job and back every day.

When Uri arrived at the RayGo headquarters building, he was happy to see that the instructions on his employment had already been sent over from the Beirut office. He was to check in here before he went over to the Cassa Carioca nightclub, which he was to manage and which had been established in the old Palm Beach Hotel, a choice beach site, where the old walled city of Famagusta abutted the Varosha resort sector.

But, while he was here, he wanted to touch base with that RayGo records system official he had met—and bedded— in Beirut and get his real agenda going.

Chris Tzavella had a small office on the fourteenth floor of the RayGo building. The glass wall gave a panoramic view that took in the entire walled city and proceeded out, over the port, to the Mediterranean.

"I said you'd be the first one I'd contact when I got to Cyprus, and here I am," laughed Uri as Chris closed the office door and approached the ruggedly handsome Russian.

"I know you really came to see my files," Chris whispered huskily, "but first I want a bit of what you gave me in Beirut the other night."

The next few minutes were taken up with a hurried sampling of what the two had shared at greater length, depth, and with lustful ingenuity in the fourth-floor Holiday Inn room overlooking the Beirut corniche three nights previously.

After a bit Chris pulled away, walked over to a computer station, and turned it on.

"I know you're trying to find someone here, and I've isolated some immigration and customs files for you to consider. It was quite an indiscretion for me to tell you that RayGo had been tapping into all of the computer files in Cyprus, but . . . it was worth it." And at this the records official turned with a teasing smile and pulled Uri over the computer.

"Since I talked with you about this, I've decided that there's a particular file I would like to see."

"Name it, lover, anything on Cyprus is yours."

"What about Beirut? Can you get me into the files of the Beirut office of the Piccard Shipping Corporation."

"Ah, the Piccards," intoned Chris. "The personal favorites of Ms. Isaksen for the past several weeks. Let's see. I know the Piccard files here in Cyprus were an early target for acquisition. Ah, yes, here they are. What exactly are we looking for?"

"The Beirut Piccards' connections with the Hizballah terrorist group. Specifically names and whereabouts of individuals and dates of operations," responded Uri, as he walked up very closely behind Chris and looked into the computer monitor.

Chris whistled and swung around until the two were eye-to-eye and belly-to-belly. "Hmm. Very special. And not just a little dangerous. I may require some intensive tension-releasing sessions to be able to provide this information. How about tomorrow evening?"

"How about right now?" Uri answered huskily, as his arm swept the top of the desk clean.

* * * *

All conversation stopped and all heads snapped too as Iranian General Ujay Khahalbi entered the intelligence service's main computer room. Of all of Iran's military leaders, he was probably the one that dealt out the roughest—and the most capricious—punishment for infractions real and imagined. And he had such strong connections with the clerics and was involved in so many different favored foreign operations that it was unlikely he was to fall from power any time soon. Not, of course, unless his scheme to undermine the economies of the Americans and the Europeans fell through, and that didn't presently look like it was likely to happen.

He strode to the center of the room and, without having to ask, was handed the reports that had been sent in over the past several hours.

"Ah, the report on the American," he mused as he leafed through the reports. "The Cyprus agent was right. The American is well-placed for this. I wonder, though, if it would be wise to use her again. Perhaps she is too close to the hive. I'll have to take the issue up with the others."

Turning to his aide, he tossed the sheaf of reports, which was dexterously caught, and then moved on down the aisle to his favorite computer hacker. There was the other matter to attend to. The agent had been missing now for over two months without reporting in. Khahalbi was not at all comfortable with loose ends. This one would have to be put back in place or snipped very soon. Khahalbi didn't care how senior or necessary she was.

* * * *

Andre Piccard drank another cup of coffee as he finished dressing. He still had to finish packing and to have the porter summoned to take his luggage down to the marina. Ingrid had already left for Famagusta. Their parting had been a bit perfunctory on both sides. Andre hadn't been in the mood to play the role of boy toy today, and Ingrid's mind had already been racing ahead to the agenda of her day.

As close as either of them had gotten to emotion was as she was finishing her breakfast and tried to connect to Uri Lukenov's lower-floor apartment to offer him a ride to Famagusta. The servant had informed her that Uri had already left a couple of hours earlier for Famagusta. She was visibly disappointed and Andre could hardly keep a sad face. She might eventually rein the handsome Russian in, Andre thought, but it would be a contest. The realization, however, that he had not made—correction, had not been permitted to make—a contest of his own subordination to Ingrid soured his morning, and he decided to go directly back to his own company headquarters in Limassol for the day.

He declined Ingrid's offer to accompany her to the RayGo headquarters building in Famagusta and to work on his Piccard Corporation affairs from there. She, with exaggerated generosity, offered him the full use of a complete business suite, with assistant and secretary, saying that she could hardly bear to part with him for even a couple of hours. Andre had earlier accepted Ingrid's offer of the use of an office near hers, but he knew that she was primarily interested in snaring his company for RayGo—or, more likely, for herself—and he also knew that any secretary or assistant assigned to him would really be working for Isaksen.

Therefore, Andre kept his distance from Ingrid as much as possible on business affairs, and, while Ingrid was motoring up to Famagusta in her private Mercedes limousine, Andre was preparing to take a hydrofoil to Limassol, whose declining commercial center his family had thus far refused to abandon as its Cyprus headquarters. Andre thought bitterly that as a mark of RayGo's control, he'd probably be forced to move the company headquarters to Famagusta soon. Already most of the shipping was operating out of Larnaca or Famagusta and all of the family-owned hotel and export-related businesses in Cyprus that were still profitable were located outside Limassol.

This couldn't go on much longer, Andre thought. He had promised to attend an important dinner with Ingrid in Nicosia tonight—and he would go there straight from Limassol. But he wasn't sure he would return here with her tonight. He might be willing to go through with this if he really thought this would save the independence of the Piccards' Cyprus—and even their Lebanese—holdings, but he was not so convinced. He would almost rather fight RayGo and Isaksen in the open.

"Yes, maybe instead of coming back here with Ingrid tonight, I'll go on up to Kakopetria and try to talk some sense into the old man. Someone has to try. He has no reason to care about the Piccard holdings much longer. But I do."

* * * *

"There, I think that may get you what you want."

In a very business-like manner, Chris exited the computer file, turned to the printer, and handed Uri several sheets of paper.

Uri was almost immobilized with nervous tension. He tentatively held out his hand and took the papers. So long. He had been searching so long, and it had been this simple. Of course, he realized that maybe it wasn't really that simple after all. Perhaps this was a red herring and that the one he sought was somewhere else altogether. But these had been the innermost of the Piccard Beirut headquarters' files. Chris had been sure that they had no idea their files had been compromised, although the records official had emitted a worrisome "uh, oh" while the file was being accessed.

Now that Uri remembered this, he had to ask. "What seemed to be wrong while you were in that file just now?"

"It's probably nothing. Don't worry."

"I was raised to worry. What did you see in the file?"

"It wasn't really what I saw in the file," Chris replied. "It was what I saw in the access symbol."

Uri was lost, and he looked the part.

Chris walked around, pushed him into a chair and started massaging his shoulders. "The access symbol started blinking while we were in the file."

"So?" Uri responded in exasperation.

"Well, that means someone else was in the file too."

"Someone else was in the file?" Uri exploded.

"Yes, but it could have been only a coincidence."

"A coincidence!? Didn't you see what was in that file and all the explosive operational material? Nobody else would be accessing that file just for browsing purposes. They probably were in it for the same reason we were. Hold on a minute. If we could tell they were in the file, could they also tell that someone else was in the file?"

"Certainly, unless their equipment was really primitive," Chris replied, "in which case they probably couldn't have accessed the file at all."

All of this computer security mumbo jumbo was giving Uri a headache, and the records official didn't seem particularly upset, so Uri refocused on his own concerns. "Thanks, Christiana, you're a doll," Uri said with genuine thanks as he strode toward the door. "You have been a life saver—and I may, unfortunately, mean that quite literally. I've got to go now and follow up this lead."

"And this is probably the last I'll see of you?" Chris asked poutingly.

"Hell no," Uri responded as he walked back to her and gave her a deep kiss. "The night after tomorrow—my place. Just as we agreed."

Uri had not lasted this long without having had very good survival techniques. Christiana Tzavella had been quite a big help, but she also was now quite a big encumbrance, especially if she became displeased with Uri and chose to share with others what she had found for him in the Piccards' highly classified Beirut computer files.

Chapter Six

Caitlyn Koniotis's Interior Ministry–sponsored lecture that evening at the presidential palace for an exclusive high-level audience had promised to mark a major transition in Cyprus' ambitious archaeological program, and Caitlyn didn't disappoint. In cooperation with Dr. Andriko Visiliou, Cyprus' long-time Archaeology Department director, and her old friend, Maria Mattas, who had risen to the position of interior minister, Caitlyn had spearheaded the reasoned, comprehensive exploration and preservation of Cyprus' prodigious archaeological heritage on the one hand and the tasteful and protected melding of the accessibility of these treasures to visitors to Cyprus on the other hand.

Here a visit to one era of the past was never a great distance from either the site of another era or, for that matter, from one's hotel or a restaurant, shops, the sea, or the mountains.

Caitlyn's vision and her strong sense of organization had served her in good stead in this endeavor. She often was heard to say that it was only the "primary perplexing problem" of archaeology that plagued the development of Cyprus' archaeological heritage in such a way that balanced preservation with discovery, research, and public accessibility. Cyprus was, in fact, almost too rich in history.

Throughout her years of work on the island, both she and Andriko Visiliou continuously struggled with the double problems of what to claim in the name of heritage and how far down—and through what other historical eras—to dig. Caitlyn was a realist. She lived in the present and she enjoyed modern life. She soon discovered when she arrived in Cyprus, however, that there likely was a rich archaeological treasure trove under every existing building—and sometimes there was more than one down there, at different layers of time.

She herself had once discovered an ancient royal tomb complex in the hillside lot across the street from Takis's family home in downtown Nicosia and had had to endure the understandable opposition to preserve this site that had come from her neighbors, who simply wanted to build their dream house on the lot they owned. If everything on Cyprus of historical interest was preserved, there would be no room left for current habitation, they reasoned.

The other dilemma was that previous eras had also constructed their lives on top of the remains of their ancestors—more often than not even putting the building material of their forerunners to new uses. Once the archaeological authorities had successfully designated a site as a historical preservation site, they themselves faced a serious decision concerning just what historical era was to be preserved. It was always painful to have to destroy the discovered site of an ancient habitation to reach down to another era—even if you were able to save the artifacts associated with the site. But it was doubly painful to reach farther than the actual habitation of the site, to dig through several layers of important archaeological eras only to reach virgin bedrock before reaching the era you had chosen to unearth.

Facing such dilemmas, one natural and far cheaper response, especially if archaeological funding is scarce, is not to excavate at all. And this essentially had been Cyprus' response to the issue since its independence in 1960. Most of the archaeological excavation projects in Cyprus prior to the twenty-first century had been conducted by foreign investors and expeditions and had been isolated to areas that could easily be marked for historical preservation. In many of these cases, the fruits of the excavating had been carted away from Cyprus. That was no longer tolerated by the Cypriots.

With Caitlyn's help, the Cypriot authorities had coalesced to approach the exploitation of the island's archaeological heritage in a logical and creative—and, as she was able to prove to them, profitable—fashion. The Ledra Foundation, the philanthropic charity that had been formed by Eleni Piccard with Piccard family financing to support the exploration and resurgence of Cyprus' heritage, had helped. Not only had it helped underwrite Caitlyn's original Fulbright grant research tour to Cyprus, but it had also actively backed her efforts to organize the reasoned archaeological exploitation of the island. Most important, it had existed, along with the work of Andriko Visiliou, as the manifestation of Cypriot interest in and ultimate control over this endeavor. Although she was the inspiration and bellwether in this process, Caitlyn was careful not to claim center stage and to point to and applaud the genuinely central role the Cypriots themselves were taking in this program. The reformation of the island into a unified federation—albeit still a little tenuous—had also helped tremendously in the process

As the culmination of this several-phased approach to archeology on the island, the Cyprus Museum had developed an exhibition model plan—largely with the help of developing computer technology—to tackle the nagging problem of having to sacrifice the preservation of subsequent layers of significant civilization to reach the chosen era. Although only the chosen era could be preserved in situ, careful excavation and computer assistance had permitted the precise databanking of the foundations of each era of habitation as layers were stripped away at archaeological sites. In all cases new computer graphing permitted a visitor to visualize what existed at each level as it was stripped away. These computer modules were available either at and within view of the site itself or in the expanded Cyprus Museum's library. For some of the most important sites, life-size dioramas, which included the actual artifacts unearthed from each era, of each unearthed and subsequently bypassed layer, had been created.

Two even more impressive—and highly successful tourist-drawing—uses of this model now existed on the island. In the ancient Greco-Roman cultural capital of Paphos, on the western coast, one site had been occupied by places of worship from the current era, represented by an Anglican chapel, all the way back to animistic worship at the dawn of time. This site had long been recognized as significant. This was based primarily in modern time on its biblical connection with St. Paul, who had journeyed to Cyprus, had been scourged at a pillar of the temple that had then been located on this spot, and had eventually converted the governor of Paphos in the first-recorded Christian conversion of a ruling government official.

In recognition of the importance of various eras at the site, the archaeologists of the mid twentieth century had valiantly tried to compromise with the dilemma of what to preserve and what to destroy in search of the most important—but by whose definition?—era. They had excavated the site at an angle, digging at one end, and progressively leaving layers intact toward the other end upon which the Anglican chapel currently was perched. In this approach, every era was represented, but none—other than the most recent house of worship—was completely exposed.

In recent times, technology had come to help, if not to the rescue, because, having been partially excavated already down to beyond the Greek era, comprehensive rescue was no longer an option. Using a nearby site, educated guesses, using computer reconstruction techniques, were made in the construction of full-size replicas of the structures that had stood on the original site during the various high points of history. This was done, of course, following the heart-rending decision that anything of archaeological value under the exhibit's site would now be lost. Treasures existed under every square inch of Paphos. The result was a virtual theme park that delighted the tourist interested in traveling back in time—which constituted the bulk of the tourists who now came to Cyprus—while serving as a serious classroom for serious students of archaeology, who also were now coming to Cyprus in droves from the four corners of the earth.

The other theme-park use of the model in Cyprus was even more inventive and impressive. Following the freedom from virtual international isolation of the Turkish-held portion of Cyprus by the island's political settlement, a major new, multiera archaeological site had been found on the island's east coast. The archaeological interest in this area of the island had long been focused on the sites at Engomi and Salamis, so the site at the hilltop above the traditional smuggler's port of Bogaz farther north, on the eastern coast at the base of the long Karpas Peninsula jutting into the underbelly of the Turkish mainland, had gone unnoticed for centuries. Engomi, on the east coast of Cyprus about six miles northwest of the present-day Famagusta and about two miles inland, had once been a major city state of the late Bronze Age (2700–1050 BC), at which time it was known as Alasia. It had been excavated in the late nineteenth century by British archaeologists, who had also discovered that it had been the center of a major Mycenean settlement engaged in metals trade throughout the eastern Mediterranean. Using modern computer-assisted seismic methods to probe even deeper into the site without disturbing the Greco-Roman excavations, however, Dr. Visiliou and his team had been astounded to find layer after layer of civilizations that extended back to the Paleolithic Period (prior to 7000 BC) and possibly even earlier into the era of unresearched human time. This had extended the advent of the civilization of Cyprus farther back into time than had been found anywhere else on the island.

In the most daring, modern, and ambitious excavation process that was now being used anywhere in the world, the Cypriots, with the new-found funding of the RayGo multinational corporation, had constructed a multifloored exhibition hall directly at the site and had, using new processes, managed to literally separate and lift the various major levels of civilization at the site to different floor levels, twelve in all, that enabled researchers and tourists alike to view any and all levels of the site in as close to an in-situ condition as probably would ever be possible, at the press of an elevator button. The curious and studious alike were descending on this site in droves from all corners of the world, and the southern coastal area of the once nearly deserted and isolated Karpas Peninsula was now enjoying the fastest growth rate in tourist dollar and beach resort hotel construction of any sector of the country.

The planned commercialization of the island's archaeological heritage within the bounds of proper preservation and good taste had constituted the third phase of the development plan devised by Caitlyn and Dr. Visiliou in cooperation with the Ledra Foundation. With the help of the interior minister, Maria Mattas, and enhanced financial backing from RayGo, the government planning and tourist development sectors had been brought into the plan and had been convinced to cooperate with each other to revive the island's seriously depressed tourist industry on the basis of not just the island's not-so-sandy beaches but also on a coordinated offering of beach, mountains, friendly and good service, a developed—thanks to the Ledra Foundation—handicraft industry, pleasant scenery, relaxed ambiance, *and* the most understandable and readily accessible trip into the rich archaeological heritage of Western Civilization. Despite the unexpected competition for Cyprus to urbanize beyond touristic interest that had resulted from the phenomenal success of RayGo's discovery and marketing of the solar energy storage capabilities, this coordinated plan had been successful beyond anyone's dreams.

And now here, tonight, on the rostrum in the presidential palace ballroom in the Strovolos suburb of Nicosia, Caitlyn Koniotis was unveiling the fourth, and final stage of the plan. The lecture tour around the rim of the Mediterranean, with Andriko Visiliou, Bill Burch, and Demetris Mattas in tow, had been the stage setter. Her husband, Takis, was looking up at her in adoring approval, and her colleagues, long-time friends in Cyprus, government officials whose programs had been aided by this process, and those from the business community whose pockets had been lined deeply with euros with the help of this process were all looking up at her with various degrees and aspects of respect, anticipation, and hope—and possibly of envy.

Although the very select audience was relatively small, both local media journalists and networks and those of Greece, Turkey, Lebanon, Egypt, Iran, and of various international media organizations were on hand to broadcast any interesting nuggets of information from this ballyhooed lecture to the world.

And there were more than enough nuggets The first nugget came in the research section of her speech, where Caitlyn proposed—not as a publicity-hungry crank but as one of the most respected, archaeologists in the world—that evidence existed that the cradle of civilization, whether or not it was the Garden of Eden, may have been located on the island of Cyprus. Not on the island of Cyprus as we know it today, she went on to say when the gasps and murmurings of the spell-bound audience had died out, but on the island that had existed where the Kyrenia Mountains now were and in the eons of time before soil from the Kyrenia mountain range island to the north and the Troodos mountain range island to the south had silted down and formed the Mesaoria Plain area between them.

Into the fascinated silence, Caitlyn revealed to the public for the first time that, following the discovery of the archaeological site at Bogaz that was eventually dated to an earlier era than had previously been known on the island, the Archaeology Department had taken two initiatives. It had, first, revisited most of the known sites around the island with its new computer-assisted seismic equipment and had shown that many of the established historical excavations, in fact, actually dated back much farther than was previously thought. This study had been revealed to the public.

The other study, however, was being announced tonight for the first time. A few years previously—the last time Caitlyn herself had visited the island in a visit that was publicized as a low-key private trip—Andriko, Caitlyn, and the senior excavators of the Archaeology Department had taken their new equipment up into the Kyrenia Mountains from the Bogaz site. They had done so on a hunch, albeit a highly educated hunch, by Caitlyn, whose hunches had previously proved to be uncannily accurate. There, outside a village now named Ardhana, on the slope of the Kyrenia mountain chain as it descends to hills and peters out at the base of the Karpas Peninsula, the team had found a promising site. They had dug in secrecy, their equipment having given good indication that they would find evidence of human habitation that went back farther than current records of human existence. They had found more or less what the new computer equipment said they might find. They found evidence of a time, beyond known time, when this area, now high on the mountain slope, had actually been at sea level. Geologically, this did not surprise them. However, what surprised them was the evidence of human habitation at the same time.

While telling her audience—which would now be the entire world—that there was no claim that this was the cradle of civilization, she strongly and authoritatively asserted that the research was finished and in hand that would now require other areas considered for the honor, including an area of China, an area of India, the delta between the Tigris and Euphrates Rivers in Iraq, and the island of Bahrain in the Persian Gulf, to push their evidence of habitation back even farther than they had to this time. She urged this work to proceed, using the same highly sophisticated tools the Cypriot archaeologists were using.

On the more human side, she said that the centuries of discussing the island of Cyprus as either a stepping stone or enslaved possession of the other major civilizations of the region, as well as the historical propensity of its own major ethnic groups to consider themselves as either Greeks or Turks rather than Cypriots, had probably colored its role as receiver rather than originator. She asked her audience to look at Cyprus afresh in considering whether it could have had a foundational role in human civilization. She noted that it was one of the largest, most easily habitable, and most strategically located islands in an area of a protected sea that had long been acknowledged to have been the development cradle of many of the more complex, sophisticated civilizations of the world. In addition, popular legends still lived that linked human civilization with the island as far back as Noah and the flood. She did not ask her audience to believe human life had started in Cyprus; she merely pointed to the scientific evidence that the Cypriot archaeologists had constructed to indicate that other contenders had their homework cut out for them.

As she turned in her lecture from the world of scientific research to real-world applications, Caitlyn dropped her other golden nugget, which electrified her entrepreneur-heavy audience. The lecture tour around the rim of the Mediterranean had not only been conducted as a stage setter for her revelation about the foundational archaeological site at Ardhana, a name that was remote no longer but would now, overnight, enter the vocabulary of most of the literate portion of the world's population. In the primary archaeological centers of the region, Caitlyn, Andriko Visiliou, and head of the American Archaeological Institute in Cyprus, Bill Burch, had also been privately revealing their research concerning Ardhana and making offers.

Tonight, in the second half of her lecture, Caitlyn formally proposed the formation of a major—probably *the* major—international archaeology teaching institute in Cyprus. RayGo and the Ledra Foundation had pledged more than sufficient financing, and Caitlyn, Visiliou, and Burch had tentatively recruited what would be the world's foremost faculty and research staff. Caitlyn herself would hold a professorship—with the permission of Colombia University, of course, which did not fancy the prospect of losing her altogether if they did not agree—but she planned only to be in Cyprus for one semester each year. If Cyprus wants to, Caitlyn offered demurely, with a look toward the Cypriot president, Cyprus can now become the premier archaeological study center of Europe, possibly of the world.

If Cyprus wanted to? The president had, of course, already been informed of the events and certainly wanted the center. The eyes of the entrepreneurs in the audience, blinded by visions of money that would result in many strange and wonderful ways from such a development, bugged out in assent. The CEO of RayGo looked up from her front-row seat with considerably more control. But, of course, Ingrid Bittmann Isaksen was just as pleased as the rest of the entrepreneurs as she laced her fingers through those of Andre Piccard—whose position with the Piccard holdings on Cyprus also made him the chairman of the sponsoring Ledra Foundation—and sighed a contented sigh. Not only was this good for her ego and, secondarily, in her concern for RayGo's business, but she also had already obtained agreement the archaeological center would move into the Middle Eastern University compound outside of Famagusta that she had bought and would now clear and that was very much under her control.

Caitlyn was radiant during the cocktail hour that followed her lecture and that preceded the even more exclusive dinner that the Cypriot president was hosting for Caitlyn and her friends and for the Cyprus Archaeology Department's benefactors. Her presentation had been an unqualified success, and the establishment of Cyprus at the center of the archaeology studies world was a culmination of a dream that she had had for many years. It was one that she had once discussed with her friend and mentor during her first year in Cyprus, the tragic Eleni Piccard, who had founded the Ledra Foundation based on just such dreams for Cyprus and who had suffered cruelly from political events in Cyprus and had been murdered brutally by her own former lover.

Although Caitlyn and Eleni had not known each other long enough to become best friends, and Caitlyn's eyes had not been closed to Eleni's own schemes and cruelty toward others, in terms of vision about Cyprus and its historical heritage, the two had quickly become as one. This had been a bond that had resulted in Caitlyn having inherited Eleni's Cypriot handicraft-filled villa on the Makedonitissa hilltop. The besmirching of the villa's ambiance by the progress of time and the settlement of political differences from which Eleni herself had cruelly suffered only heightened Caitlyn's frustration that she had lost her love for the house.

In any event, nothing that was happening in her life was intruding in Caitlyn's focused enjoyment of her hour of triumph and congratulations following her presidential palace lecture. Nothing, that was, until Andriko Visiliou inadvertently caused her smile to freeze and lines that were beginning to intrude across her brow to deepen when, during a lull in her chit chat with adoring colleagues and acquaintance, he said that he certainly hoped her announcement would not be linked with and tainted by her mistaken arrest the day before at the Larnaca sea terminal for passing counterfeit U.S. banknotes. Caitlyn willed the remark away, however, banishing it from consciousness as only a strong-willed person can do, and pretended she had not even heard Andriko's remark. Immediately shocked himself by what he had blurted out, Andriko was greatly relieved that Caitlyn apparently hadn't even heard him.

But if Caitlyn had heard the conversation that was transpiring even then not more than twenty feet from where she stood, even her unusually strong will would not have been able to banish the concern. One that could now be called a colleague of hers, even if perhaps not in quite the same terms as the others who were swirling around her at this moment, sharing the glow of her success, was receiving instructions that were being delivered in quiet tones by the on-the-spot commentator of the Iranian television crew that had been sent to cover the event, at some surprise to the president's security detail. General Khahalbi wanted one outlet pressed into service again and he wanted another one reactivated or terminated.

The interior minister, a brilliant former police investigator in her own right, had ordered that the actions of the Iranian media crew should be watched and that anything suspicious should be reported back to her, but the Iranian commentator had proven to be such a friendly, outgoing, and loquacious chap that one of his short conversations with a business person, a government official, or a diplomat looked much the same as the next.

One opportunity to cut painlessly to the chase down— unless the surveillance agent should become more analytical and reflective over the next couple of days, which he had been trained to do before he was entrusted with this line of duty. If Maria Solonos Mattas herself had been conducting this surveillance, matters would certainly have taken a different route.

Chapter Seven

"A euro for your thoughts."

"Not a counterfeit one, I hope," Caitlyn responded wanly, as she turned toward the approaching Demetris Mattas. Mattas offered her a cigarette and she declined. She had not come out onto the stone balcony of the presidential palace to indulge in nicotine, although her nerves definitely needed easing. Andriko's remark on her brush with the police authorities the previous night had come back to haunt her, and she had wanted to be alone for a few minutes to calm herself. The stars in the clear sky of the Nicosia suburb had almost done the trick. And then Demetris approached with another innocent comment that had, instead, cut her to the quick.

"You mustn't let what happened yesterday disturb your night of triumph, Caitlyn," Demetris spoke to her in a fatherly fashion, although she was a bit older than he was. "That was just a fluke that could happen to anyone and won't touch your life again. In fact, I know for a fact—because of *Semerini*'s news coverage—that many quite respectable and well-placed people have been used to pass counterfeit money in this current case."

"Is it . . . a fluke? Has nothing to do with me? Or perhaps it has something to do with who I'm married to? I wonder," Caitlyn responded almost absentmindedly, as she dug a finger into a crevice in the stone pillar she was leaning against. "Hmm. It looks like they need to do a patching job on this stonework."

"That's there on purpose," Demetris smiled, "as an illustration for history—and it can serve nicely now as a reminder that all problems are relative."

Caitlyn looked up at the journalist with curiosity.

"That's a bullet hole, Caitlyn. You may remember that there was a mainland Greece-inspired coup against the Greek Cypriot president, Archbishop Makarios, just prior to the 1974 Turkish invasion of the island. This palace was completely burned out then. They have since rebuilt and restored within the existing stone shell of the building, but they have kept these stone pillars the way their own folly in turning away from democracy had left them. Now, in comparison with the folly that this building has seen, how does your brush with the police in an innocent misunderstanding stand up?"

"Thanks, Demetris, that helped," Caitlyn smiled as she pushed away from the stone railing. "Now, put out that disgusting cigarette, and let's go back in. I can see through the windows that the chosen few are pointed at the dining room."

* * * *

Caitlyn looked timidly up from her soup course and tried to focus on Takis, who had been seated across from her but many miles down the legendary mahogany table that had seen nearly as many negotiating sessions as state dinners. She could see her husband, but she could also see that he was just as awed and as flustered as she was. The reason for that, or rather half of the reason, sat at one end of the table and immediately at Takis's left. The other half sat at the other end of the table and immediately to Caitlyn's left. Caitlyn was an honored guest of the president, but Takis was an equally honored guest of Cyprus, so he had been seated by the vice president.

The president and vice president of the FSC, the Federated State of Cyprus, could not have been any more different if they had set out to represent opposite visages and viewpoints, which, as a matter of fact, may have had a large ring of truth to it. And the basic difference was their ethnic origin. Neither Takis nor Caitlyn had ever imagined they would live to see a Greek Cypriot president of Cyprus sitting at the same table and sharing a meal with a Turkish Cypriot vice president of Cyprus, even though this did not set a precedent. Rather, for the entire period of the previous republic's history, that arrangement had been a constitutional stipulation, which nevertheless had been honored longer in the breach than in fact.

The relative young—meaning not yet quite fifty—Greek-ethnic Cypriot president was the vivacious, outgoing daughter of a Cypriot president and granddaughter of an anti-British colonial revolutionary hero. What was really amazing was that she was just in the middle of her first term as the first president of the fairly young FSC. Chrystalla Ioannou had risen to power on all of the wrong issues in a country where the traditions of paternalism and male dominance were never far below the surface. She had been a socialist fighter for the rights of woman and children in an era when the sanctity of the family unit was still permitted to hide a myriad of abuses. As a member of Parliament during her own father's six-year term as president, she had consistently and strongly pursued the strengthening of labor and environmental laws and had constantly pushed the agenda of settling the political division of the island nation in such a way that would protect the lives and welfare of both the majority Greeks and the minority Turks.

Her father had also been known as a good-faith negotiator for the unification of the island, but he never quite had been able to compromise in either his own mind or with the cooperation of his party and supporters to the level of serious unification talks. It had been largely skill and perseverance that had brought Chrystalla Ioannou to the political forefront, with, admittedly just a slight touch of nepotism—which was quite acceptable in Mediterranean politics. However, it had also come about with a large dose of irony. Although Ioannou prepared her political strategy well and had the support of both her own reform party and the strong party her father led, almost as many ballots of ill will as of support had been cast in her name. Throughout her political career she had been plagued by old-line politicians who refused to take her seriously and who, at her own election time and without strong candidates of their own, had voted in the "uppity little bitch" to see her fall on her face once and for all. But she hadn't fallen on her face; she had forged a political settlement. However much preparation and skill had played in her rise to political power in the Cyprus Republic, luck had played a bigger part in Ioannou's ability to spearhead the (somewhat) peaceful reunification of the country.

Behind the scenes had been an old friend of both Takis and Caitlyn. The preeminent Near East negotiator for the United Nations, Eric Isaksen, had shuttled quietly between all of the capitals of the region and of Europe and the United States, deftly weaving possibilities with promises until the threads of external influences on a Cyprus settlement had been woven into whole cloth. In front of the scenes, taking all of the credit, with the full cooperation of Eric, had been his wife, the UN undersecretary for political affairs, Ingrid Bittmann Isaksen.

In the end it was neither the Turkish troops nor the collapse of the Turkish economy that provided the catalyst for the move toward settlement within Cyprus. It was the collapse and death at the dinner table one night of the 350-pound, long-time Turkish Cypriot "president." Settlement via cholesterol. Some say it was a cream cake that killed the Turkish Cypriot "president." Those who were present, however, knew that between the meat and desert courses he had received word that the bulk of the Turkish troops were being withdrawn, as they were needed on the mainland. The decision was presented convincingly as irrevocable, and, although it might have looked like the "president" was choking on whipped cream, he actually was enjoying the last of a series of irritation-induced coronaries he had managed to keep secret.

His successor, Lala Hatan, the only businessman of any wealth left in the north—and the successor by right of the number of loans he held in the Turkish Cypriot community—sold concessions in a political settlement with the Greeks on the basis of turning the economy around with the clearly evident support for life and limb openly offered by various major powers, NATO, and the United Nations. This was a reasonable gamble in faith, he told his constituents, who were already tied to him by impossibly high debt to the point that they had little other choice. He failed to tell them that he—and they—also faced a firm and not-too-distant deadline to protect their own futures before Ankara withdrew its troops from the island.

Thus, the Turkish Cypriot north made the first substantive concessions. The two sides agreed to reopen the Nicosia International Airport, then locked in the UN-guarded buffer zone in the west of the capital city, which was effected when the Turkish Cypriots agreed not to shoot down planes landing there. The most substantive trade-off had come in an exchange of land for an agreement of a local self-rule arrangement that would go a long way toward protecting the lives of the minority Turkish Cypriots. The Turkish Cypriots turned over to the Greek Cypriots the towns of Morphou, the center of the citrus industry near the west coast, and Varosha, the former tourist resort area immediately to the south of the eastern coastal port of Famagusta. In return, the Greek Cypriots agreed to a confederal system of government that permitted Turkish local self-rule in a northern segment of the island and combined Turkish and Greek rule in two other cantons and in the national government.

Having established these agreements, the other major forces then came in to provide the cement for settlement. The final agreements were guaranteed, as had the earlier ultimately broken agreements been, by the Greeks, the Turks, the UK, the United States, and the Cypriot factions themselves. But in a solidifying act, NATO and the European Community also signed as guarantors.

In spite of these initial agreements, the pressuring of the UN, the World Bank, the EU, and several major nations, the talks between the two Cypriot factions, held, as all such talks were, at the historic Ledra Palace Hotel that had been locked in the buffer zone near the old Nicosia city walls, had been tough going. Moves toward settlement were opposed by the entrenched of both sides, which refused either to forget the despicable acts the other side had inflicted on their relations and friends in the past or to venture out of their ethnic strongholds.

Even though the mainland Greeks and Turks kept their word and stayed out of the struggle, other elements in the region did not. Many nefarious forces, the same organizations Takis Koniotis had been fighting for years, first as a Cypriot police official and later as a UN official, fought hard behind the scenes as well as in front of them to prevent unification. And they fought dirty. It was not in the interest of such forces as the Iranian-backed Hizballah guerrilla organization based in Lebanon and the Russian mafia that had infiltrated Cyprus for the north and the south of the island to unify. Both—the Hizballah for political terrorism purposes and the Russian mafia for illicit money-making purposes—wanted the island to remain divided so that their activities could take advantage of the limited cooperation of the two belligerents and the dearth of information that flowed between the two.

What these forces couldn't affect in influence, they tried to affect in action. Thus, it was during this period that the Hizballah attacked and nearly wiped out the workers in the headquarters of the United Nations International Crimes Investigation Service, the office Takis Koniotis had established in the UN buffer zone several years earlier near the abandoned Nicosia International Airport runways.

However, under the open guidance of Ingrid Bittmann and the unseen hand of Eric Isaksen, the Greek Cypriot and Turkish Cypriot negotiators persevered. The many years of building contact between Greek Cypriots and Turkish Cypriots who shared interests and visions eventually paid off.

Both the most tragic and the most unifying event of the settlement talks had come on a beautiful April morning after the signing of the education section of the agreement when all had gathered on the front steps of the Ledra Palace Hotel for photographs. The historic photograph of the occasion would show many happy faces with just one tragic flaw. Near the center of photograph would appear what might have been taken as a domestic dispute. Ingrid Bittmann could be seen pushing on the sleeve of her husband, Eric Isaksen, as if objecting to him trying to upstage her on this important occasion. Her permanently recorded look was venomous, and those who had known both

Ingrid and Eric well took some satisfaction that her true nature was revealed in this way in an historic photograph. Eric's face was more focused. He was looking intently up and to the left and was elbowing himself in front of his wife.

What the fast film on the camera did not reveal were the two bullets that entered Eric's body immediately afterward, or the body that had shielded Ingrid Bittmann from harm slump lifelessly to the entry stairs to the Ledra Palace Hotel, or the UN soldiers storming the Mula Bastion on the Nicosia old city walls in a vain search for the assassin or assassins, later identified via the cooperation of the worlds' crime-fighting organizations as paid assassins of elements of the Russian mafia.

The death of Eric Isaksen, who selflessly saved the key UN negotiator Ingrid Bittmann but never was fully credited in public—although certainly credited by those leaders who were directly involved in the process—as the real force behind the Cyprus settlement, steeled the will of the Cypriots of both the Greek and Turkish communities to effect their settlement. They had both come to recognize that this move was in their mutual and separate interests. And they were determined that they would live henceforth as Cypriots, not as pawns of Greece or Turkey, and certainly not as the puppets of terrorists or international criminals.

Looking toward the other end of the table at Vice President Lala Hatan, Caitlyn was struck again by the differences between the two leaders of Cyprus. Whereas Chrystalla Ioannou had inherited her position in politics and had worked hard to reach the political pinnacle while training to remain a champion of liberal causes, Hatan had started at the top in politics. While Ioannou was a trim, vivacious, relatively young intellectual, Hatan was heavy from overindulgence, with a swarthy complexion, a ready sneer and insult, and a gimlet eye that sought out and followed the movement of any beautiful woman—any beautiful woman, that is, except Chrystalla Ioannou, whom he openly detested as a "bleeding-heart socialist."

This did not mean that Hatan was stupid or obstructionist, however. He had been a brilliant entrepreneur, who had grown up in London (no one could actually be sure he actually had any Turkish or Cypriot blood in him); had built an empire of interlocking citrus export houses, savings and loans institutions, and resort hotel complexes; and had escaped the UK with all of his empire's liquid assets as his house of cards was collapsing.

He had withdrawn to the Turkish Zone of Cyprus, where he had already become far wealthier and more in control of the economy than either the Turkish Cypriot pseudo regime or the Turkish Government itself could claim. Although the British authorities tried to recall him to the UK to answer reams of criminal charges and lawsuits, he was too deeply entrenched in the splendid isolation of a Kyrenia mountaintop villa to be dislodged. When he had become president of the Turkish Cypriot pseudo state, the British conveniently forgot he was a wanted man, and when he became a key player in the Cypriot political settlement, the major sponsoring powers and the World Bank quietly paid off all of his claimants and acted as if he were a prince among men.

Caitlyn couldn't help but admire him, but she knew that Takis had been livid at having been placed at his right hand, supposedly a place of honor only second to where she herself had been placed to the right of the president. But it was an honor she knew her straight-laced policeman Greek Cypriot husband could barely tolerate.

In an effort to stifle a giggle, Caitlyn looked around the table for the first time. Some of those at the table were obviously there because of their key involvement in or sponsorship of the Cyprus' archaeological endeavors—Ingrid Bittmann Isaksen because she was CEO of RayGo; the Piccard man, to whom Caitlyn had not yet been introduced, either because he was Ingrid's escort, or, if he really was a Piccard and was head of the Piccards' Cyprus operations, because that also would make him head of the Ledra Foundation; the Visilious from the Archaeology Department; the Mattases because Maria was the interior minister; and Bill Burch from the American Archaeological Institute. Ellen Larkin obviously was there as

Takis's representative on the island and because she was a personal friend of both of the Koniotises.

The presence of two of the other dinner guests in this exclusive group, however, had knocked Caitlyn back on her heels when she had first seen them. Both of the diplomatic agents who had interrogated her at the Larnaca sea terminal, the American. Wilhelm Jacobs, and the Australian, William Stevens, were in attendance. At first she had feared that they were there to observe her activities and to ensure she didn't steal the silver candelabra, but President Ioannou had put that to rest early in the meal by referring to the "unpleasantness" she had heard that Caitlyn had suffered the previous day and hoping that that had not upset the archaeologist too much.

President Ioannou's concern had been very comforting—right up until Caitlyn indulged in a chance glance down the length of the table only to encounter a very intense and disapproving stare from the most challenging of the interrogators she had encountered the previous evening, William Stevens. The Australian diplomat obviously was not convinced of her innocence.

Chapter Eight

With the soup course at the presidential palace dinner in Caitlyn Koniotis's honor completed and the salad course appearing, Caitlyn and her hostess found themselves looking at each other expectantly in search of a new topic of conversation. Caitlyn took pity on the president, realizing that there was only so much a politician could consider interesting to talk about on the topic of archaeology.

"What an elegant house this is," Caitlyn ventured. "Did you live here during your father's term as well?"

"No," Ioannou smiled, "and I don't live here now, either. I'm afraid my father broke with tradition. When he was finally elected as president, he and my mother had just moved into a house that they had recently built, the first house, in fact, that they had ever owned. My mother wanted to live there and the house was on a street that had been named for my father's father, so for these reasons he decided not to live here and to use the palace only for his office and for cabinet meetings and social events. At least that's the reason he gave the public. By the time I became president, tradition had been set, and I didn't have to give a reason for not living here."

Caitlyn looked quizzical.

"You see," Ioannou continued, "the palace had come to symbolize much frustration and pain for my father. First, it had the connotation of the failure of our system. Father was a close friend and confidant of President Makarios. He said he never was able to walk out to the portico of this building without surfacing the image of Makarios—who represents to us Cypriots what George Washington represents to you North Americans—being gunned into exile by his own people. Beyond that, my father had been Makarios's selected successor, but the archbishop died in 1967 before he could anoint my father as such. My father had to fight and claw with the other Cypriot politicians for twenty-five more years before his single term in office. For that whole time, this palace represented for him what was unattainable."

"As for myself," the vivacious president concluded, "I don't want to attach myself to symbols of the unattainable as my father was prone to do. I always push the limits of the benefits that government can provide for its people . . . just as you do in what we can learn from our historical heritage. In that, we seem to be quite similar."

Caitlyn had always been prone to be wary of political leaders, but she felt both flattered and honored to be in the presence of Chrystalla Ioannou as those at the table finished their salads and rose to help themselves to a buffet main course from the adjoining room. As Caitlyn took a tissue from her purse, blotted her lipstick, and then draped the purse's chain over the back of her chair, she managed to figure out for herself the answer to her early quandary concerning why William Stevens had been invited to this exclusive event that clearly was outside his area of interest.

Caitlyn had paused long enough to see the petite, porcelain-doll-like blonde, Ellen Larkin, rise from her chair, put her arm through Stevens's, and, while squeezing his arm, look lovingly up into the eyes of the much taller, rougher-looking Australian spy chief. Caitlyn had seen that look in Ellen's eyes before. It had been the way that she had looked at her lost fiancée, the American diplomat Paul Conte, years ago before he died at an Amman reception while saving the Jordanian king from an assassin's bullet. Stevens obviously was Ellen's escort for the evening—and quite evidently was much more than that to her as well.

"Good for Ellen," Caitlyn thought, as she paired up with her less-than-thrilled husband and cruised the offering at the buffet. "She deserves whatever happiness she can find. She has mourned Paul too long already."

It was Bill Burch who cleared up the presence of Wilhelm Jacobs for her as they were returning to the table with their desert plates.

"Oh, didn't you know? Jacobs is a U.S. embassy representative on the Fulbright Commission Board. The board's chair couldn't make it tonight, and the president wanted someone from Fulbright here, because your original presence on the island had been as a short-term Fulbright scholar."

"Ah, yes," Caitlyn laughed, remembering how she had been tempted away from her studies of American colonial archaeology on an historical Virginia plantation to be introduced to the far older study of ancient civilizations by the U.S. government educational aid organization. "That all seems so long ago."

"So long ago and so much worthwhile work since," Burch said with admiration. "Still I think you need to be careful. You could—"

The two were separated as Ingrid swept in, took Caitlyn's desert plate from her hands and banged it on the table, lifted Caitlyn's purse off the back of her chair, and announced a tad louder than necessary that they were going to the ladies' room to freshen up and to have a nice chat. As a surprised Caitlyn was being hustled across the room, Ellen Larkin fell in step, divested Ingrid of Caitlyn's purse, and draped the chain across Caitlyn's shoulder.

When they entered the powder room, they saw that it already was occupied by yet another guest Caitlyn had not been able to identify. She probably was the youngest of the guests, a very pretty girl with a deep tan whose dress, although almost presentable at such an occasion, looked slightly disheveled and seemed to have been just pulled out of a suitcase where it had been tossed for a long journey and had been shaken just once before she put it on. Bright red with a purple scarf was not really Caitlyn's idea of a good color combination, but somehow the carefree young spirit seemed to carry it off well. Not even her frizzy auburn hair seemed to destroy the overall intriguing effect. Although Caitlyn had seen her earlier with Wilhelm Jacobs and had thus assumed she was his date for the evening, now that she was able to focus on the young woman, she realized that she had previously seen her during the last day on the *Daphne*.

Was there no end to people turning up who had been on the *Daphne* yesterday, Caitlyn wondered.

As the three woman entered the ladies' room and placed their bags on the vanity shelf, the younger woman popped up in embarrassment, almost as if she had been caught in some illegal act—and, indeed, the slender white tube Caitlyn saw her sweep into her own purse looked like it might have been useful for inhaling something potent. The young woman's eyes were focused on those of Ingrid, and there was a hint of fear behind them. She backed toward the door, awkwardly sweeping Caitlyn's purse off the table in her hurry to escape.

"Oh, I'm so sorry," she exclaimed, as she bent down, picked the bag up, and replaced it on the shelf. And then she was gone from the room.

"Who was that?" Ellen asked of no one in particular.

"Gladys Holiday," Ingrid sniffed in explanation. "A nuisance of a substandard archaeologist who is more of a camp follower than a scientist. She's been working on a dig outside Tripoli, Lebanon. I have no idea what Will Jacobs sees in her, but she's his current flame."

The three sat down at the vanity. The presence of Ellen clearly displeased Ingrid, and her "chat" quite evidently did not cover the topic she had wanted to bring up. Caitlyn assumed—and Ellen agreed later—that Ingrid was suspicious of Takis's presence on this visit to Cyprus. Caitlyn had been coming alone on her archaeological jaunts here in past years, and Ingrid knew that Takis was too busy to take a vacation. Evidently Ingrid was concerned that Takis's trip had something to do with her own activities, and she had planned to pump Caitlyn for information that would shed light on that. The presence of the chief of UNICIS, Ellen Larkin, had put a crimp in her plans.

"What a pretty shade of lipstick," Ingrid finally opened with a topic as the three were sitting at the mirror. "Much better with what I'm wearing than what that sweet boy picked for me."

With this statement, Ingrid opened Caitlyn's purse and started pulling out objects, obviously in search of the lipstick tube.

"Speaking of the 'boy,'" Caitlyn interjected, as she handed the lipstick tube Ingrid was searching for to her in exasperation and gathered up her belongings—it never was a good use of time to challenge Ingrid or to "compliment" her on her manners—"who is your escort? Or at least I assume that handsome young man is your escort. I saw the two of you together at the rail of the *Daphne* yesterday."

Caitlyn could almost have kicked herself for launching into a conversation with Ingrid at all. Although the former UN official always was very careful to be gushingly sweet to Caitlyn in public, she made no effort to sheath her talons when they were alone. They had been friends initially, but that had all changed. As Ellen clearly knew the score in Ingrid's regard for Caitlyn, Ellen operated this evening as a buffer to the older woman's attacks.

Caitlyn had never been sure when the animosity had first surfaced, but she knew why it had surfaced. Several years earlier she and Ingrid's husband, Eric Isaksen, who Bittmann had married only a few years before he had been killed, had been kidnapped by Hizballah terrorists here in Cyprus and had endured several days of fear and uncertainty together. In this time they had formed a bond that the maniacally possessive Ingrid had never been able to break, even though Eric obviously had worshipped his wife, if not all of her actions. Ellen—the deceptive delicate blonde who had then been the Canadian high commission's well-trained spy chief—had been the one to have found and rescued the pair. This fact did not, of course, curb Ingrid's resentment or tongue this evening.

"Ah, yes, yesterday," Ingrid said with a hoarse laugh and what almost could pass as a snigger in Caitlyn's direction. "That's Andre Piccard, the Cypriot CEO of the Piccard holdings. He's a patron of yours now, so you probably should learn who he is. You remember the Piccards, don't you, Caitlyn? You were always holding hands with or being physically attacked by a Piccard. Even managed to inherit a Piccard house. I've always wondered. What did you do for Eleni, actually, to inherit her house?"

"Careful, Ms. Bittmann, your true personality is showing," Ellen said quietly, as she pulled away from the mirror and stood. "I think it's time we returned to the dinner table. I have to get back to work tonight. There are a lot of questionable business activities I need to run through the UNICIS computers."

"A special project for Takis?" Ingrid queried as she too stood up.

Ellen gave no response, appearing to act like she hadn't even heard the question.

Caitlyn attempted to ease the tension by returning to the topic of Piccard. "Andre Piccard? I knew he looked like Eleni the first time I saw him. Somehow I knew he was a Piccard."

Ingrid gave Caitlyn a long, strange look. Then she opened the lipstick Caitlyn had given her, looked appraisingly at it, closed the lid, and tossed the cylinder on the vanity top. "On second thought, the color looks too tawdry for me. Something a cheap bottle blonde would wear."

She strode to the door and turned toward the other two women. "Come to lunch tomorrow in Varosha, Caitlyn. And bring Takis."

"Thank you for the invitation, Ingrid," Caitlyn responded politely, "but we have other plans tomorrow."

"Cancel them. We need to talk about the opening of your archaeological institute. We need to make plans soon if you plan on opening your doors with RayGo money anytime in the near future." The threat hung there in the air for a few minutes.

"I'm happy you brought the subject up, Ingrid," Caitlyn answered sweetly. "I've been thinking about the institute's location and sponsorship. I think Paphos might be a better location and perhaps the Costas Marine Corporation might be a more appropriate sponsor. They are doing significant research in ancient sunken ships in this area of the Mediterranean. We have enough publicity now that we shouldn't have trouble putting together a consortium of sponsors. Anyway, I'm sorry to say we're already committed to going up to Kakopetria tomorrow."

Ingrid opened the door and then turned around. "Kakopetria? The scene of multiple crimes you conveniently brushed against, including the murder of your benefactor? You'd best be careful of your extracurricular activities in Cyprus, such as your arresting appointment with the police authorities yesterday. It might be harder for you to find sponsors for your ambitious plans from prison. Who would invest in a counterfeiter? But, fine. I just remembered that Andre and I had very intimate plans for lunch tomorrow already. And I wouldn't want to disappoint the boy. Shall we say Wednesday evening at the new Cassa Carioca in Famagusta, then?"

And then, the parting shot, even as Caitlyn was forming another rebuff. "Oh, by the way. Did you know RayGo owned the Costas Marine Corporation? You've been gone for some time, you know. As a matter of fact, RayGo owns Cyprus."

And she was gone with a peal of throaty laughter, leaving both Caitlyn and Ellen speechless. Ingrid usually did have the last word; she had not risen to the top of world politics and international business on luck alone. Caitlyn found that her cheeks were burning. And then the worst insult hit her. Now, just how did Ingrid know she had been arrested last night at the Larnaca sea terminal—or that the arrest had had anything to do with counterfeiting? Or had Ingrid just seen her being carted off and the reference to counterfeiting had been a lucky guess—or knowledge based on subsequent research? In any event, Ingrid required special care. Her support obviously was vital to the success of Cyprus' archaeological program plans.

"If only RayGo didn't control the solar energy storage technology, and if only Ingrid weren't the CEO of RayGo," Caitlyn thought. But such dreams were undreamable, she knew. She had always been prepared to face reality, and Ingrid Bittmann Isaksen was just one more unpleasant reality. A particularly unpleasant reality, however, Caitlyn had to admit to herself.

Later, at dinner's end, Caitlyn and Takis began to gather the friends who had promised to return to their Makedonitissa villa for a few hours of shared memories following years of being apart. The group included the Visilious, the Mattases, and Ellen Larkin. Ellen's escort, William Stevens had gotten bored with talk of times and people he knew nothing about and had excused himself to go out on one of the presidential palace's balconies for a cigarette. The group was at the door saying their good-byes to President Ioannou, Stevens still not too happy at not being included in the conversation and Bill Burch offering to take Ellen back to her office if Stevens didn't want to take the side trip from his own drive home, when Caitlyn's purse flew open and the contents scattered across the foyer's stone floor.

"I thought you had put that purse aside," Takis commented, a bit of pique showing in his voice.

"This isn't the same purse," Caitlyn responded. "I must not have gotten this one completely shut when I was in the ladies' room with Ellen and Ingrid. I just must be living under a black cloud this week."

As the group made a game of crawling around the floor and gathering up the contents of Caitlyn's purse, Ingrid Isaksen and Andre Piccard swept past them and into the night. Caitlyn looked up in time to catch a withering look from Ingrid and a shy smile from her escort. Caitlyn's jaw dropped as did her purse once more, again scattering the contents across the floor. Caitlyn still knelt there, transfixed, as Takis reached over and tried to lift her by the elbow.

"What's the matter, Caitlyn? This really isn't the best time and place for this game."

"Piccard," Caitlyn stammered. "I've kept saying that that man looked just like Eleni Piccard."

"So. I agree. He does. So what?"

"Eleni wasn't a Piccard, Takis. She *married* a Piccard. She only had one son. If a Piccard looks like her, he should be a direct descendent of hers."

Eleni Piccard had thought for many years that her son and her husband had been killed in Kyrenia during the 1974 Turkish invasion. Caitlyn and Takis found out later, after she had died—directly from her husband, Guy—that they hadn't died then, but that Guy had used the invasion as an opportunity to escape Cyprus where he was expecting to be arrested soon for business crimes. But Guy told them that their son, Pierre, *had* died of a lingering disease soon after they escaped Cyprus. That means Eleni had no living sons.

"This boy is too young to be her son, anyway," Caitlyn now said to Takis. "But. But, how can he favor Eleni so and still be a Piccard?"

Takis had no ready answer to offer.

Bill Burch, who had approached just as Caitlyn had spoken Eleni Piccard's name, Caitlyn's infamous escaped lipstick tube in hand, started to speak, an answer to Caitlyn's query evidently on his lips. But before either Takis or Caitlyn even noticed he was there, he pursed his lips tightly, dropped the lipstick cylinder into Caitlyn's bag, and turned away.

Takis followed the Mattases toward the door but then noticed that Caitlyn wasn't with him. He turned to find her still standing in the center of the foyer, her eyes large and transfixed on an object she had been putting back into her purse.

"What's the matter, Caitlyn?" Takis asked in exasperation. "We're keeping Maria and Demetris waiting."

Caitlyn looked up and mutely raised the object in her hands. It was a passport, her passport.

"So it was in your purse all along," Takis said with a touch of irritation.

"This wasn't the purse I was carrying yesterday, Takis," was the hushed reply. "I told you that earlier. I didn't buy this purse until today—to replace the one with the broken clasp."

* * * *

William Stevens had turned down Jacobs's offer to take Ellen back to the UNICIS offices. In fact, as the couple was leaving the presidential palace in Nicosia, he asked Ellen if she really had to go back into the office right then.

"Why not?" Ellen responded. "I do have quite a bit of work I need to attend to before we start up in the morning."

"There's no way you can do that from home?" Stevens asked. "I don't feel we had any time alone at all this evening, and there's something I want to discuss with you."

"Well, yes. I can get into the UNICIS system from my computer in my apartment in Kyrenia. And I suppose you could take me home and we could discuss whatever you want to discuss while we drive." It was about a forty-five-minute drive from the southern suburbs of Nicosia to the northern harbor town if Kyrenia, where Ellen had her apartment.

They didn't discuss anything in particular—not, certainly of any import—as Stevens drove north and across the Hilarion pass in the Kyrenia range and down to the edge of the Mediterranean. Each time Ellen tried to bring the conversation around to that, Stevens changed the subject.

Having arrived in the picturesque Kyrenia harbor semicircling out from the hovering stone harbor castle, Stevens suggested that they sit at one of the cafés at the yacht basin edge and have a cup of coffee and a shot of cognac. Ellen couldn't resist. She couldn't say no to an opportunity of lingering in Kyrenia harbor at night with a special friend. That's why she lived here, well away from both her work and the capital city.

But even here Stevens was steeped in small talk, not telling her what he needed to discuss. "You said you had something important to talk with me about, Bill," Ellen final pressed him.

"Yes," he said, taking both of her hands in his and looking into her eyes. "Don't you think we need to move our relationship to a new level? Don't you think it's time to invite me up to your flat?"

Ellen blushed, but she did think it was time to invite Bill up to her apartment hovering high above the harbor. For some time now, she had thought it, in fact, was well overdue.

They made love on her platform in her glass cube of an apartment, open to the vistas down into the harbor, out into the Mediterranean, and even toward the sharp mountain peaks of the looming Kyrenia range. And Ellen did not work on her computer that night; she had to get up early the next morning to prepare the work she needed to do to start the day at UNICIS headquarters.

However, while Ellen showered after they'd made love, William Stevens did find Ellen's computer and managed to break into her files—and to start doing what he was there to do all along.

Chapter Nine

Roulla Dahir was having another bad night. Ginger Patterson had visited her Omodhos neighbor twice already in the evening and had found her to be both morose and frightened. But, although she had seemed to be comforted by Ginger's presence—after she had permitted the older woman to enter her house—Roulla had still not chosen to, or, possibly, been able to, share with Ginger the nature of the problems that plagued her so.

This evening's binge of crying and lamenting in that strange language apparently was set off earlier in the day by Ginger herself, although, for the life of her, the older woman couldn't understand what the problem was. Although she had never quite dropped her reserve and had never volunteered a fuller accounting of her background or how she had come to possess so much cash, since the night Ginger saved her from suicide, Roulla had almost clung to the older woman. She hadn't even started to attempt to make friendships, or even cordial acquaintances with any of the other villagers, even though Omodhos, like all Cypriot villages, functioned on the close ties between the residents, who, more often than not, were all linked to each other by kinship. All of her attention and energies had gone into Ginger.

Ginger hadn't found this too disturbing as yet, because, although always nearby, Roulla was not talkative nor did she interfere with Ginger's normal activities. She also didn't insist that Ginger leave whatever she was doing and visit her. In fact, the younger woman appeared intent on keeping Ginger from paying another visit to her own quarters. But during the daylight hours, Roulla was always nearby, knitting at Ginger's table while Ginger bustled around the kitchen or weaving baskets in Ginger's small, foliage-laden courtyard, while Ginger read her favorite French novels.

Roulla obviously was an expert at making tightly woven baskets and seemed happiest when her hands were busy in this activity. During these times, she often sang lullabies gently to herself. Once, when she had appeared particularly lost in her weaving, Ginger had complimented her on her singing and had asked if it had been a Lebanese tune. Roulla, still smiling dreamily, had answered in the negative and had started to identify the origin of the song. But she suddenly stopped and looked, in embarrassment and with a flash of irritation, at the basket she was making. This caused Ginger to look at the basket too.

"Oh, look," Ginger laughed teasingly in an effort to curb Roulla's mood change. "You've been so absorbed in your singing that you've been making two bottoms for that basket."

This had not had the desired effect on Roulla, whose look had unaccountably turned to one of fear and anger. With a forceful gesture, she tore one of the bottoms of the basket and threw it down at her side, and, although she continued to visit the courtyard when Ginger was there, she changed to making straw dolls thereafter.

After that first evening tea Ginger had invited Roulla to the day after she had attempted to hang herself, Roulla had never missed tea time in Ginger's courtyard—at least until today, when she hadn't appeared—and she always had something to contribute to the table.

For some reason this morning's events upset what was becoming a cozy routine of a comfortable and comforting relationship between two old widows. That morning Ginger walked into the town square area to buy some fresh vegetables and encountered a British couple she had known for years and that had retired to the island, just as she had. The couple had been showing an acquaintance and his friend around the village, always a favorite destination for visitors who had the time to spare to see more than the major tourist attractions, when they had encountered Ginger.

She had told them about the village and had volunteered to take them to its chief attraction. At the bottom of the square was located the Monastery of the Holy Cross, whose present stone buildings encasing a courtyard had been erected very early in the nineteenth century. The monastery now housed a museum, which included a relic that supposedly was from the true cross and had been bought—at least this much was documented—by St. Helena, the mother of Constantine the Great.

The couple accompanying Ginger's friends had been composed of a young American diplomat Ginger had not met before—she had withdrawn from the Nicosia-based international community several years earlier—and a pretty, but untidy young woman, who had a British accent—a strange one that Ginger could not quite identify—and who, surprisingly, had proven to know more about the background of the monastery than any of the rest, including Ginger.

While the group was entering the church, Ginger turned and spied Roulla at the gate into the compound. She had waved for Roulla to join them, but the look of surprise, fear—and what seemed to be raw hatred—on Roulla's face had arrested her movement. Before any of the rest had noticed Roulla was even there, she was gone.

When Ginger returned to her house, the residence next door was shut tight and seemed to be deserted. Roulla didn't appear in the courtyard during the early afternoon, nor did she come to evening tea. Ginger decided the woman had left the village on a trip, which was actually an encouraging thought, as it would have been the first time Roulla had ventured away from the center of the village since she had arrived, when, late in the evening, the sobs started. Roulla obviously was at home.

Ginger held out for nearly an hour before she approached Roulla's door. The sobbing stopped at Ginger's knock, but the woman didn't answer the summons. The door was locked. Ginger knocked again, and called out to Roulla, inquiring whether the other woman was well and whether there was anything Ginger could do to help. There was no response. Ginger left but was compelled to return later when the crying had abruptly stopped. She certainly hoped this was not a repeat performance of the other night, but she couldn't just sit by and do nothing if it was. This time Roulla responded to the knock. She looked past Ginger, as if she expected—or feared—that Ginger would not be alone, and pulled the other woman into the house. She unexpectedly pelted Ginger with questions on who the people were she had been with at the monastery earlier in the day and what Ginger's relationship to them was. Ginger explained in calm tones that the older couple were British friends of hers and she had just met the other couple today—that they had just stopped by while taking the scenic route from Limassol to Nicosia across the Troodos mountains to see the picturesque village square. She certainly thought Roulla's behavior was peculiar, but she didn't want to upset the excitable woman, and she had nothing to conceal concerning her friendships.

Roulla seemed to have been placated by the explanation, although her movements continued to display considerable tension, and she wouldn't let Ginger leave without joining in the tea they had missed earlier in the day. While Roulla was making the tea, Ginger's eyes traveled the room in search of the mystery about Roulla's possessions—not including the mound of cash she had stashed away—that had been teasing and eluding her since her previous visit here. The answer came to her in a flash when she saw the table on which Roulla was setting out the cups and a small plate of cookies. The woman was clearing some objects off the table as she was adding the tea things to it—and she was not watching Ginger's sudden intent stare of recognition at a photograph that had been among these objects. But Ginger had seen the photograph, one of the same ones she had glanced at on the night of Roulla's suicide attempt, just long enough to trigger her memory.

"Of course," she thought to herself. "Why didn't I recognize it the other night? I must have just been too rattled. It's so obvious, and it seems like it was just yesterday."

Roulla was too tense during their subsequently short chat to notice that Ginger too now was disturbed. And when Ginger returned to her own house, it was with trudging steps that carried the burden of a heavy and shocking secret. That night, neither woman was sleeping. The wooden floor in Roulla's house was so old that Ginger could hear her neighbor pacing back and forth even if she no longer was crying in audible tones. As for herself, although Ginger had retired to bed she couldn't sleep. Her mind was racing, remembering events and tragedies of the past and wondering what fantastic whims of fate had combined to twist and dump this old story on her doorstep. Surely Roulla—and Ginger was having trouble using that name for her neighbor now that she knew the real story, or at least some of the real story—had not recognized Ginger. And now that Ginger thought back on events she realized that they had never met, although Ginger had seen the other woman a couple of times and had known who she then was.

"Perhaps she recognized my friends this morning and that was what set her off," Ginger whispered to the darkness. "No, that's impossible. The Whitley-Strouds didn't retire to Cyprus until much later. And it couldn't have been the other couple. They are much too young to have been involved with that."

No, this was much too complicated for her and it also was much too important to keep to herself. She had to turn this over to someone else. And she had no idea whether she could now keep up her friendship with the other woman without revealing what she knew. She also was very afraid that she herself would be in danger if Roulla did discover what she knew. People had died, and there must be a reason why the woman had never come forward.

She would call someone in the morning. But who? Perhaps Maria Mattas. She would remember and they had become very close when her husband Willie had been murdered and Maria was the investigating police official. But then Ginger sat straight up in bed.

There was someone even better. She was sure that the Koniotises would have reached Cyprus by now. They had messaged ahead that they would be here and would want to see her. Takis would be the best one to tell. Maybe the Cypriot authorities would not be the best ones to bring into this. She had grown to like the other woman, and she didn't want to cause any trouble if it could be avoided. Both Takis and Caitlyn had been involved in those events. She would contact them and unburden her shocking discovery on them. They would know what would be best to do.

Wrapping her robe about her, Ginger marched off to her living area, trying her best to remember where she might have the Knoiotises' number.

For a short period, the creaking from the pacing on the other side of the wall stopped, as, Ginger tripped and stubbed a toe on a chair leg, Roulla Dahir's ears were assailed with curses that she would not have guessed Ginger Patterson even knew, let alone used in the middle of the night. Although she couldn't believe that she herself was now making enough noise to have caused Ginger's outburst, she didn't want to upset her friend— now her only friend—and so she meekly went off to bed and, to her surprise, found that she had now worn herself down enough that sleep, albeit a fitful sleep dominated by the sense of being hunted through a forest, overcame her fear and tension.

* * * *

It had been murder getting away from Ingrid when they left the presidential dinner.

"Murder, now *there's* a possibility I hadn't thought of," Andre Piccard mused grimly as he exited off the superhighway between Nicosia and Morphou and pointed the nose of the car toward Mt. Olympus. "But who would it be? There are so many worthy possibilities."

He was on his way to confront one person—about another person. Ingrid had been furious when he had instructed the driver of her old, yet elegant and head-turning Mercedes limousine to drop him off at the parking pad before exiting the grounds of the presidential palace. But he had been sensitive to her. He could just as easily have had his own car brought around to the door so that all present could see that they weren't leaving together.

And he had never told her he was coming back to Ayia Napa with her this evening. He had had enough of her—and of him—and he had been planning this trip to Kakopetria for days.

"Ingrid was just lucky I attended her precious lecture and dinner at all tonight," Andre thought angrily, as he zipped around a village tractor that was crawling along the road into the mountains—progress couldn't change all things—and started the spiral assent toward the mountain resort. Still, he had been glad that he had attended. Caitlyn Koniotis had been well worth the extra north-south trip he had had to negotiate today in order to be able to attend the affair. He had been impressed with her on both the professional and the personal levels. He had heard much about the legendary Caitlyn Koniotis and of her unusual relationship with his family during his early years, and she was everything he had been told—and more. Even when he saw her on the *Daphne* yesterday, before he had known who she was, she had been mesmerizing. She was a real gem, but he hoped she didn't get in *his* way the way she had gotten in the way of other male members of the clan.

His childhood, he thought bitterly, and he gripped the steering wheel so hard that the car made a dangerous skip

160

toward the downslope side of the road. He supposedly was from one of the richest and most indulgent of families, but the truth was that he had been locked up for much of his youth in an isolated Swiss castle, waiting for two sick men to die. But, for years, they wouldn't die, and now, after all that time, one of them still hung on to life—and, in the process, continued to make his own life miserable.

The relived misery and suppression of his early life carried him up the Solea Valley, past the now-famous archaeological dig at Kaliana and the town of Galata and to the turnoff to Kakopetria. There it was, hanging onto the western slope of the Solea Valley, bathed in the moonlight streaming down across Mt. Olympus and into the valley. The Old Mill Restaurant and Inn. It had once been a multistoried stone and wood storage building for grain when the mill at its foot and on the confluence of the valley's two small rivers was in its heyday. Now it was an exclusive mountain resort hotel, with a famous restaurant that specialized in butter-grilled trout and one of the most spectacular views, either by day or night, down the Solea Valley on the Mesaoria Plain toward Morphou Bay. And on the floor above that restaurant was located his goal—the Piccard family mountain apartment, furnished by a mourning Eleni Piccard as a memorial to her lost husband and son.

"Yeah, right," Andre spat out, as he pulled over to the side of the road above Kakopetria, not yet prepared to go into battle. "A memorial to falsity, rather." Lies and deceit. Sometimes Andre wondered if the Piccards owned these to a greater extent than all of the ships, hotels, travel agencies, and export houses in their holdings.

His eyes drifted down the valley from the Old Mill Inn and stopped at the large village church that proudly perched on an outcropping that extended into the valley near where Kakopetria above ran into Galata below. Eleni Piccard had built that church, also as a memorial to—and as a final resting place for—her family. The pained expression remained on his face. More lies and deceit. Eleni Piccard was buried in that courtyard for sure—buried there after she had been murdered by a former lover in the small elevator that had once risen from the base of the Old Mill Inn building to the restaurant above, long since replaced by a more commodious and reliable lift. But no one knew whose bones had been taken for those of her lost husband and son, presumed killed in Kyrenia Castle during the 1974 Turkish invasion of the island, and buried in that church yard twenty years later.

Andre took three deep breaths and started off on his quest. By the glow of the lights at the top of the Old Mill Inn, he knew that his quarry was still awake. The old man had been in so much pain for so long that one of the mysteries of Andre's young life was when the man ever slept—and more to the point, when he ever would take his talons off of Andre and let him live his own life.

Andre was sure that he might as well have saved himself the trip. He never could stand up to the older Piccard. In fact, he couldn't remember when he had ever been able to stand up to any Piccard. The interview was short. It had been a particularly difficult day for the older Piccard, and he wasn't in the mood to entertain a family coup this evening. Keeping RayGo at bay and fooled for the moment was vital to the Piccard fortunes.

"Need I keep telling you that keeping RayGo under control unfortunately means keeping its CEO, Ingrid Bittmann Isaksen, happy."

"I don't see—"

"Of course you don't see. You never had the depth of perception your predecessors did. It's quite simple. If she's smitten with and focused on you, she's more likely to be inattentive toward what is happening with the Piccard accounts. Need I remind you that you have the easiest . . . no, don't give me that doubting look; I know the relative cost for effort to do anything, including just struggling for the next breath . . . that you have the easiest part of the operation." The older man went on to detail how he, himself, was busy with moving accounts and assets from Cyprus to Beirut. RayGo controlled Cyprus now, but they didn't control the even more important economic center at Beirut. They had a big slice of it, to be sure, but if he could slip Piccard's holdings out of Cyprus and into Beirut, the Piccards, not RayGo would control that city.

"The Piccards and the Hizballah," Andre voiced a correction.

"One and the same thing," the other man overrode him. "Although there still aren't many who know that—which is the way we want it to remain. Without us, the Hizballah terrorists would have disappeared years ago."

"Unfortunately, Ingrid Isaksen already seems to be well aware of our connection with Hizballah," Andre shot back. "And as far as I can tell, she and RayGo have always had a strong relationship with the Hizballah themselves and are increasing those ties."

The older Piccard folded up like a spent balloon and fell into a chair, both of his canes dropping with a thump and sliding across the highly polished wooden floor. His hands went to his eyes and he looked defeated. For the first time that night Andre felt remorse and went to his father's side. The next time he spoke, it was somewhat more gently.

"But I'm beginning to learn something about RayGo that might help us. At least the company has some secret that it is trying very hard to hide."

The older Piccard recovered his composure and looked up with interest.

"I think it has something to do with the solar energy storage invention," Andre continued. "I know Ingrid has papers in her Ayia Napa flat she doesn't want me to see. I've seen her slip them away, but I haven't been left alone long enough in her bedroom to search for them."

"Then what other evidence do you need that you must continue as you are for a while?" his father asked.

There was no answer to that. Andre didn't like to admit it, but he had tried once again to stand up to his father, and once again he had lost. His whole life was wrapped up in hatred and derision. He would never be good enough to be a Piccard. Without another word, he rose and stomped out of the apartment. He had intended to stay in the apartment tonight—or at least in the hotel below, where he had booked a room, but he couldn't stay under the same roof with a father who had so little regard for him. He didn't know where he would go, but it would not be here tonight. And, by God, he wouldn't go all the way to Ayia Napa tonight just to please Ingrid Isaksen—and at the same time, quite evidently, please his father.

When the young man had left, his father rolled his chair around until he had retrieved his canes and painfully rose to his feet. Stopping at the piano to pick up a framed photograph, he moved out onto the balcony and watched Andre getting into his car and roaring out of the stone river-side parking apron five floors below. Through his pain, Pierre Piccard was smiling. He lifted the photograph and looked into the eyes of Eleni Piccard.

"You would be proud of your grandson, Mother," Pierre Piccard—the Pierre Piccard who supposed died of a genetic disease thirty-seven years earlier, when his father, Guy, had faked both of their deaths under the convenient shield of the Turkish invasion, and, unknown to a grieving Eleni, had escaped the island with his son—crooned to the photograph. "He's just like you. And he's coming along nicely. Soon, very soon, he will be able to take his place at the head of the family."

The pain that prompted Pierre's movement back into the apartment, where he would sit, eyes open and pulsating to every new scream from millions of nerve endings while he waited for the rest of the island to waken and respond to his business liquidation manipulations, made quite plain that his son, Guy and Eleni's grandson, Andre, would need to be ready quite soon for the transfer of power.

* * * *

The agent hadn't had time to report today's sighting until how. But the general in Iran didn't need to know exactly when the missing woman had been sighted—only where. The report couldn't be made here either.

The lover was just in the other room, pleasantly sleeping off the wild time they had made of it after they had escaped that lecture and dinner at the presidential palace.

Ginger Patterson didn't think that anyone else had noticed the appearance of Roulla Dahir in the gateway to the monastery in Omodhos this morning, but someone else *had* seen Roulla. It was the same person who had sent her into the tailspin that had ruined the rest of her day—and the rest of Ginger's day as well.

"Well, I'll report the sighting of the straying Hizballah agent," thought General Khahalbi's searcher, "and then I'll be out of it and can get on with my life."

But the agent was wrong. General Ujay Khahalbi never released one of his agents—he harried them to the very last ounce of their usefulness and then he discarded them without a thought of remorse. In fact, at this very moment, he was setting up delicious plans for a deadly rendezvous between this very agent and his new play toy, the American archaeologist and wife of that pesky UN international investigations official. Perhaps if Takis Koniotis was busy trying to save his wife, we wouldn't develop an interest in the world's new currency problems—at least not in time to save Europe and the United States.

Chapter Ten

The evening was just warming up at the newly opened Famagusta version of the Cassa Carioca. First launched some thirty years earlier on a hill overlooking the Amathus resort hotel gold coast just to the east of the then-major port city of Limassol to cater to the vacationing Arab sheikh crowd, the nightclub was now located in the new center of foreign wealth. Although the clientele had changed from a Middle Eastern focus to that of Eastern European and Russian entrepreneurs of questionable standing and of the ever-present Korean and Taiwanese businessmen who had displaced Japanese industrialists before the latter had been able to find Cyprus on the map, the tastelessness of the original Cassa Carioca's decor had not been changed by either the move or by the passage of time.

The club building itself, the former Palm Bay Hotel, was surrounded by a border of beautiful tall queen palms, but, in keeping with its tacky past, the main doorway to the nightclub was flanked by plastic pink palm trees. And by the time the club's new manager, Uri Lukenov, and his date for the evening, the RayGo computer records official Christiana Tzavella, had arrived, the show room was already packed. As with its predecessor, the gold lamé tablecloths and the silver and metallic turquoise chair covers sparkled in the yellow, purple, and lime green-colored search lights that jabbed frenetically from here to there between the smoked-glass mirrored walls—here picking out one of an assortment of couples engaging in surreptitious sex under a table top; there illuminating a Korean businessman volcanically losing a champagne-chugging contest.

On the stage, a slinky female-impersonator chanteuse, backed up by a forty-piece, nearly naked all-female orchestra, was losing his/her own battle of volume in trying to sell a hard rock-rhythm version of "Is That All There Is?" to a crowd that seemed much more interested in getting all they could right there. Everywhere once could look in the strobing lights could be seen customers fondling the various protuberances of an army of cocktail waitresses and, upon request, waiters, clad only in pink rabbit ears, white bunny tails, thongs, and elastic waistbands in use as cash registers.

The main show room merely set the average of what one could find in this section of the Cassa Carioca. There were, of course, more restrained entertainment areas in the club, just as there were areas that were both more unrestrained and more private. Despite the attempts of the Cypriot police to curb the excesses of such clubs, RayGo had set itself beyond the law in the Famagusta-Varosha area, and the Cassa Carioca was both owned by RayGo and served as the flagship for the "anything goes" lifestyle of the new resort coast. Interior Minister Maria Mattas and President Chrystalla Ioannou were working to close down this lifestyle in Cyprus, but RayGo's power and influence on the island ran deep, and its regular clientele included many among the country's elite, not to mention international personages of renown who the Cypriot authorities welcomed to the island's shore with open arms.

When Lukenov arrived with the wide-eyed and obviously apprehensive Christiana Tzavella, he took one look in the main show room and backed out in distaste. If Ingrid Isaksen thought that he was going to manage this decadence, she was sadly mistaken. He would hold out until his search was completed and then he would be gone. And he didn't think the search would be long now. Not with Chris to help him.

He guided his date toward another room, which proved to be a much more sedate cocktail and games room. After escorting Chris to a table and telling her that he would return as quickly as he could, he moved on to the manager's office. He first, however, ensured that the tuxedoed man at the door to the show room knew who he was and knew that he didn't want anyone bothering Christiana before he got back.

As Uri approached the manager's office, the door burst open and a young woman emerged and nearly knocked him over. She was giggling and had more of her clothing in her hands than she did on her back. Uri paused at the door and looked in before entering. The outgoing manager was standing in the middle of the room, in front of the large, ornate desk, from which most of the trappings had been swept onto the floor. At the sound of Uri's approach, he turned with a smirk. He was still rebuttoning his shirt, after which he slowly zipped up his trousers as he surveyed the young Russian who was to replace him as club manager.

Sergey Stepanov had lived long—and hard—in the Mediterranean region. One of the first of what had come to be known as the Russian mafia to take up residence in Cyprus, his association with organized crime on the island and with the Cassa Carioca operation had lasted for nearly twenty years, with a strange five-year hiatus during which he had thought it less threatening to live away from Cyprus and had taken up the position of the head of the Israeli prime minister's security detail.

Stepanov had been in Cyprus long enough that he had known—and had sparred with—the father of Uri Lukenov, who had once been the Russian spy chief on the island. Stepanov was now returning to Moscow, all of the former Soviet-regime officials of his unsavory early life with the Soviet KGB intelligence service having now gone on to their greater reward.

He had already set up a connection there that promised to be far more lucrative than his work at the Cassa Carioca.

He stood there, assessing the younger man. Lukenov apparently had no idea who he was and that Stepanov and his father had not exactly been friends. That was just as well, thought Sergey. He didn't need any complications as he withdrew from the island. The young man had much the look of his father about him. Better looking and more muscularly constructed, of course. He must have gotten his better features from his mother, but he had the aura of his father's stubbornness and singleness of purpose about him.

At the thought of Uri's mother, Sergey turned away and used the excuse of moving to the other side of the desk so as not to let Uri see his expression. Irina Lukenov had been a painful memory for him. She had, perhaps, been the only decent thing that had ever happened to him, and he had let her slip through his fingers, eventually to die a tragic death at the hands of terrorists. They had been lovers in their youth in Grozny, a city in the Caucasus mountains in the far south of the then-Soviet Union. But ambition drew Sergey to Moscow, where he joined the KGB. Sergey had drawn Irina to Moscow as well, where she found that Sergey had already married, a marriage of convenience to further his career. Irina's father had been a high-level party official back in Grozny, so Mikhail Lukenov had also thought himself lucky when he had caught her on the rebound.

The Lukenovs had been happy for awhile, and Uri had been a result of their early happiness, but Sergey, who had always had roving body parts, not only his eye, soon tired of his bride of convenience and began to look further afield. The Lukenovs' second son, Pavel, was really Sergey's son, conceived when Sergey was in Moscow on one of his infrequent visits home and Mikhail was out of Moscow on one of his frequent postings abroad. Mikhail had never bothered to take his family on his postings before coming here to Cyprus, which was part of the reason Irina was so susceptible to Sergey's renewed attentions.

It had been sheer coincidence that had brought the Lukenovs and Stepanov to Cyprus at the same time. Irina was particularly vulnerable at the time, as she had just arrived on the island after having escaped from Grozny, where the Russians were fighting a Chechen succession attempt. Mikhail had allowed Irina and her sons to visit her parents in Grozny even though he had prior knowledge that the Russians were going to assault the city and that her father was on their seizure list, information that he, as a KGB officer, couldn't share with even his own wife without facing execution.

Irina and their boys had arrived in Grozny just after her parent's house had been leveled and all of her near relatives had perished. For the following two months, the three Lukenovs were trapped in a war-torn city and only managed to escape because Mikhail used all his contacts to get them pulled out. He brought them to Cyprus, thinking that this could smooth over what they had endured on the streets of Grozny. But all three arrived in shock and anger, and Irina couldn't forget that Mikhail had not warned either her and the boys or her family of the impending military action.

When she saw Sergey in the Russian Embassy in the Nicosia suburb of Engomi during her first week in Cyprus, something snapped inside her. She went on her knees and begged him to take her and the boys away. She no longer could live with Mikhail—or without Sergey. Sergey, who was then wooing the powerful Cypriot businesswoman Eleni Piccard, was not about to become openly embroiled with the wife of the Russian spy chief in Cyprus. The rejection had served to deepen Irina's depression and retreat from the world.

Then Mikhail took the family to the Turkish side of the island to visit some remote Greek ruins, and, in a freak incident, Irina was kidnapped by a band of Hizballah fighters who had come to Cyprus surreptitiously to train in mountain warfare. At length she was transferred to a Hizballah hideout in Beirut and had reportedly been blown up by explosives when a squad of Russian agents tried to rescue her. It had only been after her supposed death that Sergey realized what he had lost by not taking her away from Lukenov and Cyprus when she had asked him for protection.

Sergey had to give Uri Lukenov credit this evening. The young man was all business and he seemed to be well prepared to take over the management of the nightclub. It remained to be seen, however, if he would be able to balance the club's "amenities" and the demands of both the clientele and the owners as well as those of the Cypriot authorities as smoothly and expertly as Sergey had managed to do. From the first that he had seen of the handsome man with the well-cut figure, Sergey had known that Ingrid Isaksen had picked him for one purpose only.

"It's just as well she's found a new manager," Stepanov sighed to himself as Lukenov finished his business for the evening and left the room. "I'm getting too old to satisfy the likes of that woman."

When Uri returned to Chris, he could see that, although several old men and one hard-looking woman had been circling the table like vultures, the assistant manager for that area of the nightclub had done as he had been told. This indicated, Uri thought, that news of his tough family connections had traveled faster than had the reality of his separation from the family. This was good, as it was obvious that it would take a reputation for brutality to maintain peace here even in the short term.

As he had hoped, he found that Chris had been hard at work in the RayGo files since their last encounter.

"No, I haven't found out any more about the exact current location of the person you're seeking, Uri. But I've begun to read into some other very sensitive files—some that I know, by the way, that are being protected, that RayGo wouldn't want anyone else to know about. And I found some files that RayGo probably doesn't realize are there and would really like to know about themselves."

"Tell me what you've found," Uri said in a soothing voice as he leaned in toward Chris over the tabletop and played with the fine hair on her forearm with his fingertips.

Chris shuddered with pleasure. "In the first category are indications that someone in RayGo is beginning to play games with the Iranians and with their Hizballah terrorist surrogates in Lebanon. There also is something funny there concerning the company's all-important solar energy storage invention that I can only surmise because I reached so many sudden blind alleys in my perusal of the files."

"You must be very careful in your searching," Uri murmured as he brought Chris's wrist up to his lips and kissed it.

"Ooo, that tickles," Chris said, her voice beginning to slur from the drink she had been more than sipping on. Without her noticing it, Uri moved the half-full glass away from her reach. He wanted her lucid and talking to him now.

Chris continued with what she was relating to him of her search. "In the second category, I've found evidence that the

Piccards were furiously dumping their holdings in Cyprus and moving assets back to France and to Lebanon. I'm sure the front office in RayGo would be very interested in this, so I'm thinking that maybe I can send this information up to them to help cover for all of the time I am spending in the computer files."

Uri's eyes took on a hard look. "Please don't do this—at least for the present."

"I don't understand. What—?"

"Just don't do it, please. It would mess up some of my own plans."

"You already knew about this? You have plans?"

"Enough business for now," Uri said. "Look, you haven't finished your drink yet and I see the waitress coming with more."

Christiana waited until they had two more rounds of drinks, danced a few intimate circuits around the floor in front of the piano—with men and women in the vicinity drooling over both according to their own proclivities—and visited one of the club's private rooms that had not yet been converted from a hotel room before she told him of her most significant find.

"Also, Uri, honey, I think you should know that I've discovered something else in the real-time area of the files."

"And what is that?" Uri asked as he nuzzled a delectable nipple.

"The other searches for your target of interest are continuing and now they are coming from four different directions—from Beirut, as before, but now also from Tehran, from Nicosia, and from right here at RayGo."

Uri turned and sat up on the side of the bed and started to gather his clothes.

"Come on, come on. Get up. You need to get back to your office and get to work on this."

Chris looked disappointed, but she also started to reassemble herself.

"Have you tried everything to find a current location?"

"Well I found the information I have already given you in the police records in Beirut and the immigration records here. I could isolate the time and point of entry. But I don't know where else I can pick information up unless one of the known aliases is used or until the marked banknotes start to appear and to be noted in official computer records."

"What are these other searches?" Uri pressed. "What does a 'real-time' search mean?"

"Well, they are records of cell phone calls that are intercepted by the RayGo collectors and dropped into appropriate read files. Since RayGo is in the hunt, too, it has a cell phone call file I have been able to access."

"Can you follow that as it is being fed?"

"Certainly. It can be done, but it's a little risky. It's easier to tell that someone is monitoring the file and to trace back to that source."

"Well, I wouldn't want you to do anything that was personally dangerous," Uri said dubiously. But then he flashed one of his golden smiles at her, lowered his lashes, and ran a strong hand inside her not-yet-buttoned bodice. "It would mean so much to me, though, to have that file monitored in case the location comes up there."

Uri was just too sexy for Chris.

"I don't guess it would be too dangerous," she responded. "And, of course, if you come over there with me tonight, I'd be protected and we wouldn't have to devote all of our attention to the terminal screen."

Unfortunately, as good at computer hacking as Christiana was, she wasn't the best at evading detection. And Uri couldn't be at her side at all times.

* * * *

Although it was a laugh-filled and congenial group that descended on the Koniotis Makedonitissa hilltop home for drinks and a reunion chat following the lecture and dinner at the presidential palace, everyone quickly sobered up as they discovered that too much of what they had to reminisce about was tragic. That they had moved to the rooftop terrace Takis had added to the house to permit them to watch the twinkling lights that descended from the villages on the slopes of the Kyrenia Range across Nicosia and down into the Makedonitissa Valley below the villa did, however, help the discussion, as it was very difficult to see the expressions on each others' faces.

Among those present, only the Visilious and the Koniotises seemed to have been largely untouched in directly negative ways by the passage of the last decade, and even they bravely bore the scars of having lost shared friends and colleagues. Maria and Demetris Mattas had enjoyed highly successful professional careers—she having risen through the police department from the one-time position as Takis Koniotis's assistant to the current position of interior minister and he having become the publisher of a very influential Cypriot newspaper—and they seemed quite happy now. But their careers had taken a demanding toll and the two had not always coped well with balancing their jobs and their marriage. They had, in fact, only come back together again two years previously following an attempt at separation that had not satisfied either.

Both had reacted to their difficulties in dangerous ways. Demetris had begun to drink to excess and gotten in with a bad crowd at the nightclubs and casinos on the southern coast, and Maria had hit the liquor cabinet a bit too hard as well. In fact, Caitlyn had already become worried about Maria's drinking this evening and had seen to it that the drink she had requested when they reached the house had far less of a kick than Maria probably expected.

"How did Ellen look to you this evening?" Maria asked when the discussion was going through the current status of their mutual friends.

"She looked happy and contented," Caitlyn answered. "I thought that when I saw her earlier—and I'm glad she's settling down after the tragedy she's seen—and I guess I saw the reason for the 'new' Ellen at dinner this evening."

"You mean that Australian diplomat? A bit of a surprise that, I think."

"Right," Caitlyn answered. "He was quite gruff with me the first time we encountered each other—at the sea terminal where he gave me the third degree on the money I'd exchanged. Quite rough around the edges. He's no Paul, but if Ellen likes him, I'll certainly do what I can to endure him."

"Yes, I suppose we must," Maria answered.

Ellen Larkin, despite her perky appearance to her friends this evening and her obvious enthrallment with her Australian diplomat, William Stevens, had had a rough life of it since she had first met Takis and Caitlyn, and some of the tragedy she had seen had hit very close to home with the Koniotises. Shortly after Caitlyn first met Ellen, who was then very competently fulfilling the unlikely role of the Canadian Intelligence chief in

Cyprus, Ellen almost singlehandedly rescued Caitlyn and the UN official, Eric Isaksen, from having been kidnapped by a band of Hizballah terrorists. Eventually it had seemed that all had settled down, when a highly talented and mutually respectful group of colleagues had come together to make a resounding success of the United Nations International Crimes Investigation Service— UNICIS—headquarters that Takis Koniotis had formed and established at the then-United Nations base in the buffer zone on the ridge just to the west of the Koniotises' Makedonitissa home. Takis had been the first director, with the brilliant criminologist Safa Ziya, who had been Takis's Turkish Cypriot counterpart when he had headed the Greek Cypriot International Investigations Unit, as his deputy director. Ziya's "special friend," the British scientist John Patterson, had been the chief of the UNICIS computer lab, Ellen Larkin signed on as UNICIS operations chief on the rebound from losing her fiancé right before they were to marry, and a very cooperative Maria Solonos—now Maria Mattas—held sway as chief of the Greek Cypriot International Investigations Unit.

The success-driven departure of Takis Koniotis for higher-level work at the United Nations Secretariat in New York City had not upset the equilibrium much. Safa Ziya moved up to be the UNICIS director and Ellen Larkin became her deputy. The relations with the host government flourished even further as Maria Mattas moved up into the position of chief of the Cypriot Republic police department.

It was the success of the Cypriot political settlement efforts, primarily by their old friend Eric Isaksen, that resulted in tragedy for the Koniotises' old friends in UNICIS. This developing success shocked the international terrorist and crime forces that had been benefiting from the political partition of the island, and it spurred them to action. Their final, unsuccessful salvo had been the assassination of Eric Isaksen, but a year before that they had attempted a fairly wide range of actions in Cyprus, including random bombings and shootings, kidnappings of leading pro-peace officials, and economic sabotage.

Their most spectacular stunt had been a full armed attack on the UNICIS headquarters in the UN buffer zone to the west of Nicosia. One beautiful spring morning, while most of the UN troops were engaged in a change of contingents ceremony on the abandoned runway of the adjacent Nicosia International Airport, two bands of terrorist guerrillas ran across the now-unmanned no-man's zone to the east of the UN base and converged on the lightly guarded UNICIS headquarters building. Several workers inside the building died as antitank missiles were fired onto the roof of the building, piercing into the upper floor. Safa Ziya died at the front door of the facility from a hail of gunshots while she was trying to prevent panicked employees from fleeing the building into the terrorists' gun sights. Inside the building, in the operations room that sat at the very heart of the facility, Ellen Larkin was calmly messaging for help. She was one of the few UNICIS employees to walk away from the carnage unscathed—physically if not emotionally unscathed.

John Patterson had been another survivor, speaking again only in terms of physical survival. The mousy, rotund little man who had gone so well together with Safa Ziya despite her overpowering bulk and intellect, had left the headquarters building only a few minutes before the attack and was doomed to watch the entire action from a distance. He had been close enough to clearly identify his dearly loved companion cut down by bullets and yet far enough away that he couldn't help and was forced to sit in his automobile and watch in stunned paralysis as if seeing a particularly gruesome action film.

Ellen Larkin eventually recovered to the point where she would take on the directorship of the UNICIS and supervise its move to the western neutral-canton town of Morphou as part of the UN agreement to the Cyprus settlement.

John Patterson never set foot in the UNICIS building again. He moved to the Troodos Mountain resort town of Platres and returned to miscellaneous tinkering in his private lab. Over the next few years he increasingly came into contact with an old acquaintance, Ginger Hamilton, who had moved to the nearby village of Omodhos and who had also tragically lost her journalist husband in recent years. They had slowly grown close in their grief and eventually married, to the surprise and delight of their friends, many of whom knew both but in separate contexts and few of whom had even realized a relationship had been developing.

Ginger had been a good influence on John. He began to take increased interest in his scientific tinkerings and, at various well-placed suggestions of the highly practical Ginger, had begun to concentrate on advancements that were marketable. He gained the interest of businesses in Cyprus and the region and even sold a few inventions. It was while he was on a business trip to Beirut that he unexpectedly died of a heart attack. Ginger had not even known he had heart trouble. However, although the outcome saddened her, she steeled herself to the possibility from the start that John might predecease her. She had outlived a good many husbands—all but the first, although, since she hadn't heard from the groom in her first, short-live marriage for over fifty years, as far as she knew she had outlived him as well.

All of these events and the shared knowledge of the activities of a few other mutual friends and colleagues had taken up nearly two hours of discussion on the Koniotises' darkened roof terrace. As the more painful memories surfaced and began to predominate the conversation, the intervening silences began to lengthen. At one point, Caitlyn tried to brighten the evening by asking about how Ginger Patterson was doing in Omodhos now and declaring that they all should troop up together to-surprise her with a picnic in the famous anemone-drenched meadows that dominated that area of the island at this time of year. The cheery suggestion did not seem to take, however, and it was becoming obvious that the evening would soon end, and that it would end on a downbeat.

Thus, the shrill ringing of the outside phone alarm seemed to shock everyone out of lethargy, and they all began to rise and say their good-byes, while Takis was off taking the call.

When he returned, he looked a little off balance.

"Speaking of coincidences," he relayed to Caitlyn, as they were following the others down the stairs and to their transporters, "That was Ginger. She wants us to come up to Omodhos as soon as we can. I told her we were going to Kakopetria for lunch and the early afternoon tomorrow and that we'd come on over the mountain in the late afternoon to see her."

"Fine with me," Caitlyn said brightly as she waved at the departing guests. "But why the questioning face? We were planning to go and see Ginger anyway, and my idea of a reunion picnic just fell flatter than our earlier discussions of pains best left unpoked. Why did she say she wanted us to come up as soon as possible?"

"That's just it," Takis responded. "She wouldn't say. She said she couldn't say over the phone. Ginger seems to have a little mystery to share, and it has been years since Ginger was mysterious."

"I'm not sure I'm ready for the return of the old Ginger," Caitlyn yawned as she started carrying glasses into the house. "Let's hope this doesn't turn into a busman's holiday for you."

As usual, this was a bit too much for Caitlyn to hope for.

* * * *

Uri's sudden nibbling attack on Chris's left ear almost ruined the whole night's search. Luckily, the right earphone was fully in place. She was at the terminal, headset on, and was spinning through RayGo's sophisticated—but highly illegal—cell phone intercept code in search of interesting international conversations, specifically ones to such places as Beirut and Tehran. Uri had more-or-less been leaving her to her hacker's paradise, but occasionally he had gotten bored—and/or aroused—and had forced her to take a few pleasure breaks, none of which, up to now, had upset her a bit.

"No, stop that," Chris uncharacteristically exclaimed, as she went rigid and fought to keep the left earphone in place.

"You don't mean that," Uri teased, as his hands got into the act.

"No," she giggled as her body relaxed. But then she tightened up again. "I mean, yes, I do mean that. I think I've got something."

"I think you've got it all," Uri teased.

"No, I mean here on the computer, silly."

Uri stopped playing, now all business. "What is it? What have you got?"

"Shhh." Christiana was very good at what she was doing. She concentrated for a few moments and then sat back with a very disturbed look on her face.

"Well? Was something there? You look like it was a false lead."

"No, it was there all right. A connection from Nicosia to Tehran. Somebody claims they have a location."

Chris wrote a word on a slip of paper and handed it to an excited Uri, who was so excited that he didn't notice that Chris was still in a dejected mood. So involved was he with the information that she had intercepted that he didn't catch how nervous she had become or see the tear in each eye as she let him out of the high-security area and saw him on his way back to his Ayia Napa apartment in preparation for planning his next move.

When he was gone, she returned to her office and sat down in front of her terminal. After a few minutes she leaned over and switched off the pulsing amber light that had meant so little to Uri when it had first gone on. However, it meant everything to her, because it signaled that someone in the RayGo operation had latched onto her as she was intercepting the Nicosia-Tehran connection. Someone knew what she, by log-on and location, was perusing in a highly secret program, one to which she did not have official access. The detector would also have been able to access exactly the same conversation she was monitoring.

She knew she was in trouble now; she just didn't know how much trouble she was in and how soon the knife would fall.

The answers were not what she would hope them to be. They were a lot—and soon.

Chapter Eleven

The walls were shaking in the Varosha RayGo office tower in the early morning sunshine. The staff, from the cafeteria to the CEO's office suite, was scuttling around, trying to look very, very busy and very, very uninvolved or uninterested in whatever was happening on the executive floor.

Computer records official Christiana Tzavella, in particular, was cowering in her office, sure that all of the consternation was about her hacking into the company's data banks and equally sure that she was about to be tossed out on her pretty ear, which was not, in itself what was disturbing her so. She wouldn't particularly mind being fired; she really would rather be in London now, and, with the training she had had with RayGo, she could land a good job with one of their competitors even if she were fired—in fact there were plenty of companies that would hire her just to obtain information on RayGo's operations. No, what was frightening her so was that she had seen enough in RayGo's private files to know that they could really play rough, and the turmoil that was swirling around her this morning made her fear that if she was to be tossed out of RayGo, it might be from the top of the tower instead of from the front entrance.

As a matter of fact, Christiana did have quite a bit to do with the fireworks at the top of the tower this morning, but in a positive rather than a negative sense. The computer official had figured she was in enough trouble just helping Uri Lukenov find the person he was looking for with the help of the RayGo computers. Thus, she had ignored Uri's request not to pass on what she had found out about the Piccard conglomerate's secret divestiture of holdings in Cyprus and its buildup in Beirut. As she was leaving the previous evening, Chris had put printouts of several of the separate pieces of evidence in the computer on the Piccard moves in an envelope and marked them for executive floor attention. It was the only excuse she had been able to construct on such short notice to cover her presence in the building during the previous night.

The center of and cause of the explosion on the RayGo executive floor could be traced to its CEO, Ingrid Bittmann Isaksen, herself. All by herself. Ingrid needed no outside help to shake the foundations of the RayGo Tower. She had been mad enough that Andre Piccard hadn't traveled back to the Ayia Napa apartment with her the previous night, particularly since her consolation prize plan had also not worked out. No one had answered the telephone at Uri Lukenov's fourth-floor apartment in her building either. Now, thanks to some little snoop in computer records, she had learned that the Piccards were trying to slip out from underneath her control altogether. As bad as that was, they were consolidating in Beirut, where they could endanger RayGo's power there.

Oh, yes, Ingrid knew that Christiana Tzavella had been playing around in the private RayGo files, files that supposedly were not accessible by the young woman. And she had been preparing to take care of that little problem in the near future. But she couldn't take care of it now—certainly not today. And now she couldn't take care of it at all with an overt firing. Today Ingrid had to grit her teeth and thank the Tzavella woman for passing on these files, and she must be very careful not to ask the computer official how she had found the files and what other files she had been snooping in. Ingrid knew that Tzavella may have told some of her associates about finding the Piccard material, and Ingrid could hardly terminate someone for sending her information that she would want anyone else who found it to send up to the executive floor.

The general hubbub at the top of the tower started to die down, as Ingrid Isaksen regained her composure and sat down at her desk to seethe and scheme.

And then there was a deathly hush, starting from the reception entrance and rising floor by floor until it reached the open door into the CEO's office. Misunderstanding the source of the silence, Christiana Tzavella huddled in the corner of her small office and stared stoically at the closed door.

The world was topsy-turvy when Andre Piccard checked in at Ingrid's office before trudging off to the nearby office that had been assigned to him—to do what in relationship to RayGo, no one knew for sure, least of all Andre. Andre was sulking, and Ingrid was suddenly all seductive smiles. There was a minimum of meaningless chitchat as Andre avoided telling Ingrid where he had spent the night and as Ingrid avoided asking either this question or why the hell he hadn't told her his family was trying to escape RayGo's clutches.

When he walked in, she was sitting there castigating herself for wasting her time trying to use the young man as a hostage against RayGo's takeover for the Piccards' Cyprus holdings. Her worst regret was that he hadn't even been all that great of a lay. She was sure that Uri Lukenov would be quite a bit better in bed, and she could hardly wait to trade in models. For the time being, however, she knew she had to keep up pretenses with Andre until she could figure out how to counter the Piccard move.

To get rid of Andre before she lost control and strangled him right then and there, Ingrid volunteered to get his morning coffee and told him she would bring it to his office. As she wafted out of the room, Andre tried to contain his shock. Ingrid had never deigned to fetch her own cup of coffee, let alone fetched his or anyone else's that he knew of. The force of the shock sent him to the window. Would she be harder than usually to satisfy tonight, he wondered with a shudder. He certainly hoped that she wouldn't react to his absence last night as a need to intensify their relationship.

Andre turned to go to his office, and then he saw them on Ingrid's desk—the printouts on the business transaction intercepts that Christiana had sent up to the executive floor the previous night. He tried to remain calm as he shakily walked to his office and waited for Ingrid—or whatever flunky she sent— to bring his coffee. It turned out to be flunky, one who noticed without difficulty how drained and scared Andre looked but one who misinterpreted his condition, with considerable sympathy, as the result of a tongue-lashing from Ingrid Isaksen.

When Andre Piccard's hand had steadied, he picked up the phone on and placed a call to Kakopetria.

Now back in her own office, Ingrid Isaksen was grimly beginning to formulate her own plans for various people and companies—for Andre Piccard, for the Piccard company as a whole, and, of course, for sweet little Christiana Tzavella. Now that she had specific goals in front of her, Ingrid was beginning to regain control of her composure. She also remembered that she had come in this morning with the intent of setting something in motion that had struck her fancy during the ghastly dinner at the presidential palace the previous evening. Kakopetria was on her mind just as it was on Andre's mind at the very moment, but Ingrid made a call to Nicosia instead. As Ingrid hung up, her secretary entered the office and strutted his two hundred pounds of blond beefcake bulk up to her desk. As he passed a reminder of her Famagusta luncheon with the Australian diplomat William Stevens to her, their hands brushed and clutched for a moment longer than necessary.

"Yes," Ingrid thought to herself, "I really have been wasting my time with Andre Piccard."

Ingrid looked up into her very private Swedish secretary's eyes but was nonplussed by the fear and shock she saw there rather than the usual sensual smile he gave her when they were alone. For the second time that morning the walls of the RayGo office tower were shaking. But this time, the CEO was not the cause, the walls really were shaking. This side of the island was experiencing one of the slight tremors—magnified in effect here on the top of the RayGo Tower—that had increasingly been in evidence since the major shock that had destroyed the Limassol waterfront and port some years previously.

This tremor didn't frighten Ingrid. But she was, in general, very frightened of dying in an earthquake. It had been a fear that had possessed her since her childhood, even though she had never experienced an actual quake as she was growing up in

Europe. It was probably much the unknown, unexperienced aspect of such a natural calamity that was at the base of Ingrid's fear of earthquakes. This one did not frighten Ingrid, but it certainly caused her to register in the back of her mind the intent to track down why the Russian construction company that had built this building—and many of RayGo's other high-rise properties—had disbanded and its manager had been deported from the country.

* * * *

The view across the hill resort of Kakopetria from the mountain-hugging road winding up from the Mesaoria Plain to Mount Olympus never ceased to take Caitlyn's breath away. This was especially so in view of associations Caitlyn had with Kakopetria—and with the Solea Valley as a whole. It was farther down this valley, at Kaliana, where she had first pushed back time with the historical excavation discoveries upon which she had solidified her international reputation as an archaeologist. And it was at the Old Mill Inn, hanging on the slope just across the valley, as the Koniotis convertible dipped off the road and toward the town square, that Caitlyn had herself been involved in so much tragedy in the lives of her friends. Yet still, she had also known some very good times here in the company of her friends, and the valley and Kakopetria itself had a powerful pull on her. She always felt at peace when she was here.

The Old Mill Inn, with its treetop restaurant and its exclusive hotel rooms, had been the pride and joy of Caitlyn's first sponsor in Cyprus, the international businesswoman Eleni Piccard. Kakopetria had been Eleni's native village and the ancient mill complex had been in her Cypriot family's holdings for centuries. Based on her own visions of reviving the handicraft traditions of Cyprus and her husband, Guy's, interest in designing and creating a tasteful but profitable business out of the mill complex and the availability of seed money from the Piccard conglomerate's fortunes, Eleni had turned the Old Mill Inn into one of the most popular businesses in the Troodos Mountains.

Unfortunately, she had lost her husband and son during the 1974 annexation of the northern third of the island by Turkey, and so the project had been one that she had had to carry out herself. In addition to establishing, first, the restaurant in the complex's massive storage building, then a gift shop in the old mill building itself, followed by a twelve-room luxurious inn below the restaurant, Eleni had also developed the top floor of the storage building into a private retreat that included, almost in museum style, all of the mementos associated with her lost family.

What Eleni, quite tragically, had never gotten around to establishing before she was murdered in the small elevator that had then connected the restaurant and her apartment with the ground-level stone parking apron—the hotel entrance having separate access to a forecourt on the hillside the building abutted—was the working handicraft center she had planned for the ground floor of the former storage building. This had been Eleni's real passion. Her formation of the Ledra Foundation to support archaeological projects and historical building preservations in Cyprus stemmed from this passion. The highly successful handicraft center and export house she set up down in Nicosia had also resulted from this interest.

As usual, Caitlyn asked Takis to drive over to the large Greek Orthodox Church Eleni had donated and had built on an outcropping of the valley wall in the lower section of Kakopetria, where it ran into the town of Galata. Eleni had the church built as a memorial to her missing husband and son when it was thought that their remains had been found in the dungeons of the northern coastal Kyrenia Castle, and two graves for these family members were prominently located in the church yard. Caitlyn and Takis had accompanied Eleni to the emotionally packed reinternment ceremony for the bones, in the courtyard, none of them having known until a few years later that the bones were not, in fact, those of Guy and Pierre Piccard, even though they had been identified as such by the family dentist.

The dentist had lied, having been paid off by and later murdered under the instruction of Guy, who had manufactured his death and that of his son, Pierre, to cover an escape from prosecution in Cyprus for business fraud. The sickly son Pierre had, according to what Guy told Caitlyn and Takis when they encountered him years later, died soon after leaving Cyprus in 1974. Guy had never bothered relieving Eleni's grief by telling her what had really happened, and Eleni had died without having heard the truth. Guy had only told Caitlyn and Takis the story because he himself had been diagnosed as being terminally ill and had been trapped on a murder and international terrorism charge. Ironically, Guy slipped imprisonment, as several members of the influential French Piccard Shipping family had been able to do over the centuries, and lived for a further ten years, dying in the end not from the cancer that plagued him but from an accidental fall off the battlements of his isolated Swiss mountain castle.

As Caitlyn stood thoughtfully and respectfully before the graves of Eleni Piccard and the two unknown victims of Kyrenia Castle, no longer identified by their tombstones as Guy and Pierre Piccard, she couldn't help but wonder whether Guy had told even her and Takis the full truth when it seemed he was baring all in his "deathbed" confession, delivered in Eleni's apartment at the Old Mill. If so, how could the young Andre Piccard bear such a resemblance to Eleni? Eleni must have had at least one other son who had been kept a complete secret, or Pierre Piccard, who would have been a young boy at the time, had not died when and where Guy had previously revealed.

Caitlyn could tell that the same, or similar thoughts, were running through Takis's mind, but she didn't surface the questions. She wasn't sure how any of it would matter now, and she didn't want Takis working in his investigator mode while they were visiting Cyprus. She had maneuvered him into taking this trip because he needed to get away from sleuthing for a while. She would do her best to keep him from being bothered by mysteries.

Her best would not be good enough, however.

* * * *

Caitlyn was more than pleased by what she saw as the Koniotis convertible purred into the Old Mill Inn forecourt. She fully expected to see a general deterioration in the complex following years of management by less-devoted hands than Eleni Piccard's—although she also expected that the restaurant would still be living up to its reputation for buttered grilled trout, because it was still highly touted by all of the friends she had talked to in Nicosia over the past two days. What she found, however, were a building and riverside gardens that were in better shape than ever before. And to top this off, someone had carried through with Eleni's dream and the ground floor of the former multifloored storage building now contained a handicraft center.

Caitlyn started to make a beeline for the handicraft store, but Takis moved quickly in behind her and spun her around with a laugh.

"No you don't," he declared. "You promised to walk the town with me for exercise before we went up to lunch. If I let you in that store now, we'll never get the walk in."

Reluctantly Caitlyn pulled away. It was not that she was an inveterate shopper, but she wanted to see how closely they had followed Eleni's dream of featuring only the best of the island's handicrafts and to demonstrate the crafts as well as sell them. However, she was as interested in taking the traditional pre-meal walk as Takis was—not just for the exercise value but also because she wondered what had changed in Kakopetria over the past few years of galloping development on the island.

Happily, Caitlyn and Takis discovered that not much had changed at all in central Kakopetria, although the valley slopes supported far more stuccoed and tile-roofed villas than ever before. The village itself still reflected the two distinct eras of modern habitation in the Cyprus mountains. The evidence of the Greco-Roman period and earlier, although the Kakopetria area was settled at that time, was completely gone now, but, as the couple crossed the stone bridge where the mill's water wheel had once dipped into the river, they entered the "old" village of Kakopetria, located between the two rivers that met in the town and composed of buildings that were now at least a century old.

The only real differences Caitlyn and Takis initially noted as they walked the narrow cobble-stoned streets—more pedestrian paths now, because there wasn't very much room for cars between the houses—of the old village were that more water was now running in the rivers, a result of the aquification projects on the island that were creating more water for irrigation and pumping it back up into the Troodos to cascade down across the roots of plants and trees again, and the construction and more lush vegetation on the valley walls made them feel compressed in the old village streets.

When they got to the top of the old village, they crossed the other river and descended the streets of the "new" village, which consisted principally of buildings constructed in the last century without, as was normal in Cyprus, the benefit of zoning, style coordination, and preservation controls. This part of the village was now more to the liking of Caitlyn and Takis than the other. Although they groaned at the occasional eyesore and architectural "mistake," they also felt freer in this less constrained, more exuberant environment. Near the school adjacent to the town square and at the bottom of "Kato"—or "upper"—Kakopetria village streets, they came upon a fruit stand that was featuring some of the biggest and most deeply colored oranges Caitlyn had ever seen. When she opened her purse to pay for her choices, however, she discovered that she didn't have her wallet—and remembered that she had left it under her seat in their convertible. Takis paid for the fruit and the couple moved quickly toward the road access to the Old Mill Inn that ran beside the river on the other side of the town square.

As they continued down the road toward the Old Mill Inn parking apron, Caitlyn saw a familiar figure standing at the door of the new elevator to the upper reaches of the complex.

"There's Bill Burch," Caitlyn said. "I wonder what he's doing here."

She called to the director of the American Archaeological Institute, but the elevator had arrived, and he stepped in, presumably not having heard his name called. No matter. When they got up to the restaurant, Caitlyn thought, they would see him again.

Thankfully, Caitlyn's wallet was where she had left it. She looked inside and determined that her credit cards and banknotes were still there; Takis said he wanted to check his messages on his cell phone and walked over to the side of the brook by the parking apron, which Caitlyn took as a not-so-subtle demur on accompanying her into the handicraft shop.

The center was all that Eleni would have wanted it to be. Not only were the handicrafts that were on display first-quality goods, but there were crafts people on duty demonstrating the various techniques and the center had remained true, as Eleni had always insisted when she was alive, to the motifs and shapes of the traditional Cypriot styles. In one area Caitlyn found the traditional Cypriot pottery, leather work, silver jewelry, and weaving crafts. To her real delight, however, another section honed in on the specific crafts—saddle tooling and silk production and weaving—that Kakopetria itself had once been famous for.

As she reached for one silk scarf that had fascinated her, she found someone else had latched on to another end of the same scarf. Looking up in bemusement, Caitlyn started to apologize, only to find herself staring into the amused eyes of the red-headed Gypsy-type girl from the previous evening.

"Oh, I'm sorry. I didn't mean to grab onto the scarf you were looking at," Caitlyn started off, adding "But haven't I seen you someplace before? At the dinner at the presidential palace last night and on the *Daphne* the previous day?"

"That's quite all right," the younger woman said with a laugh. "I'm sure you were holding this scarf first. And, see, here's another one just like it over here. And now that I see it better, I don't think it's my style, anyway. And, yes, we've seen each other a couple of times before. I loved your lecture and admire your work. Here, excuse me," the girl gushed as she knocked Caitlyn's purse while trying to pass the scarf over, "I seem to be all thumbs today. As I was saying, I loved your lecture. I'm an archaeologist too, you know. But, then, you don't know, do you? I mean you don't know anything about me. And why should you?"

Caitlyn backed away slightly from the onslaught, but the young woman pressed on.

"OK, stop," the woman declared, presumably to herself, and she did stop and took a deep breath, although she now had one of Caitlyn's hands in her grip, so Caitlyn wasn't going anywhere for the moment. "Let me begin again. My name is Gladys Holiday—but 'Gladys' is so ghastly that my friends call me Billie—after the black American Blues singer. Not that I'm either black or American, mind you, but I *do* sing a bit—not Blues, of course."

Caitlyn was barely able to keep up with Ms. Holiday's exuberant British accent.

"I don't actually live here in Cyprus," the woman rambled on. "I'm here to visit a friend. You know, Willy Jacobs from the American embassy. I'm really an archaeologist— University of Michigan, just like you. I checked it out, of course. That makes us sisters or something, doesn't it?"

It didn't, but the mention of archaeology had, as it always did, caught Caitlyn's attention.

"I'm working at the Hisn Al-Akrad excavation. You know, the Crac des Chevaliers crusaders' castle in northern Lebanon."

Indeed Caitlyn did know about this excavation and was very interested in it. But, as her interest in "Billie" Holiday increased, Holiday's interest inexplicably waned. The younger woman let loose of Caitlyn's hand and didn't follow her to the cash register. She even refused—without much in the way of a convincing excuse—Caitlyn's invitation to join her and Takis for lunch upstairs in the restaurant.

Caitlyn received a pleasant surprise when she reached the cash register. The clerk on duty had worked in Eleni's main handicraft center down in Nicosia and remembered Caitlyn from earlier years. As Caitlyn paid for her new silk scarf, she looked around for Billie Holiday, but the young woman had disappeared. Her sudden disappearance hit Caitlyn as strange— but no stranger than her sudden appearance had been. The woman had been quite right. The scarf that had attracted Caitlyn had not seemed to be something that would appeal to the flamboyant redhead at all. Caitlyn could only wonder why the woman had picked up her end of the scarf in the first place.

Caitlyn and Takis lingered for more than two hours over their butter-grilled trout. Although, strangely enough, Bill Burch wasn't anywhere to be seen when they arrived for lunch, the restaurant manager from their earlier years, when Eleni held sway here, was still in evidence. He moved from table to table, albeit a little more slowly, greeting and chatting with his customers. He recognized Caitlyn and Takis instantly and honored them by sitting with them at great length at their choice reserved table on the balcony with unobstructed views down the valley and up to Mount Olympus.

The manager was expansive in his conversation right up until the point that Caitlyn, without any forethought, asked what Eleni's former apartment upstairs was used for and blurted out that she herself would like to have it as a vacation apartment. Although the manager didn't become unfriendly, he did become a little reserved and merely said that the Piccards still used the apartment and that, in fact, a Piccard was in residence there now.

When the manager left, Caitlyn found Takis staring at her intently.

"And just where did sudden interest in Eleni's flat surface from?" he asked pointedly, a slight edge to his voice.

"I don't know," Caitlyn answered, a bit in awe herself over her remark. "I had not been thinking about it at all—at least not consciously. I guess I was just so disappointed at what has happened around our Makedonitissa house. But now that the thought has bubbled out, it doesn't sound so odd. Kakopetria still has the peace and quiet that Makedonitissa had when we moved into that house. And I still feel a bond with this building that I seem to have lost with the villa. And an apartment would be much more sensible to keep here for our occasional visits than a separate house is."

Takis started to answer, but he was interrupted by the appearance of an old friend. At first neither Caitlyn nor Takis recognized Ahmad Jallud when he strode up to their table, but at the sound of his voice, the years were swept away.

"Ahmad!" Caitlyn exclaimed, as she rose and hugged the handsome police official. "I hardly recognized you. You've grown so." Caitlyn's delight was genuine and obvious as was only natural in response to someone who, as an Arab youth, had unwillingly been indentured to a gang of Hizballah terrorists and had kept Caitlyn, whom the band had kidnapped, alive and safe from harm, to the point of having himself been grievously wounded.

Takis also rose and gave Jallud a hearty handshake but was shaken by the worried look Jallud flashed him when he sat down at the table. Takis knew that Jallud had risen to the position of the chief of the Cypriot national police, a job he had won both through excellent service and because, as a Cypriot of Lebanese background, he was neither fully feast nor fowl when it came to being of either Greek or Turkish extraction—although he technically met the constitutional mandate for his position by being considered Turkish—so he was more acceptable to all parties than other candidates had been.

"Yes, please join us," Caitlyn smiled. "You must tell us all about how you are doing. I heard you have gotten married and that your uncle was trying to arrange to come back to Cyprus again. But we really haven't heard very . . . Ahmad, what's wrong? You look concerned."

"I'm sorry, Mrs. Kon—, Caitlyn. Yes, of course we must chat. But could I see Takis alone for a minute? We could go over there by the fireplace. You don't need to get up at all."

Caitlyn was agape. And Takis sat there stone faced for a moment, as well, although his brain was working overtime, and he didn't like what this was adding to.

"Again, I'm sorry," Ahmad looked very embarrassed and started to rise, looking pleadingly at Takis.

"Don't be sorry," Caitlyn responded. "And I see no reason why you should have to talk to Takis alone. I'm a big girl, and your reticence in telling us what's wrong is scaring me. What is it, Ahmad?"

Once again Ahmad looked to Takis for help, but Takis just shook his head and pointed to the chair for Ahmad to sit down again.

"I really don't think you'll be able to keep whatever it is away from Caitlyn now, Ahmad. You know how stubborn she is. And she's right; she's a big girl and can take bad news. I halfway expect I know what it is anyway."

Ahmad plopped down with a resigned sigh and fixed soft brown, but very sad eyes on the woman he had worshipped for years.

"I'm really sorry to have to say this, Caitlyn, but I have come here to talk to you about passing more counterfeit currency."

The volume and intensity of the conversation on the restaurant balcony rose in pitch from there, to the extent that neither of the three heard the deadly gurgling noises—hardly identifiable as human, but very definitely human—that started at that moment on the balcony to the Piccard apartment immediately above their heads.

Chapter Twelve

It was far later than they had planned for it to be before Caitlyn and Takis hit the road again for the trip over the Troodos mountains to the village of Omodhos, overlooking the Mediterranean from the range's southern slopes. However, everything is relative, and the couple realized they were lucky to be on the move again, rather than for Caitlyn to be carted down the Solea Valley to a hot prison cell in Nicosia.

The euro banknote Caitlyn had used to buy her scarf at the handicraft center had been counterfeit. Not only had it been counterfeit, but it also quite evidently had come from the same source of bills as had the U.S. bills Caitlyn had passed at the Larnaca sea terminal currency exchange just two days previously. A blue thread not used in the legal printing of either monetary unit was found running through the paper both types of bills had been engraved on. The sales clerk at the handicraft center, who quite luckily had known Caitlyn, had reported the matter to the Old Mill Inn management, rather than straight to the village police. The manager of the restaurant, in turn, had notified police headquarters in Nicosia, where he knew the Koniotises had high-level friends and then had visited at the lunch table with Caitlyn and Takis long enough to ensure they didn't go off before the police arrived.

None of this—by instructions that had been left by Maria Mattas because she feared Caitlyn was being set up—was done because anyone actually suspected Caitlyn was guilty, but because her friends thought that it meant she might also be in danger. It was evident that someone was toying with her, someone who was, at best, connected with a very nasty international counterfeiting ring. And if these people could easily get close enough to Caitlyn to slip counterfeit bills in her wallet, they could get close enough to do her real harm. As far as Maria knew—and she was sure this had occurred to Takis as well—the whole ploy was a warning to the UN security chief, Takis Koniotis, that his enemies could reach and embarrass his family at will—or worse.

Normally a person in Caitlyn's position would be in real trouble with the police. She had a considerable number of counterfeit notes of both locally acceptable currencies in her wallet both times she had been apprehended. Until now, the only time people had been stopped with both currencies and with large numbers of notes was as they were entering the country—as had been the case when Caitlyn was first stopped.

And in all previous cases, some involving people with professional backgrounds and social standing in Cyprus that rivaled Caitlyn's, the authorities were convinced they had apprehended key counterfeit couriers. The more it was occurring, though, the less sure the authorities were that these otherwise reputable people were culpable.

"You didn't have to come yourself," Takis said to the national police chief, Ahmad Jallud, after Caitlyn had answered Jallud's questions.

"Yes, I did, Takis. All of my people need to know that Caitlyn isn't a real suspect in this—and just as important, I need to know that you appreciate and understand that you're the real target. I would like to assign a police detail to you and Caitlyn, Takis."

"No, we can't let you do that. That would be a sign of weakness, and we've been on the firing line before."

"Perhaps Caitlyn thinks otherwise," Jallud said as he turned to her.

"No, Ahmad, Caitlyn doesn't think otherwise," Caitlyn answered in a determined voice. "But I'll try to be more aware and careful from now on. I just haven't understood how serious this all was and have been walking around as if in a dream."

"We do understand and fully appreciate what you're saying, though," Takis said. "We shouldn't be in country much longer and we'll both be on our guard while we are."

Takis was looking decidedly grim and Caitlyn was trying hard to appear nonchalant as their convertible chugged to the top of the mountain range and slowly passed through the town of Troodos, which, as it sat just below the summit of Mount Olympus, was the highest town in Cyprus in elevation.

To break the heavy tension in the air as the vehicle cleared Troodos and started down the southern slope of the range toward the old British hill station of Platres, Caitlyn opened her new scarf in the breeze and turned toward her husband and sweetly said, "I don't suppose you will leave all this counterfeit business to Ahmad and Maria, will you?"

"Not a chance," was the response, as Takis gripped the wheel hard and spun out around a heavy truck making the descent at a slow pace.

Just then the scarf had the misfortune of snapping out of Caitlyn's hand and flying into Takis's face. The convertible careened dangerously toward the outer edge of the mountain road. However, Takis had the presence of mind to turn the wheel smoothly enough not to skid and to take his foot off the accelerator. As he swept the scarf back toward Caitlyn, he regained control of the car and the vehicle missed the truck and stopped.

With horror, Caitlyn wadded up the scarf and buried it in the bottom of her purse.

"Jinxed scarf," she cried. "I should have let Billie Holiday have it."

"Billie Holiday?" Takis asked. "What does that scarf have to do with an American singer from the past?"

So Caitlyn told him about her unlikely encounter with the young archaeologist who had been at the dinner the previous evening. After admonishing Caitlyn for not telling Ahmad and him about her brush with Holiday, and after being counterattacked, on the basis that the men hadn't bothered to ask her anything about what happened in the handicraft center, Takis declared that they would sit down that evening and go over every move Caitlyn had made since that last time he checked the money in her wallet.

They drove off and by that time they reached Platres, Caitlyn had told her husband to shush up for a while and enjoy this unique mountain resort town whose older buildings had been constructed, atypically for Cyprus, from dressed red bricks and in the style of the British colonial Victorians who had originally established the town as a cool retreat for their families from the hot southern coast. For nearly two centuries, from the time of the British to the early years of the republic, the town had been the seat of the island's summer capital as well, and even now on any given evening in the summer months there were more national government officials in residence in Platres than there were in Nicosia.

So intent was Caitlyn on enjoying Platres, and in trying to make Takis concentrate on enjoying Platres as well, rather than on catching counterfeiters, that neither she nor Takis noticed the sedan that had fallen in behind them, at the turnoff to the road down the eastern flank of the Troodos, toward Famagusta, and that was now following them down from Platres to Omodhos.

* * * *

When Ingrid Isaksen returned to her RayGo Tower office following lunch with William Stevens, she felt energized, as she always felt after a meeting with Stevens. There was something about that man that both attracted and scared her— emotions which got her vital juices flowing. She felt that Stevens just might be her equal under his secretive, rough outback exterior. They had, in fact, been lovers for a brief time after he had come to the island, but Ingrid had found him a bit too rough in his love play even for her, and she had, regretfully, backed off and found a new level for their relationship.

She knew the Australian brought out something exciting in her, but she couldn't quite isolate what that was. She stood for some time at the floor-to-ceiling window and looked out over the fragments of the spires of more than 300 church ruins inside the old walls of Famagusta. At length she turned back to her desk and proceeded to prove that what Stevens brought out in her was probably sheer meanness.

Her first call was to that silly little snoop, Christiana Tzavella, but she was told that she had just missed her, that the computer official had just left the building unexpectedly and in a hurry. The second call was to Andre in his office, but she found that he wasn't in either. The venom was building and the targets were dwindling.

The third series of calls—one to Tehran, one to Beirut, and one to a mobile phone helped ease the ire buildup. The Piccard counterattack was in full swing. Who did that pathetic shell, Pierre Piccard, think he was dealing with anyway?

The fourth call was more delicate, again to a mobile phone in a vehicle returning from Kakopetria to Nicosia. Good, that had worked, Ingrid sneered. That should keep those two busy and out of her hair for a while.

Ingrid's testosterone level had returned to normal by the fourth call, which was just as well, as the room was being filled with testosterone from another source at just that moment. As she disconnected from the phone for the last time, she looked up into the puckered navel of her secretary. He had already taken off his shirt and tie and his muscles rippled in the effort to unzip his tight trousers. His broad smile was enough to erase most of the day's little irritations. Ingrid so loved these surprise afternoon dictation sessions. As the wall into her adjacent lounge opened at her touch of a switch, the Swede was down to his socks. He moved around the desk and behind his boss, nuzzling his face into Ingrid's neck as his hands traveled down the front of her blouse, expertly flipping open buttons in their wake. Following a very brief period of arousal, he took Ingrid up in his arms, which was no small task in itself, and padded off to the private lounge.

* * * *

When the Koniotises left the road just above Omodhos and made their way down toward the town square, the sedan that had been following them at a discreet distance pulled over to the side of the road and its sole occupant took out a pair of binoculars with directional listening sensors.

Caitlyn had never been to Omodhos before and Takis had not been there since his childhood, so this visit to Ginger Patterson's home was somewhat of an adventure for them. They parked to the east of the square, which, like several of the surrounding lanes, had been blocked off and paved as a pedestrian mall. As Caitlyn and Takis approached Ginger's house, they were oblivious to the two pairs of eyes that watched their every movement—or at least the two pairs of eyes that started by watching them and ended with one pair watching them and the other pair watching the watcher.

As dusk began to descend, Caitlyn and Takis turned to finding Ginger's house. This wasn't too difficult. The village was small and the inhabitants were friendly and helpful. Ginger gathered the couple in at her courtyard door and they proceeded to her small living room, where, breaking her recent habits—and recalling her old habits—she had laid out a tray of liquor bottles rather than her customary afternoon tea.

Both Caitlyn and Takis were happy to see that Ginger had aged well and that the mellow mood that had set in long after they had first met her had endured beyond her last marriage to their old friend, John Patterson. There had been a period in their acquaintance with the woman that, like so many others, they had been careful to avoid her because of her legendary acid tongue and quick temper.

Their initial conversation was briefly about John and his unfortunate death in Beirut. Although Caitlyn and Takis had always assumed that John would grow old with Takis's former colleague, Safa Ziya, they had to admit that his marriage to Ginger, brief as it was, had been a happy one and that he had been fortunate to find her—much more fortunate perhaps than her previous husband, the journalist Willie Hamilton, who had found and been initially married to her in her Wicked Witch of the West phase.

Takis could tell that Ginger was preoccupied and worried during their conversation, though, and he urged her to tell him what the matter was. When she told him what she had found out about her new neighbor, Roulla Dahir—both about who she was, and the money that Ginger had seen, Takis became quite concerned and suggested that, for the safety of both Ginger and Roulla, he had better be taken to see the neighbor.

The trip next door, however, was largely a waste of time. One of the pairs of eyes that had been watching the Koniotises stroll the village and wend their way eventually to Ginger's door had belonged to Roulla. She had recognized both Caitlyn and Takis instantly. She never could have forgotten them, even if she had not found and kept newspaper clippings in which the two figured prominently. Roulla had been on the roof of her house when the Koniotises arrived. While they were reminiscing with Ginger, Roulla was gathering up her most valuable possessions, including most of the photographs and money that had unknowingly brought attention to her. She then slipped out the rear door of her house and climbed the hillside to the road that ran from Limassol on the coast, to Platres in the mountains.

She was still looking from one direction to the other, trying to decide which road to take, when the watcher in the sedan, the watcher who had first been watching Caitlyn and Takis and who had then turned their full attention to Roulla Dahir in distress on her roof top, gunned the engine of the sedan, bore down on Roulla, and obviated her need to decide which road to choose.

****

The note the secretary had passed to her had told her to go immediately to the Cassa Carioca. The secretary had said that the message had been called in by a man, but she didn't know who.

It had to have been Uri, Christiana Tzavella thought. He must have realized that she was in trouble and he was going to help her. It was natural that he had told her to meet him at the Cassa Carioca. It was within a short walk, and it would be virtually deserted during the late afternoon hours. As he was the manager there now, he could help her. He could probably help her hide from RayGo for a while and then could help her slip off the island and to London, where she could easily lose herself in that metropolis.

She encountered no trouble at the front entrance of the Cassa Carioca, and there was the assistant manager who came to greet her, the same man who had been admonished to protect her the other night as Uri went off to meet with the outgoing manager. Chris briefly wondered if the outgoing manager, Sergey Stepanov, had departed the island yet. He had once made a pass at her, and she had almost accommodated him. He was pretty old now, but he still had the charisma and rugged good looks that had made him a legend on the island's southern coast over the past two decades. But then she had remembered that his reputation had included some very kinky and brutal habits and she had backed off. He had not been pleased, and she certainly hoped she wouldn't run into him here at the club today.

She was following the assistant manager, but he wasn't leading her to the lounge where she and Uri had been the previous evening—nor toward the direction in which Uri had gone when he was going to the manager's office. Instead, they angled off to the left, past the now-quiet main show room and one of the bigger casino halls, through a padded door and down some stairs, through another padded door and into a darkened room.

The assistant manager stood aside and let Christiana enter the room. Then he flipped on a bank of lights, leered at the young woman, and left the room. The door clicked decisively and ominously behind him.

Uh Oh. This wasn't the manager's office and what she saw in the glaring lights was not the Uri she had expected.

* * * *

The rest of the evening was a blur of confusion for Caitlyn, whereas Takis seemed to be in his element. When they realized that Roulla Dahir was not going to come to the door, they entered the small house adjacent to Ginger's cottage. The

222

door had not been locked, and it quickly became evident that she had left in a hurry. Drawers were open and belongings were scattered about. A small plate of cookies was on a bureau beside the door, most likely left there, Ginger surmised, because Roulla had been ready to come over to Ginger's courtyard for afternoon tea when Caitlyn and Takis appeared. Even the lights were still on in the dining area and kitchen. Ginger could tell, however, that the photographs she had seen were now gone.

Caitlyn and Ginger returned to Ginger's place, while, first, the police from Platres and, later, Ahmad Jallud himself appeared at Takis's summons and searched Roulla's dwelling from stem to stern.

Caitlyn could hardly believe what Ginger had told them. Irina Lukenov alive? After all these years. The Lukenov kidnapping and supposed murder story had also been the Caitlyn Koniotis and Eric Isaksen kidnapping story, so not only was the sudden reappearance of Irina Lukenov a shock to Caitlyn's system, it also dredged up some decidedly painful memories. Irina Lukenov had been the wife of the Russian diplomat, Mikhail Lukenov. She had been kidnapped while on a family outing, shortly after arriving in Cyprus by a band of Hizballah terrorists who were secretly training in the Troodos mountains. Caitlyn and Eric Isaksen had been kidnapped by the same band. However, whereas Caitlyn and Eric had been protected by Ahmad Jallud, at that time an unwilling member of the terrorist unit, and rescued by Ellen Larkin, Irina Lukenov had always been thought to have been transferred to Beirut and to have died in a bombing incident during a failed rescue attempt by a Russian squad.

Could this really be Irina Lukenov, Caitlyn wondered. If so, where had she been all these years, and why had she not revealed herself earlier? And what was she doing back in Cyprus now?

When Takis appeared back at Ginger's door at last, Caitlyn pelted him with these questions. Takis had some answers to give her, but his answers were far more provocative than her questions had been.

"You said you saw a large cache of banknotes next door, Ginger?"

Ginger nodded her assent.

"Well, she must have taken most of them with her. However, she didn't manage to take them all. Damndest thing." Takis looked very perplexed.

"What do you mean?" Caitlyn couldn't resist asking.

"We found a few large-denomination euro bills that had been caught in a crack in a compartment below her floorboards. They were counterfeit—the same blue thread going through them that shouldn't be there. Ahmad seems to think they are from the same lot that have been salted in Caitlyn's purse."

"That's strange," was the first thing Caitlyn could think of saying. "But what I can't understand is why this blue thread is such a giveaway. I meant to ask that back at the restaurant."

"That blue thread is part of the fight against counterfeiting. In a combined program, several countries' treasuries leaked stories that the new banknotes would have this thread and some fake sample paper was floated. But the real bills don't have the thread. So, those that do have the thread do so because the counterfeiters were fooled—and the thread aids quick detection."

"Oh," was all Caitlyn said.

"And if you think it's strange for these notes to match the ones passed through you," Takis continued, "take a look at this photograph we found buried in the back of a bureau drawer. Is this one of the photographs you saw earlier, Ginger?"

Ginger took the photograph from Takis and examined it. "I can't say for sure that it is," she said. "This one appears to be even older than those I saw in the house. But then, yes, now that I think about it, there might have been one this old. This looks like it could be a young Roulla. But who is the young man, I wonder?"

Caitlyn had come up behind Ginger and was staring at the photograph over the older woman's shoulder.

"He looks familiar," she said. And then she exclaimed: "Why, he looks like a very young Sergey Stepanov!"

"My thoughts, exactly," Takis agreed grimly.

* * * *

Ingrid Isaksen had been flabbergasted. Andre had come into her office that afternoon and had found her in a compromising position with her secretary. That didn't bother her a bit, but quite unexpectedly he had thrown himself into a jealous rage—the first real emotion she had seen the insipid young man display during the length of their relationship—and had flounced off, saying that she need not expect him to return to the Ayia Napa apartment that evening.

Fine with her, she had thought. She hadn't been sure she would have been able to keep up pretenses of affection that evening anyway. She needed time away from Andre to consolidate her attack on the Piccard holding moves. What she was not aware of, of course, was the precise reason Andre had feigned a jealous snit. He also was having trouble containing his rising hatred of the woman and needed to give his father the necessary time to ensure that the family company had escaped RayGo's clutches.

However, as Ingrid's Mercedes pulled up to the Ayia Napa Ingrid Beach Tower, she realized she would need some sort of companionship that evening. Andre had interrupted her and the Swede at a very strategic moment, and although Andre's attack had caused the secretary to finish abruptly, Ingrid had not been satisfied. She looked up at the tall block of apartments and saw that the lights were on in the fourth-floor apartment.

Ah, Uri Lukenov must be home now. Her pulse quickened and she headed straight for the elevator, her high heels playing a brisk tattoo on the terrazzo floor of the foyer.

Yes, he was home, but she was much taken aback when he answered the door. He opened the door only wide enough for her to see his face, although she could see that he was in a robe—and quite possibly nothing else—and thus appeared to be in just the right condition for her intentions. But when she saw his face, she could see it was puffy and red. Had he been in a fight or had he been crying? She didn't get sufficient time to think on that further.

"I'm free for the evening," she said in a commanding voice. "I think we should talk up in my flat about your contract."

"I couldn't possibly this evening, Mrs. Isaksen—Ingrid. I'm just getting ready to go to the club for the evening. I work at night, you know."

"You work for me and can show up at the club when it suits me," Ingrid snorted. But then she softened. She had not figured out how best to handle this intriguing young and virile Russian yet. "You can be a bit late this evening. I have some champagne on ice upstairs. I have not as yet been able to check out your, ah . . . qualifications." Her leer and the way her eyes traveled down the front of his robe, which was not completely closed, left little to the imagination concerning what she had meant by the word "qualifications."

However, at that moment, there was a sound of movement in the apartment. Ingrid's eyes flashed. "You are not alone?" It was more an accusatory statement than a question.

"No, unfortunately not," Uri said apologetically.

"You have a woman in there?" Still more statement than question.

"You might say that," Uri said mildly. But then to defuse the rising storm, he said "But then I didn't know you would be stopping by this evening, did I? Perhaps, if you aren't doing anything this evening, you could come by the club later."

Now Ingrid was smiling coyly. She reached up, took Uri's robe by the lapel and pulled him into the hallway. Using both hands, she pulled the robe open. The sash unknotted and fell to the floor. She stood there for a moment surveying the goods.

"My, my, my," was all she could think of saying.

Uri cupped her cheeks in the palm of his hands, pulled her very close, kissed her full on the lips, released her, and whispered a "later" as he withdrew into the apartment and clicked the door shut.

"Yes, later," Ingrid smiled sweetly, as she strolled to the elevator. As the doors shut, she found herself repeating her earlier observation. "My, my, my."

After Ingrid was gone, Uri closed his robe, retied his sash, and turned to Andre Piccard, who asked, "Do you think she knows I'm here?"

"Relax. I'm sure she hasn't a clue. I'll make sure she has no worries tonight and that she doesn't have time or energy for any of her scheming."

"Better you than me," the younger man shuddered. "Thanks for taking me in for the night."

"It was the least I could do after what you've done for me," Uri tossed over his shoulder as he resumed the journey to the shower that had been interrupted by Ingrid's unscheduled appearance.

* * * *

It was only hours after the last of the police investigators had cleared out of Roulla's house and locked it up and Caitlyn and Takis had departed—having tried unsuccessfully to convince Ginger to come down to Nicosia with them until the mystery of Irina Lukenov had been solved—that Ginger remembered that she had invited the Koniotises to come to Omodhos for more than just to share the secret of Roulla's past. There was also the matter of John's papers, the papers that she had secreted away in the strong box behind the fireplace.

Ginger had no idea what was in those papers. She only knew that John had told her that they were very important and for her to keep them in a safe place, away from prying eyes. He had told her this just before he had left for Beirut on the trip that had been his last. She had thought that he had been strangely serious when he turned the papers over to her. It had almost been as if he knew he might not return from Beirut. She had often wondered since if he had known that he had heart trouble and had kept that knowledge from her. If so, he had miraculously kept it from his doctor as well. The woman, who was one of Nicosia's leading general practitioners, had claimed to have been very surprised when John died from a heart attack in Beirut. She claimed that he had a very healthy heart.

Although she looked through the papers on occasion, Ginger had not been able to understand what they represented. A lot of formulas, diagrams, and very small print. The small print defeated her. Thanks to the vanities of her earlier life, her eyesight was extremely bad. In her younger days, she had wanted to hide this weakness, and she wasn't about to ruin her looks by wearing spectacles, so she had let her eyesight deteriorate. She wore spectacles now, of course, which stopped her from bumping into the furniture, but she had only been able to enjoy her French novels if she wore her reading glasses, and they weren't strong enough for the fine print.

She admitted to herself that she had become very curious about the papers John had left. They were all paper copies and she couldn't figure the print out herself, and John had been clear that she shouldn't show them to just anyone. Caitlyn and Takis weren't just anyone, of course. They had been among John's most trusted friends and colleagues. So she knew John would not have minded for Takis to read his papers and to explain the contents to her.

Thus, after she had arranged for the Koniotises to visit today, Ginger had taken the strong box out and placed it on a side table to show to Takis. Roulla's disappearance, however, and the further revelations that had come out about who she was and that the money that Ginger saw in her house was counterfeit had completely vanquished the thought of John's papers from Ginger's mind until she was waving at where the couple had disappeared into the night.

Ah, well, she thought, as she returned the strong box to its resting place and prepared for bed, Caitlyn and Takis had promised to come back and see her again before they left for New York. There was always time to show them John's papers at a later date. That's what Ginger found that she had plenty of now. Time. And now that Roulla was gone, perhaps forever, time would once again weigh heavily on Ginger's life.

Later that night, Ginger heard sounds of movement in Roulla's adjacent house. She had become aware of the movement as she was already drifting off to sleep and she was filled with a sense of well-being. She had not realized until Roulla had left how good it had felt to have found some companionship, even if they had only seen each other a couple of times every day and even then had not spoken much. The next morning, however, Ginger discovered that Roulla still had not returned. The house looked a wreck, but for all she knew that was how the police had left it. If she had been sure that the sounds she heard in the night had been real and not just the wishful thinking of a lonely old woman, she would have reported the incident to Ahmad Jallud. But she wasn't sure, so she didn't bother to call him.

Chapter Thirteen

Takis Koniotis's vacation was over. Bright and early the next morning, he reverted to being the UN undersecretary general for security affairs. Having bullied Caitlyn out of bed before the sun came up across the Makedonitissa Valley and having set her to updating her account of all the people who had come within three feet of her since arriving in Cyprus on the *Daphne* three days previously, Takis called a war counsel of his most trusted—and most powerful, in terms of police affairs—colleagues in Cyprus.

Caitlyn agreed to spend some time on her list and to send what she could put together over to Takis's meeting by e-mail, but she also said she had no intention of missing the meeting at the Cyprus Museum later that morning where Andriko Visiliou was putting together a seminar visit later in the week to the Bogaz layered archaeological time exhibit and the ancient Greco-Roman city of Salamis.

By 8:00 AM Takis had made the fifteen-minute monorail ride from the Makedonitissa station to his destination in the western town of Morphou, where the new UNICIS facility had been built because it was in a quiet area here, with a clean, inviting environment, and it was more easily accessible to Nicosia via the almost-deserted monorail than any of the other towns in Cyprus.

Ellen Larkin was somewhat disgruntled when she met Takis in the UNICIS reception and security screening area, and she barely hid her irritation. When Takis had said he wanted a war council at the UNICIS headquarters on the counterfeiting issue, Ellen had readily agreed and said that she would call the appropriate group together, which would include Wilhelm Jacobs, who was working the issue for the U.S. embassy, and William Stevens, who was his Australian counterpart. However, Takis had said in no uncertain terms that he only wanted Ellen herself, Maria Mattas, and Ahmad Jallud at the meeting. Ellen, who had become very close to William Stevens, had complained that this made it look like Takis didn't trust the Australian and the American, and, to her consternation, Takis had not demurred. Rather, he had told her that, at this point he only trusted the specific people he had invited to the meeting.

When the four were together in the UNICIS emission-secure conference room that was known in embassy's worldwide as the bubble, Ellen introduced the head of the UNICIS computer lab division, Stuart Claymore, who presented Takis with a printout of the passengers and crew for the *Daphne's* last Mediterranean cruise into the Larnaca sea terminal, information Takis had requested shortly after Caitlyn was apprehended for having arrived in Cyprus on the *Daphne* with counterfeit banknotes.

As Takis was examining this list, Caitlyn's sketchy list of her close contacts since the *Daphne's* landing came in via e-mail. The frustration was immediate.

"There are nearly a dozen people who were on the *Daphne* with Caitlyn and who came in contact with her later as well, mostly at the president's dinner," Ahmad Jallud exclaimed. "Several people could have salted counterfeit banknotes in her purse both times."

"Present company excluded, of course," said Maria. "None of us went near the *Daphne*."

No one said anything for a few minutes, while everyone was scrutinizing the two lists. Ellen Larkin looked particularly preoccupied. It was with surprise, therefore, that Takis looked up and saw Stuart Claymore looking at Ellen with speculative concern.

But then Maria spoke. "This earlier list of Caitlyn's, the one where she lists the people she saw on the ship, doesn't completely match the passenger list. Look, see. They both have Caitlyn, Andriko, Demetris, and Bill Burch—all members of the archaeological group. And they also list Ingrid Isaksen and Wilhelm Jacobs and his girlfriend, Gladys Holiday. But Caitlyn's list doesn't have William Stevens, and his name is on the passenger list."

"Well, Caitlyn didn't know Stevens then," responded Takis, "and she apparently hadn't seen him on the ship before she had found out who he was. But that does explain why he was there, Johnnie on the spot, to interrogate her after she was arrested. I wonder what he was doing on the *Daphne*."

Ellen looked uncomfortable and began to speak, but then appeared to decide not to say anything.

Looking somewhat suspiciously at her, Stuart Claymore did speak. "You probably know where Stevens had been, don't you Ellen? You went to Larnaca that day to pick him up, didn't you?"

Ellen looked embarrassed. "Why yes, now that you mention it; I did pick Bill up at the sea terminal. He had been in Beirut on diplomatic business."

"And so, you were at the sea terminal the day Mrs. Koniotis was arrested?" Stuart honed in. "The interior minister just said that none of the four of you were there that day, and you didn't say anything."

Ellen had turned red, whether out of increased embarrassment or anger was not clear. "Oh, did Maria say that? I'm sorry, I wasn't listening. Yes, I was there, but I didn't see

Caitlyn, and Bill found me before I found him. I had no idea at the time that he had been questioning Caitlyn." And then she turned to Takis and said, "Takis, didn't you say you had other things to be checked out in the computers? Why don't you give those to Stuart, and he can go run them."

Takis outlined to Claymore the various threads that he wanted checked. He asked that the prints that the police had obtained at Roulla Dahir's Omodhos house the previous night be run in the computer and asked that Stuart try to track down records of the prints of Irina Lukenov, the supposedly murdered wife of the former Russian diplomat to Cyprus, as well. He wanted verification that the two were one and the same person, he wanted to know what Dahir had been up to in the intervening years, and, in consideration of the counterfeit banknotes found in Dahir's house, he wanted to know if there might be a link between that woman and what was happening to Caitlyn.

Having seen the familiar name of Piccard stand out on both the *Daphne* passenger list and on the presidential dinner list, he asked for a background check on Andre Piccard. He also asked for a computer run on Pierre Piccard. Everyone assumed that Eleni's son had died in 1974. Now that seemed to have been a lie. Takis was suddenly very interested in where Pierre was and what he was doing. In Takis's experience, the Piccard name had always all-to-easily linked up to whatever international investigation he had been conducting in Cyprus.

For this reason, he asked Stuart to check the status of the current Piccard holdings on the island as well. It had escaped no one's notice that the *Daphne* was part of the Piccard fleet and that it was not below the Piccards—whom everyone present knew and didn't love—to use their ships to move any contraband goods, including counterfeit money.

As an afterthought, Takis asked the computer official to check into RayGo and his old friend Ingrid Isaksen as well. "I'd sure like to know what *she* was doing on the *Daphne* and what her connection to Piccard is. I know, I know," he said as Maria was about to interject a snide comment. "I know it has an aspect of robbing the cradle for her own pleasure to it, but Ingrid is rarely that single-minded. I'm sure there's some other connection as well. And it would not be welcome to any of us if it turns out that RayGo and the Piccards are combining forces."

Ellen left to check her computer and returned with yet another e-mail from Caitlyn, quickly jotted off as she was leaving for the Cyprus Museum.

"What's this?" Ellen queried. "It says 'Just a hunch. Try checking the singer. Says Michigan in archaeology, but avoided discussing topic, nice nail job, and no calluses.'"

Takis chuckled. "Caitlyn and her hunches—which, as we all know, are usually prophetic. She's suggesting we check Gladys Holiday to see if she's really who she says she is. As Caitlyn told me earlier, yesterday at the Old Mill Inn, the young woman had gushed at Caitlyn about shared archaeological backgrounds—right up to the moment that Caitlyn had started to talk about archaeology, and then Holiday, who is very much on the list of those who could have set Caitlyn up, clammed up and disappeared."

"But the reference to nails and calluses?" asked Ahmad.

"If she had just come from working a dig in Lebanon, as she claimed to Caitlyn, she should have broken nails and calluses just about everywhere that showed and some places that don't. Caitlyn says she doesn't have them—the broken nails and calluses on her hands, that is. Yes, Stuart, by all means add Ms. Gladys 'Billie' Holiday, University of Michigan graduate and presumably British citizen, to your checkout list."

As Stuart reached the door on his way to the lab, Takis appeared to have an afterthought and pulled the computer official aside.

"Perhaps you had better check out Wilhelm Jacobs and William Stevens as well, Stuart," Takis said to the young man in a low voice. "And just between you and me, please. I think Ellen is in too deep with Stevens to be objective."

"I'm already ahead of you, sir," Claymore answered as he showed where he had already written the two names on his slate. "And, sir, could I see you—in private—before you leave today?"

"Certainly," Takis answered and returned to the others with a pensive frown on his face. While they were waiting for

Stuart to run his checks, Takis told the others what he and Caitlyn suspected about the lineage of Andre Piccard and of the strong possibility that Pierre Piccard had survived and sired a son. After this they moved on to discuss the even more incredible story, particularly since all four of them had been closely involved in the Hizballah band's kidnapping spree, of Irina Lukenov's return from the supposed dead. Of her disappearance from Omodhos the previous afternoon, and of her apparent link to the international counterfeit operations they were investigating.

At length, Takis picked up the *Daphne*'s passenger list and isolated his attention on the passengers who had boarded at the stop just previous to the Larnaca landing. Caitlyn had been exchanging money all across the Mediterranean during her seminar tour and yet it had not been until she reached her final destination in Cyprus that she had been pulled aside for passing counterfeit money. Part of Stuart's check on the cruise of the *Daphne* had included a query being sent to all of the ports where Caitlyn had stopped and exchanged money, concerning whether they had received any counterfeit money during these time frames, and all had reported in the negative. It kept nagging at Takis's mind that the key to the problem must be Beirut, the stop the *Daphne* had made the evening previous to the final landing at Larnaca.

He took the passenger list back up and zeroed in on the names of the appropriate passengers who had embarked in Beirut. Ingrid Isaksen and Andre Piccard, sharing one suite; Wilhelm Jacobs and Gladys Holiday, sharing a cabin; William Stevens in a single cabin.

Takis was sure that somewhere in this short list was the answer to his mystery.

But then the mystery took on a whole new dimension and his blood ran cold. There, a name that none of them had focused on because they had all been looking for the familiar. A name, nonetheless, that was very familiar to all of them in another context—at least until yesterday's events. Uri Lukenov. Takis's mind raced back in time as his colleagues chatted about various ways to approach the counterfeit operations case. Uri Lukenov. The then-young son of the Russian diplomat, whom Takis had known to be the Russian spy chief in Cyprus. The son also of the kidnapped wife, Irina Lukenov. The son who had tracked the kidnappers across Cyprus, from the Morphou Bay Turkish zone coast, across the no man's land of the UN buffer zone, into the Troodos foothills in the Greek part of the island, for a day and a half, all by himself, only to lose the trail at an isolated and deserted monastery and never to see his mother again. Uri Lukenov—if it was the same Uri Lukenov, something that Stuart would have to check out—returning to Cyprus on the

Daphne while his supposedly dead mother was living in the Troodos foothills.

And then another name entered his mind. His old nemesis Sergey Stepanov. A former Russian Intelligence KGB agent, just like Mikhail Lukenov, and on Cyprus at the same time as the Lukenov incident, but connected at that time to the Russian mafia presence. Why had that name entered his mind? Oh yes, the shocking picture they had found at Roulla Dahir's house the previous night. A picture that could have been of a very young Irina Lukenov and Sergey Stepanov. The first suggested link between the two, although at the time Takis had strongly suspected a link between Stepanov's Russian mafia and Lukenov's supposed diplomatic activity. Takis hadn't gotten around to telling Ahmad about the picture, and it hadn't come up just a bit ago when the two of them were briefing Ellen and Maria. And maybe this was just as well, Takis thought. Maybe this was a link that Takis himself should pursue for a while.

Maria was trying to get his attention. "I said, Takis, that perhaps we should meet with the International Investigations Unit this evening and start the hunt for this woman who disappeared last night. If it was Irina Lukenov, she probably has a very interesting story to tell."

"Sorry, I can't tonight, Maria. Ingrid Isaksen has invited Caitlyn and me to dinner at the Cassa Carioca tonight."

Maria looked confused. She knew that Takis avoided Ingrid Isaksen like the plague and that he knew the sordid reputation of the Cassa Carioca. She started to speak, but Takis beat her to the punch.

"I understand Sergey Stepanov is the manager of the Cassa Carioca now, true?"

Maria was even more confused. All she could do was nod her head, as Stuart Claymore reentered the conference room.

* * * *

Caitlyn didn't even notice them as she strolled past the Garden Café, which was wedged into the corner created by the parliament building, the municipal theater, and the municipal park, and crossed over the street to the main entrance of the Cyprus Museum. It probably would have been better if she had noticed them and had said something to them and shown some sign of recognition. As it was, Wilhelm Jacobs and William Stevens already were suffering so much from mutual guilt complexes that they were meeting secretly at the Garden Café, which, had they not both been fairly new of Cyprus, they would have realized had been used for nearly a hundred years as a meeting place for the foreign spies that buzzed around the island.

When they saw Caitlyn, they both hunkered down, trying to hide behind a laptop sitting on the table. While they had been conversing in their secret talk, one of them had been working on the computer, which was attached to an intranet that was separated entirely from Internet connection to fully protect its content.

Caitlyn hadn't seen them, so she hadn't registered as having seen them in any way. The two, already feeling too conspicuous, had both assumed that Caitlyn *had* seen them and was being clever about not having spoken to them, as if they weren't there. And if she was putting on a show of not seeing them, each reasoned, she must not want them to think that she had seen them. The spy's natural conclusion from this convoluted reasoning was that Caitlyn actually walked by specifically to see them and that she must know something that they, in their separate reasoning, did not want her to know. If she knew something and was following them, she must therefore be a danger to one or both of them.

Then, on the sidewalk on the other side of the street, almost opposite to the table where Jacobs and Stevens were sitting, Caitlyn sealed her fate. As if she suddenly remembered that she had written a note to herself to take care of something while she was in the city—which was, in fact, the case—she stopped and rummaged around in her briefcase. She fished out her little silver notebook, which might have looked suspiciously like a miniature camera to professional spies, and half turned toward the café, away from the glare of the sun, while she checked her notes. She could have clearly seen the two men out of the corner of her eye during this process. She did not, however, no matter what either Jacobs or Stevens might have thought, focus on those sitting at the café tables. She was, in fact, completely occupied by her notes. Satisfied with what she read there, she flipped the notebook shut, returned it to her briefcase, and turned and entered the Cyprus Museum.

The wholly innocent Caitlyn had suddenly entered the zone of personal danger in the highly professional world of suspicion. As she entered the museum, she had no idea that her life on earth had entered a new, threatening phase. She was just meeting an appointment to go see some old pottery and stones with fellow old pottery and stones enthusiasts.

As coincidence would have it—although perhaps it only seemed to be coincidence—the director of the American Archaeological Institute, Bill Burch had also been sitting in the Garden Café, enjoying a cup of coffee before attending the meeting Andriko Visiliou had called on the special seminar trip to Bogaz and Salamis. He had seen Caitlyn's actions, just as the nearby Jacobs and Stevens had, and her presence had brought a hard look and a frown to his face.

After Caitlyn crossed the street, Burch rose from his table, tipped his head at his diplomatic acquaintances as he passed them, and followed in Caitlyn's wake.

Chapter Fourteen

The UNICIS computers, the only computers in the world that linked up all of the information databases, both public and for the use of police forces, of all UN member states and all affiliated international organizations, including the international crime agency, Interpol, had done their job again. Roulla Dahir indeed was Irina Lukenov. And, more interesting than that, she had popped up as the consort of a Hizballah unit leader in Lebanon shortly after she had supposedly been killed by explosives in an unsuccessful Russian attempt to rescue her from a shop building on the Beirut waterfront. The informant, Ahmad Jallud's own uncle, who had informed the Russians where she was being held at that time, had also told them the Hizballah unit using the shop had claimed that the woman they were holding was an Israeli spy. Just maybe they had been telling him the truth.

Irina had apparently willingly taken up with the band. The fingerprints they had run had also matched those in a case where drugs from the Lebanese mountains were being smuggled into Europe in the false bottoms of native handcrafted baskets. The computers were continuing to work on digging out more information on the woman. She apparently had arrived in Cyprus from Beirut—on the *Daphne* two months previously.

Takis was right about the Piccards. Pierre Piccard was the son of Guy Piccard—and thus of Eleni, as well. He had been raised in Switzerland and was last known, from visa records, to be right here in Cyprus someplace. No particular address was available, and the Piccards had hotels, villas, and apartments all over the island. Andre Piccard was Pierre Piccard's son. The Piccards seemed to be picking up stakes and moving from Cyprus, although they were covering their tracks in the computer systems pretty well. There was nothing in the computer system on a link between Piccard and RayGo, and the coded and compartmented RayGo background files were creating a real challenge to even the UNICIS cross-checking programs.

Knowing about Takis's background with the Piccards, who had often figured in his investigations when he was a police official here in Cyprus, Claymore had saved the most disturbing information for last. Guy Piccard had been closely associated with a consortium of international crime and terrorist organizations that had once tried to prevent a Middle East settlement and attempted to sabotage the international conference, held right here in Cyprus. At that time the fully negotiated Middle East peace plan was supposed to have been signed. Although the conference actually broke up on its own short of settlement and there never had been a "final" settlement—although tensions had been increasingly lessened over the intervening years—Takis and the then-rudimentary UNICIS organization had been able to forge the police and security forces of the region into a cooperative body and had defeated the forces that Guy Piccard had been associated with. In a face-to-face showdown between Koniotis and Guy Piccard, the Frenchman had been arrested and had appeared to already be dying of cancer—at least that was what he had claimed—and he certainly looked terminal that last time Koniotis saw him.

In the following years, Koniotis had become so busy with his new job with the UN that he had lost track of what had happened following the arrest of Guy. On the basis of the just-completed computer search on the Piccards, it was Claymore's sad duty to inform Takis that the influential Piccard had gone to a castle in Switzerland rather than to a prison hospital—and that he had lived for another decade, dying from an accidental fall rather than from cancer.

Beyond a passport and several entries around the eastern Mediterranean, Gladys Holiday appeared to have no background at all. All present agreed that this made Gladys Holiday a very suspicious person, worthy of their closest scrutiny.

Holiday and Jacobs appeared to have been on vacation in Lebanon before joining the fateful *Daphne* cruise at Beirut. The hotel and restaurant charge records checked out. Stuart voiced an interesting aside on Jacobs. Whereas Holiday apparently had no past, Jacobs had had some interesting recent assignments—Beirut, Tehran, Baghdad, and the U.S. Bureau of Engraving, during a period in which there was some sort of scandal in that department.

"Funny thing about our UNICIS computer programs," Claymore said, his face showing a grin. "They are starting to think like detectives. It's very interesting what they put together and spit out sometimes."

Piccard's stay in Beirut also checked out. However, although Isaksen's hotel records checked out—she was recorded as staying with Piccard—there were three days of restaurant receipts that were for only one person, all signed by Piccard. They might have had a lover's spat, but, if that was so, then it seemed they would sleep apart rather than eat apart. Still, Isaksen was an important business woman and had been an important international diplomat. She might have gone off for a few nights to stay with someone living in Beirut.

Ellen had excused herself to attend to a previously scheduled appointment, so, while Maria and Ahmad dug into some of the other material the computers had provided, Koniotis and Claymore drew to one side.

"What about Stevens?" Takis asked.

"That's why the Isaksen thing stands out to me," responded Claymore. "The same three days that look odd in the records the computers have put together on her so far match three days that Stevens wasn't covered by records in Beirut at all."

"Hmm," Takis murmured. "And you say Jacobs and Holiday were definitely in Beirut those same days?"

"Well, nothing is definite with what we've found so far. These are only records, not reliable sightings. Jacobs and Holiday could just have been more clever in covering their tracks. One or both of them could have been gone from Beirut for a while as well. We have more checking we can do. I wouldn't want to be too sure about anything in this vein for a while."

"Thanks, Stuart. You said you wanted to talk to me about something."

"Yes Sir. I don't want to be talking out of school, and I'd trust Ellen with my life, but . . ."

"What is it, Stuart? What have you seen? I know you are perfectly straight and wouldn't be concerned without good reason."

"Yes, sir. Thank you, sir. It's just the very peculiar thing that's happening in the computer. At first I thought it was some sort of virus or a computer malfunction. But, after this afternoon, I'm sure it's something much more serious."

"Go on," Takis coaxed.

"It's the information I've been pulling out of the files for you, sir. Specifically the information you've asked for since you came to Cyprus. Well, sir. The problem is that after I pull information for you—not always, just during certain periods, just certain blocks of time—well, the file that information comes from just disappears."

"Just disappears?" Takis didn't think he was understanding what he was hearing. "You mean, it's gone from the files we are linking into and can't be retrieved again?" Takis was no computer expert, but this sounded unlikely.

"Yes, sir. It disappears. The UNICIS computers can't find it again, and, on a couple of files, I've called the original file owner and they can't recover it either. Sir, I don't know why this is happening, but I do know that there are times when our searches for you are being shadowed and destroyed, and, sir, some of our sources are beginning to scream. They can see it happening in their systems, sir, and they can tell that it's happening when we are linked in. Sir, they are starting to threaten to cut our access links. And I don't know what to do."

"Surely you've gone to Ellen with this. What does she have to say about it?"

Claymore stood, mute and with a very pained expression.

"You haven't gone to Ellen about this?" Takis asked incredulously and with an increased volume that caused Maria to look up at him. And then in a quieter, more intense voice: "And why haven't you talked to Ellen about this, Stuart?"

"Because . . . because the deletion process shows me the source of the deletion, sir." Claymore struggled with his voice, obviously miserable. "And all of the deletions are being made with Ellen's own code, sir. You see, when we developed the linkup programs, the deep deletion capability down to the original source was a real problem, a problem we didn't bother to solve because it could only be effected by those with full access codes. That's only the computer lab staff and the director herself."

"But then anyone in the lab could be doing this, and Ellen would hardly be doing it with her own code if she knew she could be identified." Takis was still grasping for understanding.

"No, sir. I'm afraid all of the deletions are being made by Ellen's code and only her code—and only Ellen doesn't know that the code actions can't be traced back to the initiator. We never bothered to tell her that, because there never a protocol for the director to delete anything in that linked database section of the computer banks."

Takis stood there, stunned, searching madly for explanations.

"Sir," Claymore fought for Koniotis's attention. "Sir, whoever can delete the files in this way can also read them while

I am accessing them. And . . . and, it was only just now, while I was running the searches you just assigned that I was sure that this was intentionally going on. While I was running the searches, I checked back on ones I had just accessed, and the one doing the deleting was on line with me, deleting right behind me. Sir, hasn't Ellen been in here with you while I was gone? Did she just step out?" Even Claymore was still grabbing for an out.

"No, Stuart. I'm sorry to say she left just after you did and hasn't returned."

"Sir, what are we going to do now?"

"Well, the only thing we can do at the moment is close down the searches for now. I can't have the whole system destroyed by loss of trust and cooperation from our original sources. Then, after it's closed down, I want you and your staff to work overtime in changing the system so no one—and I mean no one—can delete original system files through our computers. You can tell Ellen that the system has to go down to correct a basic error, which is true enough, and that I said it can't come back up without my specific permission. The worst part is that we won't have computer support for our investigation for a while. But we solved cases before we had this system, and we can solve this one without the system."

"Is that really the 'worst' part, sir?" Claymore asked glumly.

"Yes, Stuart, I have to believe it is. I've known Ellen too long not to have faith that she has nothing to do with this. I'll certainly follow up on this issue—and you've done exactly right to come to me with this problem—but I'll work on it from here."

Ellen appeared at that moment, all smiles. Stuart turned and left the room, not able to make direct eye contact with his boss.

"Appointment over with?" Takis asked mildly.

"Oh, she canceled. So, as long as I was in the office, I cleaned up some of my computer files before returning."

Well, at least she was honest about it.

* * * *

Caitlyn was early for her meeting with Andriko Visiliou. He had been mysterious when he had talked to her on the phone about the seminar trip to Bogaz and Salamis, and she was more than mildly curious why he hadn't been willing to tell her over the line who was sponsoring this special lecture trip.

Rather than going to Andriko's office only to cool her heels in his reception area for another quarter of an hour, Caitlyn went down to the museum's basement to revisit her own former dimly lit, but comfortable and inviting lab. When she first came to Cyprus she worked here, specializing in carbon dating the artifact finds that were being excavated at various digs around the island. She had enjoyed her work and had been good at it; by that time she had already established an international reputation in the carbon dating field. Thanks to Andriko, however, she eventually was tapped to work more at actual excavation sites than in this lab, and her reputation skyrocketed on her talent for sleuthing out where ancient sites could be found.

This talent for deduction had stemmed from her vivid imagination, which permitted her to stand on a site and project back over the centuries, to become one with the people of earlier times, and thus to predict where they would have lived and worked and where they would have buried their dead. In many respects archaeology thrived on what people buried with their dead. These same powers of deduction had also crossed over into the other areas of her life over the years and had both helped her husband in his criminal cases from time to time and served occasionally to cause her to brush against danger on the basis of knowing too much—which sometimes manifested itself in subconsciously having observed more than her consciousness was registering.

It was just such an unformed hunch that began to bother Caitlyn as soon as she entered her old lab. There had been something that had happened—and most likely very recently if the patterns of her hunches were working true to form—that she had seen or experienced that seemed to be important. For the life of her, however, she couldn't surface what she might have observed. She went over her walk from her car to the museum. With the thought that what was bothering her might have something to do with the note she had written to herself and had stopped to check out across the street from the museum, Caitlyn pulled the silver notebook out of her brief case and checked the note.

It seemed innocuous enough and didn't seem to be ringing any bells of recognition, so she leafed through the notebook, checking other pages. Nothing.

The phone on her old lab table softly rang, and Caitlyn unconsciously returned the notebook to her purse rather than her briefcase, as she answered the phone.

"Ah, I thought you might have gone to your old office, Caitlyn," Andriko's voice boomed down the line. "The receptionist said you arrived in the building already, and we're ready to start the meeting if you want to come up."

"I'll be there in a second," Caitlyn responded, as she grabbed up her purse, brushed her briefcase to the side of the lab table, and moved toward the door.

The presence of all who attended the meeting was predictable, with three notable exceptions. It was natural for Visiliou, Caitlyn, and Bill Burch to meet to set up a special lecture tour of the archaeological sites, and Caitlyn wasn't all that surprised to see Demetris Mattas there, as he was still writing a series on the expansion of Cyprus as an educational center for archaeology, but Caitlyn was quite surprised to see the national police chief, Ahmad Jallud, and the maybe young archaeologist Gladys Holiday there. And then there was another elderly Cypriot gentleman in an expensive gray suit who Caitlyn didn't recognize at all.

During the introductions, Andriko explained that Demetris was present to cover the special lecture tour for the press, that Gladys Holiday had been signed on to the museum on a special research grant—a statement that he delivered in a dry, straightforward voice without looking at Caitlyn, as she had already shared with Andriko her doubts that the young woman was really an archaeologist—and that the man in the gray suit was an aide at the presidential palace.

He didn't give any reason at all why Ahmad Jallud was there, merely stating that he was sure everyone present knew the chief of police. But Ahmad's presence was quickly explained when Andriko revealed that the special lecture tour would be for President Ioannou, who had not seen the special exhibit at Bogaz as yet, and a visiting high-level World Bank official who was charged with considering the extension of loans that had helped put the Cypriot economy back on track. It was obvious to all that Ioannou was hoping that the plans to expand Cyprus' activities in the area of archaeology would help convince the World Bank of the country's solvency.

About half of the people in the room—obviously the half who hadn't already known who was going to be involved in the tour, the half who included Caitlyn—were dumbstruck. Demetris looked quite pleased, as was natural, considering that this gave him a news exclusive. For some reason, Billie Holiday looked rather concerned, which surprised Caitlyn. She would have assumed that a young, impressionable archaeologist would be happy to have the chance to rub elbows with a charismatic national leader. Bill Burch's reaction had been delayed. He obviously had not foreseen the announcement, and he was very quiet at first, but then, when he had fully absorbed the information, he became quite excited, so excited that he swallowed a mouthful of coffee the wrong way and had to leave the room in a coughing fit.

Ahmad Jallud then broke in to tell them in very serious tones that he had recommended against the trip. Bogaz was in an area where there were still some strongly anti-Greek and antisettlement sentiments, for which reason President Ioannou had not previously visited this region of the island, and the president had received some threats recently from terrorist groups linked to Iran for her strongly pro-human and women's rights stands in international venues.

Surprisingly, Billie Holiday spoke up and suggested that perhaps they should go somewhere other than Bogaz for the trip if there was any possibility of danger to the president. Caitlyn would not have thought that the young woman would bother to worry about anything as down-to-earth as personal security.

The presidential aide said that the president insisted that it must be the Bogaz and Salamis area precisely because she had not visited that region as yet and because she already was receiving personal threats. She couldn't see how she could function as president if she let threats imprison her in Nicosia or if she considered any part of the country a denied area to her. She also needed to demonstrate stability and control to the World Bank official. Mattas, almost reluctantly, as he didn't want to diminish the danger even though it would be a news coup for his paper, echoed what the presidential aide said about the importance of just such a move.

Demetris was still speaking when Bill Burch returned. The American looked a little rattled and seemed to be angry about something. Visiliou picked up the discussion.

"So, this is our dilemma. It would be very advantageous to our archaeological program to provide this lecture tour to Bogaz and Salamis for the president and a senior World Bank official, but, as the police chief has pointed out, there are physical dangers involved. To the extent that there is a threat, it seems to be toward the person of the president, but I don't wish to put anyone else in jeopardy unnecessarily. I intend to lead the seminar, which will include not only the president and the World Bank official and their own entourages, but a few leading business people on the island and a handful of diplomats as well. We're going early tomorrow afternoon. I'm sorry there isn't much notice, but that's the way the police and the government wanted it for security reasons. I could use help with the lectures and with the tours for such a large group of people, but I'm sure I could manage alone if need be."

Upon noting the composition of the group, Andriko had referred to a piece of paper. Billie Holiday asked to see the list, and, after briefly scanning it, said, "This will involve too many people for you to be able to handle by yourself, Dr. Visiliou. I'm certainly willing to help with the touring."

"And I'll be there to help with the lecturing," Caitlyn said brightly.

All eyes in the room turned to Bill Burch, who now was exhibiting a small, knowing smile, as if he had just recalled a favorite joke. He looked up to see he was being inspected. "Oh, I wouldn't miss it for the world. Count me in."

When Caitlyn returned to the lab to retrieve her briefcase after the meeting ended, she found it upturned on the floor, with the contents scattered about. As she returned everything to the briefcase, her racing thoughts about tomorrow's seminar trip only permitted her enough time to think about the upturned briefcase to surmise that she herself had pushed it onto the floor in her haste to leave, following Andriko's call to the meeting.

That certainly was one explanation, but it wasn't the only possibility.

* * * *

Iranian General Ujay Khahalbi must have had a bad day. When he received the connection from Nicosia, he broke in, with irritation, after only three sentences of explanation.

"I agree. We can't take chances. Terminate her."

* * * *

When they had both returned to the Makedonitissa house later that afternoon, and while Caitlyn was telling Takis about the planned seminar trip with the president and they were both unwinding with a brandy sour, Takis was called away to the phone.

It was the UNICIS computer lab director, Stuart Claymore.

"I think we got the problem fixed, sir. Everything is back on line now."

"Very good, Stuart. Thanks for the quick work. Does this mean no one from outside the lab can work in the computers now?"

"No, sir, we couldn't do that without reprogramming the whole system. That will take a while longer, I'm afraid—at least until our normal closing time. It does mean, however, that no one can destroy the files of the originator sources outside UNICIS now—although that wouldn't be apparent to them. The functions haven't changed. They just don't destroy the original now, and the user wouldn't know unless they thought to check and recall the original file again."

"Good. Please keep track of others who are working in the files and provide a log the next time I call. And, Stuart, you have that list of everyone who was on the *Daphne* passenger list and who attended the president's dinner party the other night. When you can get back to using the computers, please start pulling background out on all of them—and especially on the passenger whose name I underlined—Uri Lukenov. I'll check back with you first thing in the morning. Keep the night crew on the digging, please."

When he had disconnected, Caitlyn noticed that he looked drawn and worried. When she asked him what was wrong, he floored her with his response.

"Come sit down over here, Caitlyn. I think we need to talk about our good friend, Ellen Larkin."

Chapter Fifteen

Caitlyn had been quite surprised earlier in the afternoon when Takis called her from the UNICIS headquarters building and asked her to inform Ingrid Isaksen that he would be accepting her invitation to dinner at the Cassa Carioca for that evening. When Caitlyn pinned him down on why he was signing up for dinner with a woman he despised, Takis had to admit that he needed a reason to go to the club so that he could confront Sergey Stepanov with the knowledge that Irina Lukenov was alive. He strongly suspected that Stepanov had something to do with the woman's disappearance from Omodhos.

While insisting that he himself was going to endure a dinner with Ingrid to get into the club, Takis strongly suggested that Caitlyn decline for herself on some excuse. But Caitlyn wouldn't have anything to do with that idea. Takis reminded his wife of the nightclub's reputation for decadence, but Caitlyn just cited that as one more reason she wouldn't let him go there alone.

"In fact, if we have to go, let's have a little fun with Ingrid as well," said Caitlyn playfully. "If you'll clear it with Maria, I'll accept the invitation for the Mattases as well as for us. Ingrid didn't invite Maria, but I can pretend that she did, and Ingrid at least can be given the discomfort of having the minister in charge of the police forces eating dinner with her at the Cassa Carioca."

Maria loved the idea—and decided to add an embellishment of her own that Caitlyn and Takis didn't know about until later. Ingrid hated the idea. But, just as Caitlyn predicted, she didn't have the gall to say that Maria and Demetris couldn't come. In fact, Ingrid was not all that happy that Caitlyn and Takis had accepted the invitation either. She had only invited them so that she could later make a fuss, in some venue embarrassing to the Koniotises, that they had snubbed the CEO of the corporation that was funding Caitlyn's archaeological work.

She had been sure that Caitlyn and Takis would not accept the invitation, and she had already planned her evening. Uri Lukenov had been more than satisfactory the previous night, and she was looking forward to a rematch at the club tonight. She would get rid of the Koniotises and Mattases as soon as possible and perhaps the rest of the evening could be salvaged. Uri would be on duty, and he would have no more important duty than her own pleasure.

Ingrid had spent the day trying to track Andre down and somehow punish him. He had returned to her apartment while she was at the club with Uri and took away all of his things. He also, to her great anger, apparently went through the papers in the desk she kept in her bedroom. However, although he seemed to have known she had a secret compartment in the desk and had tried to pry at some of the desk's seams, she was pleased to know that he hadn't gotten to the very private papers on the RayGo formulas that she was keeping there. When she opened that compartment, everything was as she had left it. She was less pleased that he had gotten back in the apartment undetected, though, and she fired the security detail that had been guarding the approaches to the building specifically to let her know if he tried to return.

Ingrid's displeasure with her security detail paled in the face of her displeasure with herself, however, for having wasted the day on trying to find Andre. Shortly before she left the apartment to meet her guests at the Cassa Carioca, she turned on her mobile and logged on to the RayGo Tower computer center to check on how her entrapment of the Piccard holdings on Cyprus was going, only to find out that the Piccards had managed to slip her noose and were now virtually divested in Cyprus, with the exception of their hotel chain, residential properties, and porting rights arrangements.

Unlike the parts of the French corporation that RayGo's lawyers could capture through manipulation of off-shore company holdings, the hotels and residences were specifically in the names of Eleni Piccard's descendants—Pierre Piccard and Andre Piccard, both of whom, to Ingrid's consternation, conveniently turned out to hold dual French and Cypriot citizenship. They would just have to go after the port rights, she thought, which, if taken from the Piccards, would cripple their shipping link to Cyprus. But that did not involve actual property and would take more time, and a lot of bribery, to arrange.

Ingrid steamed out of her apartment and into her private elevator, punched the button for the lobby, and then, on second thought, punched the button for the fourth floor. She would offer Uri a ride to the Cassa Carioca in her Mercedes. It was a twenty-minute ride, which the chauffeur would have no trouble extending to a half hour. The vehicle's rear seat was wide and plush and purpose-designed, and she knew just how to get the greatest advantage out of its contours with a man who was as well-endowed and athletic as Uri had proven to be. It gave her an extra thrill when she knew her chauffeur, who was a good ride himself, was watching the action.

She buzzed Uri's apartment. She could hear activity within, although the sound stopped when she buzzed. There was no response. She buzzed again and rattled the door. Still no response. She dug into her purse and withdrew the master key.

This building was, after all, owned by RayGo, so naturally she had a master key. As the key went into the lock, there was a flurry of activity on the other side, and the door opened a large crack.

Ingrid stepped back in surprise. She hadn't expected to see an old crone. She expected to see Uri, and she would not have been surprised to see some bimbo, but an old lady? She immediately assumed that this was Uri's cleaning lady. Trying to look beyond her, she asked to see Uri, but the woman pointed vaguely toward the outer hallway and stated in broken English that Uri had just left for the club. Ingrid stepped over to the hall window that looked down into the parking area and, sure enough, Uri was striding off toward the tram station.

Without so much as a thank you, Ingrid spun around and headed for the bank of elevators. Perhaps she could still catch him before he reached the station.

* * * *

The recently separated manager of the Cassa Carioca nightclub, Sergey Stepanov, had no reason to be approaching the Larnaca sea terminal with all the care that he had learned in the KGB, but he was a man of habit. He had rarely left a country in the open, or unpursued, in his long professional life. This should have been a treat for him. He could have just walked up the gang plank of the *Daphne*, loudly announced his name, plopped his luggage in a large outside cabin, and headed for the bar to find a companion for the evening and, if lucky, for the night.

But Stepanov's past was quite jaded and he still had enemies, which included countries and international organizations as well as individuals. He had felt very safe in Cyprus, but he never could be sure about his safety while traveling. He had not lived this long by taking any chances.

Thus, he was approaching the *Daphne* at the peak time for servicing the ship rather than for embarking as a passenger; he was wearing clothes that would help him pass to the less-than-totally observant as a workman delivering luggage to the ship, in this case his own; and he was registered on the ship's passenger list with one of his well-documented aliases. Even he thought he was probably being overly cautious for this departure from Cyprus, but that was only until he saw the American diplomat, Wilhelm Jacobs, pacing nervously back and forth near the gangplank and taking a close look at any and all who were going aboard.

Maybe the American was looking for someone else, but Stepanov couldn't be sure. There were hundreds of reasons, based on the many illegal activities Sergey had been engaging in in Cyprus, some of them even international crimes, that the American could be looking for him to prevent his escape from Cyprus. But Sergey could hardly believe that the Americans were on to him. He was sure that he would have known if there had been even a hint that they were following his more annoying activities, such as his brokering of nuclear material sales from the old depots in Russia to the new weapons construction plants in the Persian Gulf.

Stepanov was still trying to figure out how to get past the American, when the ditzy redhead, the Holiday woman, approached Jacobs. They talked in animated tones for a few minutes, and Stepanov slipped behind a column as both of them intently scanned the terminal floor. Just when Stepanov felt he might have to give up the departure via ship and devise another escape, the couple was gone.

A frightened former Russian spy maneuvered his way aboard the ship in stages that included long halts to check for surveillance. He hadn't been sure that Jacobs had recognized him, but he knew that the man had had plenty of time to see him before he discovered the American's presence. And the woman had appeared from nowhere. For all Sergey knew, she had staked him out before approaching Jacobs.

When Sergey did reach the ship, he immediately went to his small interior cabin, immediately adjacent to one of the ship's snack bars. He intended to keep to his cabin, with only brief forays to get food, until they landed in Rome. He felt he was getting entirely too old for this life. He was looking forward to returning to Russia, which, if not the paradise that Cyprus was, at least only had the types of perils that he understood and could anticipate.

* * * *

Caitlyn was pleasantly surprised by the Cassa Carioca nightclub on the beach in Varosha and was becoming convinced that there had been a conspiracy to pull a joke on her by all of the people who had warned her in quiet whispers of all of the debaucheries that were reputed to transpire at the club.

They rolled up to an elegant building, which featured heavy oak double doors under a covered entry, with a string of six-foot Norfolk pines with small strings of white lights entwined in their branches bordering the drive. The kindly and stately looking doorman was extremely polite, as was the well-groomed young parking attendant who drove away in Maria Mattas's official sedan.

The entry foyer was circular, with floors and walls in a gray-white, heavily veined marble and teak-wood trim. There were three other doors in the foyer—one to the left to the guest toilets, one to the right to the checkroom, and a double entry straight ahead to yet another marble-floored foyer. This foyer was square, and, while also trimmed in teak wood, its walls were papered in a double trompe l'oeil design—a Greco-Roman balcony scene showing fake cracks as if it was an ancient fresco that had seen better days.

A marble staircase to the second floor wound around the walls of this foyer from right to left. Beyond this second foyer, Caitlyn could see a teak-walled cross hallway with tall French-window doors opening out onto a courtyard that looked down the beach to the Mediterranean. The walls were covered with artworks made out of brightly colored patchwork quilts, and a rich-looking Oriental rug stretched down the hallway beyond the foyers. The strains of a live string quartet, playing Mozart, drifted down from the upper gallery.

Caitlyn was utterly charmed by the good taste and looked reproachfully at Takis as they crossed the first foyer and entered the second one, where Ingrid Isaksen, decked out in a blue taffeta cocktail dress and diamonds, waited beside the staircase to greet them. Before continuing to meet Ingrid, however, Caitlyn turned back to the front entry and looked past Maria and Demetris in expectation. She had seen the American diplomat, Will Jacobs, and Billie Holiday getting out of a car in the adjacent parking lot when they had rolled up to the entry in Maria's limousine, and she had expected the couple to overtake them here in the foyer. When they didn't appear, however, she turned back around and the two couples moved toward Ingrid, whose face was plastered with a formal, obviously contrived smile and whose twitching eye revealed that she was fuming beneath the surface about something. Caitlyn so hoped that it was because they had accepted her invitation and had brought the Mattases with them.

Ingrid led her guests to the hallway behind the central foyer and turned toward the right, where a series of tastefully decorated lounges ranged off into the distance and where they would be served a drink before returning down the hallway to the dining wing.

Caitlyn jabbed Takis in the ribs as they eased into a Chippendale sofa in a room decorated with Chinese porcelain and modern abstract paintings and hissed that she would really "get" him when they returned home that evening for letting her worry about encountering scenes of shocking behavior at the club. Takis tried to suppress a chortle and whispered back that they would discuss the issue later. He didn't have the courage to tell her at that point that the club had two entrances and more than four different levels of entertainment areas, gauged to the decadence level of the specific guests. He had seen Jacobs and the Holiday woman outside the club as well and assumed they had entered through the entry for the less-inhibited patrons.

Ingrid was making a valiant attempt to be a good hostess but her heart—assuming she had one—obviously wasn't in the effort, and she continued to be preoccupied except during the periods in which she, Caitlyn, and the Mattases were discussing the new archaeological university that RayGo was going to sponsor. Ingrid quite evidently really did believe in the financial and prestige benefits of this venture and was quite interested in the development issues concerned.

For her part, Caitlyn tried to develop the conversation toward the archaeological venture, because, in the lull periods of the conversation during a delicious European-style fare dinner, served impeccably and accompanied by a small orchestra, Ingrid gravitated toward baiting Demetris Mattas. It became painfully evident very quickly that during the period in which Demetris and Maria were having marital difficulties, it had been the Cassa Carioca—the other wing of the Cassa Carioca—where the newspaper publisher had come for comfort. Not only had Demetris been encouraged to drown his troubles in liquor at the club and to gamble away his concerns in one of the club's casinos, but Ingrid quickly let it be known by innuendo and double entendre that Demetris had found his way to her bed during this backslide.

Maria took Ingrid's baiting very well. She probably already had known all that there was to know about this period of Demetris's life—this not being the first such period—but Demetris became very uncomfortable. As he became increasingly uncomfortable, he decreased the time between his drink orders. Sensing his discomfort, Ingrid egged him on. At length, unfortunately before any of the rest had finished their meal, Demetris said he had to go to the men's room, and he disappeared. When he didn't return after a reasonable amount of time, all at the table assumed that he either had left because he felt sick and needed to purge himself of drink or that he was hiding in one of the lounges, unable to face Ingrid's comments.

But he was gone so long that surely someone would have remarked on his absence if Maria had not gone on the offensive as soon as he left. She had just been biding her time as Ingrid was toying with Demetris. Takis unknowingly set the stage while Demetris was still departing the dining room. Into the silence occasioned by the departure, Takis inserted the question of where the club manager, Sergey Stepanov, was and whether Takis might have a few words with him. Ingrid was fully aware from her earlier years in Cyprus as the UN political coordinator that Takis and Sergey had known each other and had been on the opposite sides of several criminal investigations when Takis was a Cypriot police official.

However, Ingrid completely surprised Takis when she shot right back with the information that Sergey no longer was the club manager and was probably already gone from Cyprus, en route to Russia, where he had found another job. While Takis was absorbing this, Maria surprised him even more by continuing the question and asking, "Then could we please talk with the new club manager, Uri Lukenov, who is, I believe, the son of the Russian diplomat Mikhail Lukenov, who we all once knew here in Cyprus."

Now everyone else at the table was taken aback. It hit Caitlyn for the first time that the young man who had intrigued her on the *Daphne* had been Uri Lukenov, who she had never seen when he was a boy but who did, in fact resemble his father. The comment caused Takis to rise to a new level of respect for his former police assistant, Maria. She had not shown any signs earlier in the afternoon of having recognized the name of Uri Lukenov on the *Daphne* passenger list, and she was several miles ahead of him in knowing that the man had been engaged as Sergey Stepanov's replacement at the Cassa Carioca.

But the most surprised of all was Ingrid Isaksen. Beyond being amazed that Maria would already know Uri worked for her here at the club, the primary reason for Ingrid's anger this evening was that she had not seen Uri since she saw him stride off toward the tram station in Ayia Napa in the late afternoon. She had not caught up with him then, and he had not appeared at the club this evening. And beyond that, unlike the others at the table who hadn't actually conversed with Uri yet, she had had no idea that he was the son of Mikhail Lukenov. She had hired Uri in Beirut simply because Andre had recommended him and because he had had a gorgeous body. His last name had not been of any interest to her.

When his mother, Caitlyn, and Eric Isaksen had been kidnapped by that Hizballah band all those years ago, Ingrid had not been particularly interested, even though she had been the one to give all of the press conferences on what the United Nations was doing to solve the problem and had taken much of the credit herself when the Cypriot police finally solved the issue itself—with the help of the various diplomatic missions on the island.

Ingrid was about to respond to the question when Maria, having looked at her wristwatch, pressed in, and started to ask Ingrid very pointed questions in quick succession about illegal activities in the club. Ingrid turned beet red, and then they heard the rise in the noise level from elsewhere in the club and the orchestra stopped playing.

Ingrid started to respond, but red lights that had been unobtrusively located in various corners where the wall met the ceiling came on and began to throb. Ingrid flashed Maria a bald look of hatred, spat out the curse, "You're going to regret this," and sprang toward the hallway through which they had entered an hour earlier.

Takis turned an amazed and amused eye on his former colleague. "You are pulling a raid on the club the night Ingrid invited us to dinner here?"

"It seemed appropriate," Maria answered. "You said yourself that you wanted Demetris and me along to irritate Ingrid. I thought it would pin her down as well. It took a long time to set up a raid her friends in high places wouldn't tell her about, and what better way to keep her from noticing the noose tightening than to be eating dinner with her? Now if you'll excuse me," the interior minister in Maria took over, "I have a woman to catch." Maria rose and strode after Ingrid.

"And I don't want to miss the fun, either," Takis tossed over his shoulder as he followed Maria. "Stay here, Caitlyn, and make sure no one eats my dessert. This is as good a place to ride out the storm as any."

Caitlyn was not at all pleased about having been left alone and that it was presumed she should—or would—stay out of the action. She only took long enough to eat both her own dessert and Takis's and to take a swallow of rich Colombian coffee and then she rose and followed the others.

Maria and Takis had given Ingrid too great a head start. When they got to where the hall met the central foyer, they couldn't see the RayGo executive or decide which direction she had taken. Neither were they sure what they would say to her and whether they would try to arrest her even if they were to find her. She was still one of the most powerful women in Cyprus, and she probably had her tracks at the Cassa Carioca covered very well anyway. She probably had all the cover she needed to show that she was not connected with any illegal activity that may be in progress in the club's other wing. Deciding that it would be best to find out just how much illegal activity they could find, Maria and Takis turned their attention to finding the police chief, Ahmad Jallud, and the other officers conducting the raid.

The two had no trouble finding how to get from the sublime wing to the ridiculous one, as a stream of well-dressed and terrified patrons were hurrying past them from the far end of the lounge areas. Although Maria recognized many of those who ran past, her purpose tonight was not to embarrass the cream of Cypriot society and politics but to uncover hard evidence of crime, so she pretended not to recognize a soul— and the favor was gratefully being reciprocated by all those who flowed around her.

When they entered the other wing, they found that not all of the better known of the patrons had fled. A good many patrons, including Wilhelm Jacobs and Billie Holiday, had gathered in one of the more innocent of the bar areas of the nightclub wing—the same bar that Uri Lukenov and Christiana Tzavella had frequented a few days earlier, where they were being guarded by a pair of policemen. Maria murmured some instructions to these guardians and the patrons were politely escorted to their vehicles and released. Maria noted both Jacobs left somewhat reluctantly and that Billie Holiday was being unusually calm through the whole process.

The scene on the main show room floor was quite a bit less sedate. The raiders had obviously found a good many statutes being broken there, and various vignettes of arrests were taking place against a backdrop of pandemonium. Even farther into the chaos and beyond the legal adult video rooms, Maria and Takis started to wade into the less-legal casino operations. Although some games of chance were now legal in Cyprus and perfectly acceptable at a nightclub such as the Cassa Carioca, some others—principally those that were being controlled by the Russian mafia at the time that the betting controls had been relaxed in the country—and high-stakes gambling were still illegal. Both the sale and use of drugs were also still illegal in the country, and it was obvious as soon as they entered the area that the Cassa Carioca's casino rooms had been floating in drugs this evening.

This, to Maria's immediate chagrin, was where they found the police chief, Ahmad Jallud. It was not that Maria didn't want to see Jallud. She just was shocked to see him in the company of her own husband in this area of the nightclub. Demetris was even drunker now than when he had left the dining room—at least Maria hoped and prayed that it was only liquor that was making him belligerent and oblivious to the raid that was going on around him—and he was holding a couple of high-stakes gambling chips. To the surprise of both Maria and Takis, Caitlyn was protectively huddled over Demetris and had, it turned out, held the police at bay until Jallud had been summoned.

Jallud turned to Maria and said: "It's all right, Maria; we'll have someone take him outside until we're finished in here and then you can take him home."

Maria looked defeated. "You know we can't do that, Ahmad. You found him in here; he's holding evidence of illegal gambling in his hand. He'll have to be arrested with the others."

"No," the police chief responded emphatically. "His arrest would be blown up in the press, and we'd lose the focus for our raid here. We can't let that happen."

Maria began to argue, but Caitlyn cut in. "I don't think an arrest should be necessary, Maria. Demetris didn't have these chips when I came in here and he wasn't standing at any of the tables. I think he was too drunk to be doing anything at all except trying to stand up. I'm sure someone from the club handed him the chips precisely to embarrass you. Let's do what Ahmad thinks is best in this."

Maria looked less sure of herself, and Takis whispered to a policeman, who led Demetris off toward the main entrance, as the attention of the rest of those assembled was claimed by a senior detective who had just appeared with what looked like a cash drawer under his arm.

"Pay dirt, Chief," he proclaimed loudly. "Guess what club had two separate cash drawers at its pay window?"

"Significance?" Jallud liked to get right to the point.

"One of the drawers had good money. The other drawer was stuffed with the funny money we have been looking for."

Takis laughed out loud and the rest turned surprised expressions toward him.

"Now that *is* clever," Takis managed between chuckles.

The expressions turned in unison from surprise to confusion.

"Don't you all see? How better to insert counterfeit money into a country than to salt the illegal gambling winnings of very important people. You yourselves have commented on how the counterfeits you have traced have often led back to important people whose reputations could not easily be sullied with charges of intentionally passing counterfeit bills. This scheme was perfect. Slip in counterfeit bills in the winnings of prominent people who, if caught passing the banknotes themselves, cannot acknowledge that they received them from illegal gambling winnings. I think now we do have something to talk to Ingrid Isaksen about."

But, instead of finding Ingrid, the group's attention was once again arrested by more important—and shocking—news. The body of a young woman had been found in a basement room. She had not been dead very long, but she quite evidently had been subjected to considerable sadistic torture before she had died. Although it would be some time before those assembled realized it, they had found the RayGo computer hacker, Christiana Tzavella.

* * * *

Instead of moving toward the noise, Ingrid Isaksen had slipped into the central foyer of the innocent wing of the Cassa Carioca after roaring out of the dining room and zipped up the marble stairs and across a floor of unused hotel rooms to a set of back stairs that put her on a terrace at the seaward side of the former hotel. She knew, just for this purpose, where there was a bougainvillea-covered hidden gate in the southern wall of the nightclub's compound that would get her out onto a quiet street and within a fifteen-minute walk to the RayGo Tower in a section of town that was virtually deserted at this time of night.

As she was rounding the empty swimming pool of the former hotel complex, however, the moonlight struck another fleeing figure at the other end of the compound, and she instinctively withdrew into the shadow of a trellised bar area. To her eye in this light it looked like the Australian diplomat, William Stevens, fleeing the raid on the club just as she was. It looked like he was carrying a heavy suitcase that was slowing his progress toward the compound's northern wall.

Ingrid stepped out of the shadow and started to move toward Stevens, but then she saw other figures spill out onto the grassy verge between the back of the club and the sandy beach in pursuit of the Australian. With this incentive, Stevens's burden appeared to become much lighter, and he had attacked the stuccoed compound wall and was over and gone before the pursuers reached him.

Ingrid waited for the searchers to return to the club and then she made good her own escape, albeit in a more stately manner than Stevens had shown. Still, she thought, as her high heels started clicking into the nearby Varosha commercial center, seeing the power and grace with which the Australian had moved reminded her of the things she had like the best about him as a bed partner. Too bad he had displeased her in other ways.

And then she forced her thoughts to turn from Stevens's talents toward the troubles that were being caused her through tonight's raid. She was furious at Maria Mattas both for daring the raid and for conducting it while she was being entertained in the club. Ingrid didn't feel in too much danger herself. She had too many connections, was too important to the economy of the country, and she had built firewalls between herself and the running of the club. She'd let Uri Lukenov take the heat for whatever they had found at the club tonight. It was regrettable to sacrifice such a luscious example of manhood to the prison system, but he had already shown himself to be unpredictable and hard to control and had hidden important information about his past from her, so perhaps it would be best to give up on him and try another manager. Maybe her secretary was ready of a promotion. He had proven both very satisfactory and very cooperative.

But then, as she entered the RayGo Tower—her sanctuary for the moment—Ingrid dragged her thoughts back to preparing battle plans. She was sure she was in no personal danger, but she couldn't fully assess and start to counter the danger until she knew what had been found in tonight's raid. She first needed to pull all of her executives in to the Tower and secure her center of operations so that not even the Cypriot police would dare try to enter, and then she and her staff must start placing their phone calls and calling in all the chits that the important families of Cyprus owed her.

A couple of connections she would make herself. One of these would most certainly go to Demetris Mattas. She wasn't finished with Maria yet, and Demetris had more than a couple of chits on file with RayGo. It was time to really make some people sweat.

Chapter Sixteen

President Chrystalla Ioannou was pleased, amazed, and fearful all in one go as she rang off on the all-important call she had been gathering strength to make for several days. This decision to take the World Bank official to Bogaz and Salamis the next day was not a sudden whim. Ioannou had been planning for many months the best possible way and the best possible time to demonstrate that she was president of all of Cyprus, of its Turkish as well as its Greek citizens. The trip to Bogaz would be her first to any predominantly Turkish ethnic sector of the island.

She rose and walked to the large wall map in her father's house, where she had chosen to come for the evening. She had made her fateful telephone call tonight following several hours of talks with him concerning what would be best for her country. Her father, a former president in his own right, had also been an EOKA—a Greek nationalist—guerrilla fighter in his youth, followed by decades of trying to find a common solution

286

to the Greek and Turkish split of the island nation—but always one that would demonstrate that the Greeks would retain the upper hand.

Following prolonged discussion, it had been the old man himself who said that, although there was likely always to be resentment and strife at some level between the strongly Orthodox Greek majority on the island and the Muslim Turkish minority, it was indeed time for Chrystalla to make the first move to show that she would be the leader who would rise above these natural divisions and provide justice and security for all Cypriots. He further agreed that a visit to a Turkish stronghold on the island as a president bringing the message of development plans for that specific region, plans that would principally benefit the Turkish areas of the eastern coast, would constitute a good first step.

He had been unsure of the wisdom—and particularly of the success—of the rest of her plan, but he had sat there, holding her hand while she had made the call, and he was there to give her a reassuring hug when the call was complete.

President Ioannou rarely saw her vice president, Lala Hatan. They were two very different people completely irrespective of the realities of security that generally kept him in the northern, Turkish sector of the capital of Nicosia and her in the southern, Greek sector. She was relatively young, had been raised to privilege and education, and was a humanist. He was old, had scratched his way to the top—not always very ethically, and was a grasping entrepreneur.

Before tonight President Ioannou had little idea of whether Vice President Hatan accorded her any respect whatsoever or was capable of sharing, let alone pursuing, mutual goals with her. Thus, it had taken her days to build up the courage to ask him to accompany her to Bogaz and Salamis to start, together, the task of solidifying the settlement agreements that had been signed more than a decade earlier. But he had totally amazed her by readily agreeing, without hesitation, to join her on the seminar trip.

It was only after the telephone call with Hatan had dimmed and after her father had released her from his arms and left her alone momentarily as he went in search of two glasses of brandy, that the seasoned politician in her started to take hold. Hatan had accepted quickly. Perhaps too quickly. Perhaps he had a self-promoting motive. There would be many from the media on this trip. Perhaps he only wanted the opportunity to try to embarrass her before the country's press. Perhaps, indeed, half a decade was too short a time to have waited to move toward the genuine consolidation of the country. But she was a leader, and leadership involved taking risks and laying her principals on the line.

* * * *

It was probably a cruel joke for Uri Lukenov and Andre Piccard to steal Ingrid Isaksen's own hydrofoil to escape her clutches, but it wasn't really stolen; she had told Andre he could use it any time he wanted. Of course that was before she found out that he had only paid attention to her to cover his family corporation's move from Cyprus. The hydrofoil's crew had seen no reason to question the request for a lift from the pier at RayGo's Ayia Napa block of seaside condos to the yacht marina on the Larnaca waterfront. However, if they had been as sharp as Ingrid was paying them to be, they probably should have been suspicious of the number of passengers they were transporting and the luggage that was involved.

Uri had not actually gone to the tram to leave for the Cassa Carioca that afternoon. When Ingrid had pounded on the door of his apartment—and then opened it with her own key— Uri had left by the rear door and had run down the stairs. Ingrid's attention had been purposefully drawn to his disappearing figure. He had doubled back to the apartment while she was looking for him on the street and at the tram station, and then he and the others had just hidden in the apartment with the lights off until effecting this late-night escape.

Uri and Andre had met only a week previously, in a dark Beirut bar, where Andre had gone to celebrate Ingrid's three-day absence from Lebanon on business and Uri, who was actually managing the small nightclub, had gone to soak his sorrows and his frustration. They had started talking and had struck up an immediate friendship based on shared sorrow. Both were suffering, and suffering badly, from feelings of prolonged abuse and abandonment by their parents.

Andre, who even now was being forced, by family order, to act as a young boy toy to a grasping woman he could not stand, was locked in a deep love-hate relationship with his parents. His mother, who was only a misty remembrance of softness and bedtime caresses, had abandoned him in the Piccards' isolated and bleak Swiss mountain castle and had escaped back to her aristocratic origins in Paris, only to be killed in an auto accident. It had been obvious that she had not married Andre's perpetually sickly father for love, but as a family-to-family business arrangement, to give the Piccards a title and to provide his mother's family with capital. Pierre Piccard had not even told the boy of his mother's death until two years after the event. Pierre had always been a reclusive, crippled, cold, disapproving parent. The only other presence of authority in the environment in which Andre was raised was his grandfather, Guy Piccard, who was a cruel and manipulating tyrant. And, still, Andre would have loved either or both of these men if given half the chance. He still, to this day, despite all of Pierre's demands and cutting criticism, loved his father as much as he despised him.

Amazingly, from the moment they had first spoken to each other, it had been clear to Andre that Uri Lukenov understood fully how he felt. And well he should. He had lost his mother when he was a young child, shortly after having lived with her for two weeks in a war-torn city where they didn't know from moment to moment what they would find to eat, where they could sleep, or even if one of them would be struck by a stray, or not so stray, bullet. He had lost her, or thought that he had lost her, in a most terrible way. She had been kidnapped while the family was on an outing and had reportedly later been blown to smithereens in an unsuccessful rescue attempt. It was only years later that he began to hear family rumors that it had not been she, but a shop girl, who had died in the rescue attempt, but that she had, rather, joined the terrorists who had abducted her and was living among them in the mountains of Lebanon.

When Uri at last became convinced that she was truly alive, he possibly should have rejoiced. But, although he loved her still and wanted to find her, the dominant emotions he felt were confusion and abandonment. The woman who had fought and schemed like a she wolf to keep Uri and his younger brother alive and safe in the battle-scarred city of Grozny had, just weeks later, walked away and left the boys to the father, without subsequently ever having tried to contact them.

Uri's father had been much like the father Andre had described to him. A professional soldier and spy, Mikhail Lukenov had only thought of toughening his boys up. He had been proud of Uri when the nine year old had tracked his mother's kidnappers across a belligerent border for nearly a day. But he had shown his pride by letting the boy participate in the slaughter of the band of terrorists on the high seas. Mikhail had thought that this revenge bloodletting had made a man out of his son, but the main thing that it had done was provide Uri with the nightmares of distress and guilt that had plagued him for the next two decades. When the motherless family had returned to Moscow, Mikhail had done Uri the dubious favor of abandoning him to the spy and thug schools that were meant to train him to follow in his father's questionably exalted footsteps.

But Uri had never forgotten his mother and, for some reason, had never been freed of his guilt about how he had been raised. When he gained some degree of independence and the belief that his mother was in Lebanon, that was where he had gone. He had been working in this Beirut club in which Andre found him for nearly a year and had spent his off hours and his covert training in trying to locate his mother. Just the day before Andre appeared in his life, Uri had learned that his mother, still associated with the Hizballah terrorists who had originally abducted her, had been sent back to Cyprus, where his troubles had begun, on a mission.

The meeting of the two young men was like the igniting of a forest fire. It had brought instant understanding, liking, and empathy. Theirs was a normal, natural friendship, built on mutual pain and support. The friendship also brought instant hope and answers. Ingrid had left Andre a task to perform while she was gone. He was supposed to find her a new Cassa Carioca club manager from among the Russian Mafiosi that buzzed around Beirut, and Andre's own requirements for such a man was someone who might relieve him of Ingrid's attentions. Uri met both of these bills. In turn, Andre provided Uri entry into Cyprus to continue the search for his mother. Andre had promised to get Uri to Cyprus, to help him find his mother, and to get them both safely away.

And here and now, as the hydrofoil glided into the Larnaca marina, Andre was delivering on his promises. As Uri helped his mother, Irina, whom he had tracked to Omodhos and picked up on the road as she was fleeing the village during the visit there of a couple she recognized from the past, Caitlyn and Takis Koniotis, up onto the dock, Andre was directing Ingrid's crew to return to Ayia Napa. When the hydrofoil had retreated over the eastern horizon, the three travelers and their luggage were stowed aboard a dingy from the *Daphne*, the flagship Mediterranean cruiser of the Piccard shipping empire that had been left at the marina at Andre's direction. Then they motored out to the *Daphne*, which had departed the Larnaca sea terminal on schedule, but was floating not far off shore to take on special passengers, again at the direction of Andre Piccard.

After the three were quietly brought on board and while they were being silently escorted down a darkened corridor toward the staterooms Andre had reserved for Uri and his mother, the excited and somewhat out-of-breath Irina Lukenov bumped her knee on a cart sticking out of the doorway of a small snack bar room and nearly fell to the floor of the passageway. She was lifted by the four strong arms of Uri and Andre, but she had exclaimed a few curse words from the pain and had done so in her native Russian.

As the three friends continued down the corridor, the occupant of the small cabin adjacent to the snack bar moved restlessly in his sleep. Sergey Stepanov was dreaming of the lost love of his youth. It was almost as if he could hear his Irina; almost as if she was just next to him, providing one of the earthy and pithy commentaries on life in general that he had been fascinated to hear incongruously coming from such lovely and sensuous lips. It was a pleasant dream. Thoughts of Irina were almost the only aspects of life left to Sergey that could soften him and make him melancholy. He found he was awake. It was strange how he could be dreaming about Irina, dreaming about her being almost within touch and yet not really being asleep. He turned his face to the wall and willed peaceful sleep, a sleep that would return his Irina to him if only for a couple of hours.

After settling Uri and Irina in the owner's stateroom, saying his good-byes for now, and checking with the captain to ensure that all of his instructions were understood and would be followed, Andre returned to shore. Uri had exorcised the demon of his love-hate relationship with his mother; now it was time for Andre to try to do the same with his father.

Although some time later, Takis's UNICIS computers were able to triangulate on the Lukenovs and to spit out the new base of their lives in the Swiss town at the base of the Piccard family castle, by the time their location was identified, Takis no longer felt inclined to disturb the new lives they had created, thanks to an understanding and empathetic Andre Piccard.

It also would have been a strange coincidence if Sergey Stepanov and his lost love, Irina Lukenov, had encountered each other while the *Daphne* sailed to Rome. Stepanov was determined to stay in his second-class cabin and then to leave the ship as covertly as possible, and the Lukenovs had no intention of being social butterflies either and would be disembarked by the crew in much the same way that they had embarked, avoiding Immigration and Customs officials at both ends of the cruise. And the two probably would not even have recognized one another if they had collided in the corridor. Sergey didn't realize that Irina was still alive. However, strangely enough, Sergey Stepanov never cleared through Immigration in Rome either, and he never arrived in Moscow to take up his new position there. So it's just possible that Sergey and Irina did encounter and recognize each other on that voyage.

Even more strangely, Uri's younger brother Pavel, who had been placed in a New York City-based multinational banking corporation by the Russian secret service, mysteriously disappeared just a few months later somewhere between Paris and Brussels while on a business trip to Europe—and was never heard from again.

* * * *

Ingrid Isaksen, arrayed with her RayGo executives at the top of the RayGo Tower like a general preparing for battle, had made all of the calls she could to strengthen the protective cordon around the RayGo-dominated commercial center of Varosha against encroachment by Maria Mattas or her Cypriot police forces. The conversation with Demetris Mattas had been tough. The man was drunk and obviously was only understanding half of what she said, but she was fairly sure she had gotten her point and instructions across before Maria had reached the phone and cut them off.

Ingrid was saving the call that she dreaded and feared the most until the last. She activated her highly controlled communications system and specified the special channel. It had taken her time to phrase the situation so that he wouldn't panic and she wouldn't be in grave danger. She had been contemptuous of Maria's raid earlier that night, but now that she had received a full report of what had been found in the special wing of the Cassa Carioca, Ingrid was shaken and scared. But she couldn't show this to the world. She couldn't show this to the executives who were buzzing around her, bolstering RayGo's defenses, and she most certainly couldn't show this to him.

* * * *

Ingrid Isaksen was not the only woman who was concerned and who was even then using a special communications channel to try to contain damage. In a restored village house in the old walled city of Nicosia, Gladys "Billie" Holiday was speaking on her phone in a shaky tone that had lost all of its British polish and was clearly coming out as a Midwestern American twang.

Gladys—or Ann Wynette to be more correct—could legitimately have been shaken by her brush with the law earlier that evening in the Cassa Carioca, where she very luckily had been in the company of an American diplomat and even more luckily had not been near any illegal action when the raid came down. However, Gladys (Ann Wynette) Holiday had a long history of contact with the law, and such brushes didn't frighten her.

What was in the works tomorrow was what frightened her, and she had to make this rare, dangerous, direct connection to ensure that everything was in place for an event that would be earth shattering—in more ways than even she guessed.

* * * *

The presses in the basement of the Tehran Central Bank were, one by one, being brought to a halt in the early morning hours for the coming weekend. Production had been good that week. The workers were tired, but they knew that they had earned their two days of rest.

The dying of the noise of last press into an eerie silence only served to accentuate the wild, strangled cry and the sound of metal hitting concrete, as General Ujay Khahalbi punched the phone to the ground. That was not what he was in the mood to hear from the woman tonight. Feeling all eyes staring at him and the sweat level in the room rising significantly, Khahalbi screamed, "Well, don't just stand there. Get those machines going again. We've lost a week's worth of production. I don't want these presses stopped again until we're back on schedule."

"Stupid slut," he was muttering to himself, as he strode down the aisle and out the door, all eyes turning to raw hatred in his wake—but not, of course, to his face. "She'd better not screw up tomorrow; she said it would all be fixed tomorrow."

As he passed through the door at the top of the basement stairs, he changed expression instantly. He took on an air of confidence and high spirits. It was unlikely that any of his own superiors would be around this time of night, but it would be just his luck to run into one of them—one of them who was not all that sure that they should be backing his venture—when his guard was down. And, although he prided himself in being one mean bastard, he was not, by any means, the meanest bastard in Tehran.

Chapter Seventeen

His belabored breathing almost sounded as if he was being strangled. He had moved out onto the balcony of the apartment, high above the Solea Valley, because the pain had been so intense that he couldn't sleep in the bed and the air in the room had been so close that he felt like he was suffocating. Once he had settled on the balcony the gentle cool breeze that was drifting down from Mt. Olympus and through Kakopetria and the sounds of the gurgling running water several floors below had lulled him into one of his rare sleeps, albeit more of a stupor than sleep. In any event, even a stupor represented a temporary release from pain and the constant battle to find the next breath.

Pierre Piccard turned a bit in his chair, and, as a result, his lungs filled with a fluid that brought on a hacking, choking cough and brought him back to full consciousness. He needed water to try to stem the coughing fit, and so he struggled up to the chair and hobbled on his two canes across the threshold back into the interior of the apartment above the Old Mill Inn. His eyes were arrested by the visage of his son, Andre, sitting on the sofa and watching him in aloof speculation.

Pierre went to the kitchen, drew his water, and gulped down mouthfuls of liquid until the coughing was stifled. The retreat of the coughs, however, was accompanied by an increase in the pain. He knew he didn't have long to wait now. No matter, he had accomplished what he had needed to accomplish and he had set in motion his last act to protect the safety of the family holdings. He turned and hobbled back to the lounge.

"So you've come to be at the finish. How long have you been sitting there?"

"Not long. I decided not to disturb your sleep. What do you mean by finish?" Andre was suddenly alert.

"The assets are moved and I've ensured their safety. My turn has come to a close."

"Ah, I didn't know you had managed to get everything essential moved to Beirut. I was afraid you might not have done that yet, and I've broken with that woman. She evidently found out what was going on and was already turning from me. I couldn't hold her. Once again I have failed. It's good that you managed your end, but I suppose that doesn't lessen my failure in your eyes, does it?" Andre had his chin stuck out in defiance.

Silence, as Pierre studied his son intently. Andre looked abruptly away, unable to maintain eye contact. And then the father backed toward a lounge chair and more or less collapsed at the knees and into the chair.

"I know you had the harder part of the bargain," Pierre wheezed. "Still, even though we have escaped RayGo's clutches for now, I hate to leave you with Ingrid Isaksen as an enemy."

A fearful look came to Andre's eyes as his father spoke these words. As if to change the topics from something he didn't want to face, he reached for his briefcase.

"I may have found something to keep Ingrid and RayGo at arms' length."

There was a glint of interest in the sick man's eyes, however short, before it was replaced by a flash of pain.

"Look at these photographs. The papers they depict must be very important, as Ingrid had them hidden in a secret compartment of her bedroom desk. She even had what looked like decoy papers planted in the locked drawer in front of the compartment. Although I left some scratch marks when I found these, I don't think she will suspect I reached the secret compartment. I took photographs rather than the papers themselves, and I was careful to leave them as I found them. They are formulas and descriptions of some sort. Presumably the solar energy storage formulas that have made RayGo wealthy. But the process is patented and isn't all that complicated, so I wonder what the secrecy of these papers is all about."

Pierre took the photographs and studied them at length, and then he emitted a raspy, but very satisfied laugh.

"You found something?"

"Oh, yes, I found something. Come here. What do you see in the bottom corner of these photographs?"

Andre walked over and took a look. "Initials. So? That doesn't mean much to me."

"No, I dare say it doesn't mean much to you. But it means a great deal to me, and it means a great deal to Ingrid, and it would mean a great deal to the Cypriot authorities, I'm sure. I always wondered. At the time it looked a little too contrived."

"Are you going to explain?" Andre asked archly.

"No, I'm not going to explain if you use that sort of tone with me. You can discover what this means easily enough yourself if you ask the right people. But if you just mention the formulas and those initials in the same breath whenever Ingrid shows her claws, I'm sure you'll see a dramatic change in her attitude."

"Then perhaps that will help explain the meaning of some of the other material I found in Ingrid's desk and photographed," murmured Andre.

"What is that you said?" Pierre asked excitedly.

"I found some sort of diary and photographed what appeared to be particularly interesting pages until I ran out of film. I haven't had a chance to read much of it very carefully

303

myself. But, here, you may take a look yourself. I think it's Ingrid's diary."

The father grabbed at the pile of photographs eagerly and poured over them voraciously for some moments.

"Here, take them back," he said had great length, full of satisfaction. "And protect them well. They do indeed help explain a lot, and these should be all the protection you will need against future takeover attempts by either RayGo or Isaksen. If you are clever, perhaps you can do some taking over of your own. And that," Pierre said, as he slowly emerged from the chair, "more or less takes care of my last care. Shall we have a little family ceremony on the balcony?"

"No!" Andre declared, taking a step further back into the interior of the apartment. "I've always told you I wouldn't be a party to that infamous family tradition. Besides, you haven't told me everything I need to know. What do you mean by having assured the safety of the family holdings you moved? You moved them to Beirut. You know I've always said I wouldn't agree to be any part of the Beirut end of the operations—not since the associations grandfather established there; associations that you perpetuate."

"You know we haven't been able to operate in Lebanon without the cooperation of the Hizballah, Andre. Until now we haven't been able to deal with them on equal footing."

"Then when I have control, we will move out of Lebanon. I will not be linked to the Hizballah."

"That, of course, will be your decision to make and your responsibility to realize—when you are the head of the Piccards. However, very soon I don't think you need worry about the quality of support from the Hizballah. Now, shall we repair to the balcony?"

Again the resounding "No!" as Andre moved farther away from the door to the balcony. "I won't be a party to that. What do you mean about improved support by the Hizballah? What have you done? What had you agreed to do to assure the safety of our holdings in Beirut?"

"It's all right. We were leaving Cyprus anyway. I am giving them what they have wanted here in Cyprus for some time, and, in turn, they are giving us what we want in Beirut. The world does not revolve around one life."

Andre gaped in horror. "I thought such dealings as these went out with grandfather. You know I won't perpetuate such acts. I've told you time and again that if and when I take control, we are going completely legitimate."

"And I repeat that that is your choice. I've made my choices on the basis of reality and the needs of the Piccard fortunes. I am old and tired and far past caring any more. Come, the ritual."

Once again the defiant "No! Not me, not that way. And the ritual has been broken anyway. Power did not pass between you and grandfather that way."

Pierre smiled a little bitter smile and said softly. "Have you truly raised your protective walls to the point that you've really convinced yourself that Guy Piccard's fall from the castle battlements was an accident? How quaint."

Andre was at a loss for words. He stumbled backward toward the entry door to the apartment, eyes wide in terror and filling with tears. As he turned to flee his father's presence, he heard his father speak in quiet, but very clear tones.

"I respect your decision son. Know that I love you and have always loved you and that I am proud of you."

Andre rushed out of the room and stumbled down the stairway toward the ground floor, careening off the walls as he went, blind from the tears in his eyes.

Pierre calmly shuffled over to the grand piano and picked up a photograph of Eleni Piccard.

"He's ready, Mama. You would be as proud of him as I am. He has steel and will make his own decisions. Not the decisions that I and Father would make, but probably the decisions that you would have made. Good-bye."

He kissed the photograph, gently returned it to the piano and moved painfully toward the beckoning door onto the balcony.

Andre had slowed his movements as he descended the staircase, not ever wanting his downward journey to end, knowing what he would find when he reached the stone parking area below. And, as he surmised, his hesitancy to reach the ground floor enabled his father to reach the stones before him.

Andre only stayed with his father briefly, only long enough to permit his pent-up hatreds and accumulated hurts to drain out onto the soil of Cyprus. The orange and purple glow of the morning sun was outlining the eastern wall of the Solea Valley as Andre reached the church his grandmother had built on the eastern slope and knelt at her grave. He would go down into Nicosia to talk with someone at the police division as soon as he felt strong enough to do so. But now he had to finish his good-byes. He was truly alone now. The last of his branch of the Piccards. But somehow he felt stronger and more in touch with his ancestors and with his responsibilities to the Piccard holdings in his current aloneness than in the aloneness he had felt for the previous twenty years.

* * * *

Ellen Larkin had been a maverick when it came to choosing living accommodations when the UNICIS headquarters had moved to Morphou. A few of her colleagues who lived and breathed their exciting and demanding professional lives chose to live in sleepy provincial Morphou itself. The more social among her fellow workers lived in Nicosia, which was only a short monorail ride away from work. Ellen Larkin, however, who was really a romantic at heart, had decided to move into the old harbor town of Kyrenia, the ancient northern coast castle town that remained the most picturesque settlement on the island. And, although she received many gibes of having peculiar tastes, in truth, nearly all of her colleagues envied Ellen's choice.

Located only a few miles—over the most-used pass through the Kyrenia Range—due north of Nicosia, Kyrenia was the best-preserved of the island's harbor towns. Dominated by a massive triple-walled castle—a Byzantine castle within a Lusignan castle within a Venetian castle, the town's snug little harbor had been developed into a semicircle of restaurants, shops, and hotels fronted on a stone-paved street supporting umbrella-covered terrace café tables streaming down to a yacht basin. The fronts of the buildings that now faced the harbor were actually the backs of the ancient stone and stucco three- and four-floored attached buildings that rimmed the harbor.

In centuries past the little harbor had been a major Mediterranean export center for the shipping of carob, the long, black, edible pods that grew on trees indigenous to the thin northern Cyprus coast that sloped down from the rugged Kyrenia mountains to the Mediterranean. The ground floors of these buildings, facing the harbor, had been the warehouses for carob awaiting shipment, and the upper stories, facing a narrow street away from the harbor, had provided the dwellings for the rich merchants who could afford to lodge within the city proper's walls that backed onto the next row of houses.

Ellen Larkin didn't live in one of the buildings immediately facing the harbor. Better than that, she lived at the top of one of the houses in the next row of buildings away from the harbor, at a higher elevation. The city wall having crumbled with the exception of a single corner tower many, many years previously, Ellen's approach to her apartment was almost directly from the town square suspended high above the level of the harbor. From a parking pad large enough for two vehicles and a small enclosed courtyard that was assigned to her fourth-floor penthouse apartment, a private foyer and elevator brought visitors to her level without revealing to them the treat that was in store at the end of their journey.

At the penthouse level, visitors exited the elevator and were faced with a single large living space floating above and looking out over the Kyrenia harbor through floor-to-ceiling windows across the eastern, northern, and western walls. The kitchen, the bathroom, and a combination dressing room-closet extended across the single stone wall on the southern side of the apartment. The apartment wasn't set squarely on the points of the compass, however, so the western vista looked up into the

Kyrenia Mountains toward St. Hilarion castle and the eastern wall provided a mountain view of the artists' village of Bellapais, its medieval abbey and the Buffavento crusaders' castle. All in all, Ellen Larkin might have the most beautiful view in all of Cyprus.

However, although Ellen was home as the sun was rising in the east down the face of the Kyrenia Mountain chain, she was not enjoying her spectacular view at just that moment. She was sitting motionless in front of the computer that was hooked up to the UNICIS computer banks in Morphou and that had been provided for her at home so that she could remain current on what was happening in the world of international crime fighting without leaving her lovely rooftop nest. She was sitting there—and had been sitting there for some time—printout in hand, computer screen aglow, waiting for something, waiting for what she suspected and feared to be confirmed without a shred of doubt.

And then there were murmurings of sounds from below. Something more distinctive and more familiar than the usual sounds of the busy little tourist harbor awakening to another beautiful day in paradise. The scraping of a door closing, the sound of the elevator doors parting and then shutting, the whir of the cage rising, ever nearer. The little clumping noise as the elevator reached the penthouse, and the smooth, gliding sound as the elevator doors opened.

And then there he was, her lover. The Australian diplomat—and spy chief—William Stevens was home from a long night on the prowl. Tired and drawn, all he wanted was a quick beer and several hours of sleep. He saw Ellen sitting there, staring at him, printout in hand, and there seemed to be no reason to speak—no hope of anything as comforting and simple as a cold beer and a couple of hours in the sack. It was back to business. All of his careful work had obviously reached critical mass.

The heavy suitcase he was carrying hit the floor, as he reached inside his jacket. A sharp noise accompanied the snapping shut of the elevator door. Two other sharp noises followed in quick succession. But these were very loud noises and no one would have mistaken them for anything as innocent as the closing of an elevator door.

Chapter Eighteen

Takis Koniotis couldn't quite remember what had ever tempted him to leave this building. He had been happiest when he had been working for the Cypriot national police more than a decade and a half earlier—or at least it was easy for him to imagine that this had been so. Life seemed so uncomplicated then. The crimes were relatively simple, the hours had been more regular, and he had not had to fight the traffic and pollution of New York City or face the frequent trips abroad— or so he remembered it in very rosy retrospect. As a matter of fact, crimes had not been simple then, and he had driven himself night and day to solve them—just as he did in this UN position, which was why he had moved up the ladder to become the world's premier police official.

He was sitting in the office of the Cypriot chief of police—now the office of his long-time friend, Ahmad Jallud— in the old British colonial-style military barracks that had been turned into the national police headquarters, located just outside the old city walls of the capital, Nicosia. It was a corner office, and the late-morning springtime sunshine invaded the thick-walled room from two different directions, dispelling the mustiness that pervaded such old buildings overnight and bringing intense light to the most-distant corner of the dusty chamber. Takis had enjoyed this office when he himself briefly had been the police chief, but it was the smaller, dirtier, and dustier office down the hall, which had not let in nearly as much light because it overlooked the close-by blank wall of the homicide division annex, that Takis remembered the best and thought he missed the most.

It had been there that Takis had sold and developed his idea of a separate international crimes division, which he had led and the success of which had catapulted Koniotis into leadership of a United Nations version of his unit design. If only he could regain the past, Takis thought. And he wondered if Ahmad and Maria Mattas would let him return to Cyprus and take up his old divisional responsibilities if he decided he wanted to do that—and if Caitlyn was willing to move back permanently. A big "if" that.

Koniotis was brought back to real life, as he was handed a cup of coffee and Ellen Larkin was putting the finishing touches on the story she had been relating to him and to Jallud. Takis sat up in his chair and smiled warmly and with comforting concern at the Cyprus UNICIS division chief. He was quite openly delighted that all suspicion of Ellen had been dispatched by the previous night's events, while he was concerned how Ellen was being affected by having what she knew in heart confirmed—that her lover had merely been using her to get at secret information in the UNICIS computers and that he had been prepared to kill her to cover his tracks. But Takis need not have been too concerned. Ellen Larkin had once again proved that the small, delicate-looking package in which she resided concealed an iron will. She looked much the worse for wear at the moment and in the strong morning light, but, then, she hadn't slept and had spent all of the earlier hours of the day pursuing loose ends and coping with the various levels of officialdom in the Stevens shooting. By all evidence she would be back in fighting form by the next day.

Bill Stevens had been very careless at the Kyrenia apartment, and Ellen seemed more perturbed that he had taken her for granted and had underestimated her Intelligence abilities than that she had had to put two bullets in his heart to save her own life. Stevens had quite evidently wormed his way into Ellen's life and into her Kyrenia apartment to obtain entry to her computer code accesses to the UNICIS computer banks, which existed as perhaps the most complete and complex cross-referenced data bases in the world. Not only had he found her access code and had been using it on her computer in the Kyrenia apartment, but he also had managed to establish access from his own laptop computer and thus was able to—and actually did—get into the UNICIS databanks from wherever his computer could link with Morphou.

It had been Stevens, of course, who had been erasing the original files that fed the UNICIS computer. He had been destroying files that touched on the counterfeiting operation he had been charged by the Australian High Commission to investigate as well as files that related to the Hizballah terrorist organization and to the RayGo Corporation. And he was so unwisely disdainful of Ellen Larkin's abilities as an investigator that he was making printouts of the erased files and, the last time he used her Kyrenia apartment computer, had just shuffled the printouts in with others at the bottom on one of the desk drawers.

When Ellen returned to an empty apartment late the previous afternoon, she first found her access code carelessly lying next to the computer and, upon further investigation, found the computer printouts and discovered that the files had been erased from the UNICIS system. These discoveries were somewhat of an anticlimax for her, because she had known something was wrong and had already pretty much isolated the source of the breach as being Stevens—through her. For the rest of the evening, she herself had used the UNICIS computers to illuminate William Stevens's life as an Australian master spy, and she didn't like what she was finding out by the time he returned to the apartment in the early morning hours.

Stevens's realization that Ellen was on to him was instantaneous as he exited the elevator and saw her holding his printouts and fixing him with a steely gaze. Unfortunately for the Australian spy chief, however, his earlier evening's activities at the Cassa Carioca on the other side of the island and the heavy suitcase that he was holding—one of two he'd left the club with, having dropped the other one in a dark garden in his escape— had slowed his reflexes, and he barely revealed his intention to shoot the UNICIS director when she beat him to the draw.

The evidence Ellen had already accumulated exonerated her of her own actions and had even been convincing enough to the Australian high commission that, with considerable embarrassment over what they hadn't known about their own intelligence officer, they were being very cooperative in the initial Cypriot police and official UNICIS investigation. It had been obvious that the cat had been let out among the canaries in the ongoing investigation of the use of Cyprus to distribute high-quality euro and U.S. banknote counterfeits into the European and, eventually, the American economies. Stevens, who was a key figure in trying to stop the operation, had obviously been, instead, a key figure in promoting the operation—and of protecting it from the authorities.

Even with Ellen's information, it was obvious to both Takis Koniotis and Ahmad Jallud that it would take some time to follow all of the threads leading from Stevens in various directions. What fascinated and perplexed them right now, however, were the contents of the suitcase Stevens had been clutching when he reached Ellen's apartment and that very likely had cost him his life. Takis had been particularly interested in Stevens and this suitcase even before the shooting incident had reached his attention, because someone at the Cassa Carioca the previous evening had declared that they had seen the Australian diplomat, with suitcases in his possession, sneaking out of the nightclub's business office in the early moments of the raid. Stevens had obviously escaped arrest at the Cassa Carioca, only to make his appointment with death a few hours later on the other side of the island in Kyrenia. The suitcase he had dropped in flight had some very interesting contents.

Like that suitcase, the one Stevens brought to Ellen's apartment had been full of money—of high-denomination euro and U.S. banknotes, all counterfeit. It was becoming obvious that Stevens had been part of the operation of distributing counterfeit notes in the form of illegal gambling winnings at the Cassa Carioca and that he had been trying to ensure that the counterfeits were not seized during the raid on the nightclub. Unfortunately, he had missed a tray of bogus bills in his flight from the club—which pinned down the relationship of all of the bills.

Even more damning for Stevens personally, however, than the find of counterfeit bills in his possession was the other object that had been found in the bottom of the suitcase. It was a purse. A purse with a bit of blood on it and covered, the police lab soon determined, with Stevens's fingerprints. It was the purse of the young woman, Christiana Tzavella, whose brutally tortured body had been found in a basement room of the Cassa Carioca a few hours earlier. If he had lived, Stevens would have had far worse charges to answer than international conspiracy and counterfeiting.

After Ellen Larkin finished giving her disposition on the shooting death of William Stevens and had been given a few minutes to relax with a cup of coffee, Ahmad Jallud invited her and Takis Koniotis to a nearby conference room, where the most recent reports on the UNICIS research into the list of suspects in the attempts to frame Caitlyn in the counterfeiting operation had been gathered for Takis's review. Ahmad was really supposed to have gone out to Bogaz and Salamis with the president's archaeological excursion party, but everything was happening so fast with the counterfeit ring case here at headquarters that he had put someone else in charge of the security for the trip and would be going out to the coast later in the day to help escort them back.

As the three police officials got comfortable around the conference table, Takis began to review what had been found thus far.

"The UNICIS computer research process is really quite amazing," he said. "Its computer banks have come as close to replicating the human mind as is currently possible, and as the computer programs work away on a query, they keep refining what they query and what they report based on earlier information received and earlier links to other targets of interest."

"We here on Cyprus are quite fortunate to have this research available to us," Ahmad said. "What new information do you have for us?"

"The most disappointing report I have is the one on Gladys 'Billie' Holiday. She apparently just appeared in Lebanon one morning three months ago with no past. There is disagreement among the archaeological institutions in Lebanon where she came from, who verified her credentials as an archaeologist, and even whose dig she supposedly is working on in Lebanon. All the archaeologists there seem to know is that she was working in the country. She's a very vivacious young woman, and apparently a most unforgettable character in Lebanon. But no one is claiming she worked on *their* project. All anyone could say to our questions was that it didn't take her long to latch onto the American diplomat, Wilhelm Jacobs, and she had fought off all competition for his affections. Her fingerprints were obtained by a UNICIS agent, but the computers had yet to trace them. This, in itself, set off alarm bells."

"That's rather intriguing," Ahmad. "and I think she should be looked at more closely. To you have anything else?"

"Yes. We've done some research on Wilhelm Jacobs too—the U.S. Secret Service agent assigned to the American embassy. In contrast to the Holiday woman, her constant companion—as constant as one could be when the man worked in Cyprus and the woman supposedly worked in Lebanon— apparently has led a very open life and a relatively uneventful career considering the very interesting assignments he has had of late. He spent most of his career in Washington, D.C., working with the U.S. Treasury, including a couple of years with the Bureau of Engraving, which prints the country's currency. Prior to this Washington assignment, he worked in several countries of the region, including Iraq. He had only had one previous tour after Washington before being assigned to Cyprus, however. He had a one-year assignment in Tehran as a member of an international delegation examining Iran's attempt to improve its standing with the World Bank to qualify for more development loans."

"And anyone else of interest you wanted us to look at today, Takis?"

"Yes, a couple more. There's the American Archaeological Institute chief, Bill Burch. He was with an archaeological institute in Paris before arriving in Cyprus. As far as she knows, Caitlyn had never met him before he joined her recent lecture tour of the Mediterranean, and nothing has been surfaced in his background that would link him to any part of this inquiry. But, like some of the others, he always seems to be on the periphery of events we are investigating.

"And the, also, there's the Russian, Uri Lukenov, who I'm itching to track down and interview, not only because of his new connection to the Cassa Carioca but also because of the recently discovered bombshell information that his supposedly murdered mother, Irina Lukenov, is alive and probably connected to the counterfeit operation. The computers had an especially interesting time unearthing information on Lukenov. He has a decidedly murky background. The computers connected him with several Russian mafia-style organizations in Russia, something he shared with his Intelligence operative father. However, Uri doesn't seem to be in very good standing with some of the shadowy Russian organizations he was linked to in the Moscow area. He only appeared in the Mediterranean region—in Lebanon, to be exact—in the past couple of months, and all of the evidence points to him having learned his mother was alive, first in Lebanon and then in Cyprus, and to him being primarily here to search for her. Still, there is question how he had gotten the job of manager of the Cassa Carioca—and why."

Takis put his folder in the "intensified research" pile along with that of Gladys Holiday.

"What about the Piccards?" Ahmad asked, as Takis was shuffling around with other files on his desk.

"Ah, yes, the Piccards," Takis said, and he extracted a file from the pile on the desk and opened it. "There hasn't been much information surfaced yet on the young scion of the Piccard Shipping empire, Andre Piccard. Any Piccard is highly suspect because of the family's historical ties with the international underworld, and Andre is doubly suspect now because of his connection with the ever dirtier-appearing Ingrid Isaksen. However, the young man himself seems to have a basically clean and restricted past to this point.

"Andre's father, Pierre, conversely, has proven to be another matter altogether. I must admit that it was a shock to me that the sickly and presumed dead son of Eleni and Guy Piccard has actually been alive all of these decades and has been guiding the family business for the last couple of years. However, I'm not all that surprised that Pierre has been functioned as a traditional-style Piccard and had his fingers in many dastardly plots, including helping to fulfill the financing and transportation needs of the Hizballah terrorist organization. If he hadn't jumped to his death from the balcony of the apartment above the Old Mill Restaurant and hadn't left a suicide note—and hadn't telephoned his intent to his Limassol offices—I wouldn't hesitate in putting his file into the 'intensive research' pile."

"You don't think that his death clears up many of these matters?" Ahmad asked.

"Pierre was genuinely ill," Takis answered. "I don't think he could have been physically capable of much of the counterfeit operation under his own steam. And he almost certainly could not have been directly involved in trying to implicate Caitlyn, as he was not known to have been on the *Daphne* with her and had not been present at the president's dinner. From everything noted in the file, he'd been too ill to leave the confines of his apartment for a couple of years."

"I feel I must ask," Ahmad said. "What about Andriko Visiliou, the Cyprus Archaeology Department chief? I know he's a friend of yours and Caitlyn's. But he was physically present at some of the events we're scrutinizing."

"Yes, we looked into him too. We're trying to be as thorough as possible. He came out squeaky clean in the UNICIS computer check."

"And the *Semerini* publisher, Demetris Mattas. Quite a delicate matter, since he's married to the interior minister, but—"

"Maria made quite clear to me that he needed to be investigated along with the rest," Takis said. "It's true that he's had had several questionable dealings in the past and a shocking number of bad gambling debt brushes with the underworld in Cyprus while he and Maria were going through the bad patch in their marriage, but the computers found no derogatory information of late, and I see no reason to pursue his file further at this time.

"So, that's it then, is it?" Ahmad asked.

"No, not by a long shot," Takis responded. "The UNICIS computers have been super busy. Irina Lukenov, or the Lebanese terrorist Roulla Dahir, as she has been known for the last decade and a half, is a more intriguing case. According to Ginger Patterson, Roulla had a considerable amount of currency in her Omodhos house, and we discovered a few bills that she had left behind there that proved to the counterfeit euro notes. The computer research ties her to the Hizballah and to drug smuggling operations as well, and, more interestingly, the computer also tied her to the activities in Lebanon of MEIAC, the organization that had predated the RayGo Corporation. But, *most* interestingly, she surprisingly has been linked to the name of Sergey Stepanov earlier in her life, under her Irina Lukenov personality. And we found a photo of the two of them together in the long ago past when we searched the Omodhos house.

"And this leads us to Sergey Stepanov. More than half of the printout material we have here to look at today details the very extensive and highly illegal activities of Sergey Stepanov over a long and varied career. It's frustrating to me that Stepanov wasn't still there at the Cassa Carioca last evening and wasn't swept up in the police raid net. Whatever the plot list might be for an international counterfeiting ring, there was no doubt that Stepanov's name appeared prominently and in dark letters."

As Takis continued the perusal of the printouts, he decided that Stepanov's name probably didn't appear any higher than third from the top on that list. These computer check results showed Koniotis that his former UN colleague and old nemesis, Ingrid Bittmann Isaksen, had been a very bad girl—and for an amazingly long time. The computer had picked up hits that went all the way back to her days as the UN undersecretary for political affairs, where it had become obvious that she had been suborned by the Lebanese and their questionable bedfellows during the Middle East settlement talks that had led up to an international conference on Cyprus' Amathus coast. It was also now beyond question that Ingrid, as RayGo CEO, coupled with the Australian diplomat William Stevens, had been the kingpins of the Cyprus end of the international counterfeiting operation.

Increasingly, the UNICIS computers had zeroed in on links between Isaksen and Stevens. Stevens had served in Lebanon before coming the Cyprus, and the computer was finding progressively more frequent hits on the combination of the terms "Stevens," "Ingrid Isaksen," "Hizballah," and "MEIAC." One of the most interesting hits had Ingrid and Stevens on a plane together from Tehran to Beirut just a few days before they met up with Caitlyn on the *Daphne*. One of the most disturbing hits was a matchup between Stevens and John Patterson in Beirut at the time of Patterson's unexpected death.

In the group's further discussion, Takis agreed to leave instructions at the UNICIS research office for the computer to further pursue the Stevens-Patterson matchup, but he said he didn't think UNICIS needed to waste any more time on linking either Isaksen or Stevens to the central counterfeit operation case for the present. It was obvious that both had been up to their necks in the operation. Stevens was now beyond questioning, but Isaksen was still in Cyprus, albeit holed up in her RayGo Tower in Varosha with the drawbridge raised. But she couldn't hold out forever, and all of her high-level Cypriot and international connections would not be sufficient to save her from this particular rap.

Ahmad Jallud had reached the door to place an arrest warrant out for Ingrid Isaksen, when a haggard-looking Andre Piccard staggered into his path. Jallud added several jugs of coffee and a platter of kebabs to his "to do" list and left the conference room, while Takis and Ellen helped the young man into a chair.

When Ahmad returned to the conference room, Takis and Ellen were pouring over a series of photographs and emitting various sounds of amazement and disgust.

"These were photographs of papers and of some pages of a diary Ingrid Isaksen had kept locked up in a secret compartment in her Ayia Napa flat," Andre informed Ahmad.

"These are revealing and very, very helpful," Takis said, looking up from the photo copies into Andre's eyes. "I'm not sure why you are showing these to us, though. What do the Piccards gain from revealing all of this?"

"My father is dead," Andre answered. "The means I am head of the Piccard shipping empire now. I represent the Piccards, and I want to clean up the family name. I want to start putting the company back on the right side of the law. I decided that turning these photographs over to the police would be a good start. I haven't had time to read much of what is in them myself, but what I have shows much that is illegal and unconscionable, and I'm sure the documents are incriminating for both Ingrid and RayGo."

"And ever!" Ellen exclaimed, and all four started to unravel information that added to and deepened what the UNICIS computers had already provided them.

Uppermost, the papers, in conjunction with what they had learned elsewhere, showed that the RayGo Corporation and its predecessor MEIAC—and centrally Ingrid Isaksen—had joined with William Stevens to run the Cyprus end of a Hizballah-controlled counterfeit distribution operation. What the photographs revealed that went even further than the computer records had explicitly proved, however, was that the counterfeit money could be traced all the way back to Iran, which undoubtedly was trying to undermine the economies of the part of the world—much the largest part of the world—that did not meet Tehran's approval.

The notes revealed that Roulla Dahir had indeed been one of the couriers into Cyprus for the counterfeit bills but that she had disappeared after arriving in Cyprus—along with the money she had been carrying. Ingrid's diary indicated that someone had been assigned to track Roulla down, but it, curiously, didn't appear that either Ingrid or William Stevens was responsible for that activity. When hearing this, Takis had the chilling thought that there may be more agents of this conspiracy wandering around Cyprus than he had previously assumed.

Ingrid's diary also exonerated Uri Lukenov of being involved in the operation. He apparently had been picked up by Ingrid in Lebanon, at Andre's instigation—a fact that Andre confirmed, although he was being quite reticent about either Uri or his mother—and had been hired for his personal attraction to Ingrid and his shady Russian mafia background. Ingrid had fully intended to indoctrinate him into the Cassa Carioca laundering of the counterfeit money but had not yet had a chance to do so.

Ingrid had further gloated in her diary about having set Caitlyn up with counterfeit money on the *Daphne,* primarily for the enjoyment of seeing her arrested. However, her diary also made clear that she and Stevens more than halfway believed that Caitlyn's archaeology trip to Cyprus was really an elaborate ruse to cover Takis's own quiet return to the island to help with the investigation into the counterfeiting operations. (Takis smiled at this suggestion and reminded himself to tease Caitlyn about it when she returned from her tour of Bogaz and Salamis later this afternoon.) Thus, Stevens had extended the toying with Caitlyn, including the theft and return of her passport, to keep Takis busy trying to protect his own wife.

"Oh, my God, we've got him!" exclaimed Ellen, who was reading one of the other recent entries. "Listen to this page from her diary, Takis. 'Had lunch with Bill S. today. Let slip that I thought the Tzavella girl was playing around in our secret computer files. He went into a rage. I know that look. Think I'll be in the market for a new records official soon.' That, coupled with Stevens's prints on the girl's purse shouldn't leave much doubt about who murdered Christiana Tzavella."

Takis was only half listening. He had just discovered a bombshell of his own. But it wasn't among the diary pages, it was by way of the other pages Andre had photocopied.

"Why, I'll be. Do you have any idea what you've photocopied here, Mr. Piccard?"

"Yes, I think so," Andre responded faultingly. "My father was very excited when he saw that. He said it would mean the end of RayGo."

"Without a doubt," said Takis with awe and a whistle.

"He also said the initials at the bottom of the documents were significant. 'JP.' I wonder what is significant about those."

"We'll have to discover that," Takis said. "If Pierre said they are significant, no doubt they are."

The mention of Pierre Piccard had sobered Andre up considerably.

"But that's not all my father said to me last night, Mr. Koniotis. He said something else that really disturbed me and has caused me to come in this morning. I'm not sure I would have brought this material in this soon if I didn't feel there was something else I should tell the police quickly."

Andre instantly held everyone's attention.

"You see," Andre continued, "my father has been moving the family assets to Beirut to escape the clutches of Ingrid Isaksen and RayGo. He finally succeeded, but last night he revealed that he had to make some sort of deal with the Hizballah to give the family holdings full protection from RayGo in Lebanon. I think he had to arrange something for them here. He said something very strange to me when I objected to his dealing with the Hizballah. He said something about one

330

person's life not really making that much of a difference. Do you have any idea what he could have meant?"

Takis and Ahmad stared intently at each other and rose in unison. The thought had hit them both at the same moment.

"The president," said Ahmad as Takis was saying "Bogaz." And then both were gone from the room as if neither had been there at all.

Chapter Nineteen

They had found the body hidden in the marshlands. Those who had killed him undoubtedly intended to take the body away and dump it into the sea in the dark of the night, for, although the authorities didn't really approve of what he and Paul had been doing, only his own people felt threatened enough to have silenced him irrevocably. But she had seen them hide the body, and, when they had departed, she told her friends, who helped her carry him off to a safe place. A mile away from the coast they found what they had been looking for—the small entrance to an underground cavern in a glade of carob trees. Someone had brought his book, the one handwritten personally for him by Matthew to help in his work. They entombed him with the book and then did what they could to cover over the entrance to the grave site with rocks. The last rays of the sun had set over the ruined city of the ancients by the time they had finished and were returning to the new city. As they approached Saint Catherine's prison in the royal burial grounds, the murderers saw them from a distance.

Then she was running from her pursuers. It seemed she and her friends had been fleeing for hours, parallel to the mountains and toward the city on the central plain. Some of her friends had fallen behind, and she had heard their strangled cries as the pursuers fell upon them. She had almost reached the Paraskevi Caves, where she knew she could find safety and shelter, but then she slipped and fell. She knew that she was too exhausted to go further. One of the pursuers had seen her and lunged at her as the earth opened below her trembling knees. . . .

"After the body of the apostle Saint Barnabus was entombed, the survivors of those who had hidden the body fled to Egypt by way of what is now Paphos," Andriko Visiliou was telling the president's party as Caitlyn drifted back into consciousness. She sat up on the blanket in the grove of trees near the gateway into the monastery compound, where they had stopped for their lunch break. As was often the case, Caitlyn's vivid imagination and her ability to identify with events and peoples of the past had come into play when she had become drowsy while Andriko was telling the official party the story of the Saint Barnabus monastery compound, of the journey of the saints, Paul and Barnabus, across the island and how, when Barnabus had returned later to his native Cyprus, he had been martyred and buried with a copy of Saint Mark's Gospel in an unmarked grave. Or, so the legend went. The grave had been discovered and this monastery had been built over it. While Andriko was telling this tale to the visiting dignitaries, Caitlyn, as she often had, drifted back to a time when some earlier "her" had moved inside events on the island of Cyprus.

"Well, enough of our stay here, I'm afraid," announced the professor. They all gathered up their luncheon gear and prepared to go their separate ways for now. Professor Visiliou had decided that the group had grown too large. Thus, he himself was taking the president, vice president, and World Bank visitor and a very few of their close retinue to the Bogaz exhibit site several miles to the northeast for a tour, while Caitlyn was charged with taking the rest of the group just a mile to the west for a tour of the ruined Greco-Roman city of Salamis. Later, the groups would change places. It meant that Andriko and Caitlyn would each have to give their lectures twice, but neither particularly cared.

Caitlyn, however, was concerned at what she had seen as she was returning to the vehicle to which she had been assigned for the short ride over to show the visitors the royal tomb area before going on to Salamis. President Ioannou had wanted to take the World Bank official back to the museum in the monastery compound to look at a motif on an ancient ceramic jug that they had been discussing during lunch, and so Andriko's group was hanging back. The American diplomat, Wilhelm Jacobs, had been a little less than diplomatic when he had been assigned to go to Salamis first and thus was no longer in the president's truncated party.

Just after the president, her guest, and Andriko moved through the gate into the monastery compound, Caitlyn spied Jacobs's friend, Gladys Holiday, stealing around the side of the compound wall—Caitlyn couldn't have described the movement in any other fashion—and into the side door on the northern wall. Moments later, she and Jacobs came striding out of the front gate. He was red-faced and obviously unhappy.

The last Caitlyn saw of the two before reaching Saint Catherine's prison was a highly vocal altercation, as they moved to the vehicle that had been waiting for them. Caitlyn was quite glad the couple had been separated from the president's party for having shown such poor manners.

She would have reason, however, to be less than happy that they were coming with her to Salamis.

* * * *

Demetris Mattas had been avoiding Caitlyn all day. He seemed a bit sullen and probably was both embarrassed and hung over from his experience at the Cassa Carioca the previous evening, but Caitlyn couldn't figure out why he was being so standoffish toward her. She hadn't caused his problems of the previous evening; she had helped get him out of the club without his having been arrested. Conversely, she also found it hard to understand that he had connected himself to the group that came with her first rather than staying with the president's party, where one would think any news reporter would want to be.

At Salamis Caitlyn gave her lecture in the reconstructed amphitheatre to her first set of visitors, explaining to them how Salamis had been founded by warriors returning from the Trojan War, colonized in the eleventh century BC, by survivors of an earthquake in the nearby older city state of Engomi, and, in turn, deserted after the fourth century AD, by a series of earthquakes, the silting of its harbor, and raids by Arab pirates. After this, Caitlyn had let the group roam freely in the gymnasium area before taking them to see the basilica by the water's edge.

It was during this period that she caught Demetris alone near the ruins of the baths and tried to ask him what was wrong. At first he was angry and defensive, but then he said that it would be best if Caitlyn just stayed away from him for awhile. He started to tell her something, but Will Jacobs and Billie Holiday unexpectedly appeared in a doorway, apparently having made up with each other again and looking very much like they had been seeking their own very private spot. The two looked a bit startled at having happened upon Caitlyn and Demetris, and, as Billie Holiday very pointedly pulled Jacobs away from the doorway and into some shadows, Demetris seized this moment to disappear through another opening in the stone wall.

En route to the basilica, Caitlyn had the touring vehicle stop briefly at an off-the-track site that, in antiquity, had been a typical middle-class Roman villa. In more recent centuries the site had been used as a winery, and, since the compound had remained in continuous use much longer than the surrounding area, it had become one of the few sites in the Salamis complex that had been extensively excavated during the previous century. Wilhelm, Billie, and Demetris, presumably all having seen the villa before, had stayed near the vehicle while Caitlyn walked the rest of the group into the site.

It was while they were here that Caitlyn had her first premonition that something was wrong. She had been standing next to a covered stone passageway in the villa, giving a short talk on how the complex had been used in Roman times, when she saw Wilhelm hurrying toward the group, with Billie following along a bit further back. When Wilhelm saw that the group was gathered together around Caitlyn, he pulled up. Billie, whom Wilhelm had apparently not seen following him, came up close behind him. Caitlyn could see that the young woman had a concerned expression on her face. But her gaze appeared to be targeted above Caitlyn's head. At nearly the same instant, Caitlyn felt some dust and pebbles hitting her head and shoulder, and this sensation, plus the Holiday woman's expression, caused her to look up.

Demetris had climbed to the top of the stone passageway and was leaning on a rock that appeared to be wobbling toward the edge just above Caitlyn's head.

Caitlyn gave out a sharp expression, informing Demetris in no uncertain terms that the structure wasn't stable enough for visitors to be climbing around it. Demetris returned an apologetic smile and a shrug and raised his camera as an explanation for why he was perched above her. Something about his expression as well as those of Wilhelm and Billie, however, raised alarm bells in the back of Caitlyn's mind, although she couldn't understand why they had done so—or what this all meant.

As they returned to the vehicle, Caitlyn sensed that there was a tension in the air that had even affected the animal life. Usually when she came here she didn't notice the wild life at all, but this afternoon she could hear movement in the brush about them and even the birds were chirping louder and flitting about more nervously than she had previously been aware of. She herself felt tense and tingly. This seemed to be developing into a high-irritation day for no particular reason that she could imagine.

* * * *

The presidential party arrived in Bogaz. While the touring vehicle was driving up the eastern coast, to the base of the Karpas Peninsula, Andriko let the American Archaeological Institute's director, Bill Burch, tell the visitors of the history of the area. In tones that Andriko found surprisingly nervous, the American archaeologist described the progression of the main body of the area's populace from the ancient city state of Engomi westward to the coast at Salamis, and then, according to popular history, southward down the coast to the Famagusta area.

After the group had reached the impressive, multifloored exhibition hall at Bogaz and descended from their vehicle, Andriko took over the lecture to explain how, more recently, they had been discovering that a significant proportion of the population had spread along the coast north from Salamis as well and that their remains were only now starting to be discovered.

Visiliou stopped the group a good distance from the exhibition hall, whose separate floors, each representing an era of ancient habitation at the nearby excavation, were open on the sides and marked at floor level with the names of the eras represented. The professor was standing on the hillside below the hall and was faced toward the Salamis area toward the south. From where he was standing, he could, on this very clear day see the ruined church steeples of the walled city of Famagusta and the modern commercial skyscrapers of Varosha even further down the coast. The more important of the VIPs were arrayed just in front of him, with their entourage fanned out just a bit further down the hillside. As Visiliou took over the lecture, Bill Burch drifted back to the line of the entourage.

Only Vice President Lala Hatan caught the look of horror that came across Visiliou's face, as his voice died away into a croak and an in-take of breath. President Chrystalla Ioannou and her World Bank guest were a vital split second too late in picking up what was happening, because they had been talking to each other in quiet tones about some point that had been made and the World Bank official had not caught. Although the horror of what had caught Visiliou's attention had little to do with the event that launched Hatan into action, it had been responsible for providing the signal for action.

What Visiliou saw was a roaring surf at the very limit of his vision down the coast and back out to sea that led up onto land in a series of rips into the earth and a rumbling under foot that left little doubt that the southeast coast of Cyprus was experience one of its rare, but history-altering major earthquakes. The source of most of the horror in the professor's eyes was the reflection of the far-off skyscrapers of Varosha folding up and imploding like flimsy cardboard boxes under the impact of the rifts that had apparently come aground just where old Famagusta and new Varosha met—most likely right across the old Palm Bay

Hotel, which until seconds ago had been the new Cassa Carioca nightclub.

What had caught Lala Hatan's own attention when he turned his gaze to see what had horrified the professor, however, was the gun that he saw in Bill Burch's hands. The Cypriot vice president had had no time at all before the bullets started to fly to decide on his action.

* * * *

At that instant, in the ruins of the fourth-century Kampanopetra basilica of Salamis, which had once been some distance from the sea but which was now perched just above it thanks to the last major earthquake that had hit this coast, Caitlyn Koniotis had her tour group gathered around her in the mosaic-floored area that had once surrounded the church's altar. Demetris Mattas, Wilhelm Jacobs, and Billie Holiday were all within arm's reach of her, and her glazed, slow-motion impression, as the ground started to rumble and move below her was of both of the men reaching out toward her and the woman pulling on one of the men. But the woman lost her grip, and one of the men seemed to surge toward Caitlyn and give her a glancing blow as he continued on—and mysteriously disappeared into the ground.

It suddenly occurred to Caitlyn as if in a muddled dream that this was possible because the earth behind her, just across the altar line, had parted—and then was gnashing back and forth like the masticating jaws of a giant. Even the sulfurous smell and roaring noise went with the giant's maw image. She had the brief sensation of teetering on the brink, the heels of shoes supportless over the void, and then the woman was upon her, Caitlyn was falling, and the world went black.

Chapter Twenty

Ginger Patterson was the picture of great sadness as she stood in the courtyard doorway of her Omodhos home several days after the tragic earthquake on Cyprus' eastern coast and watched Takis Koniotis and Andre Piccard trudge toward her. When the men reached the gate, she turned, and the three entered her house and sat in introspective silence, all eyes involuntarily drifting from time to time to the strongbox lying on the coffee table, while Ginger bustled around serving drinks and refreshments. After Ginger had folded herself into a comfortable chair, the three engaged in small talk, in anticipation of the opportunity to be able to move into more serious discussion without causing undue pain.

The conversation inevitably centered on the recent earthquake that had virtually destroyed the newly built Varosha and had raced up the coast, doing minimal damage to the ancient walls of Famagusta, thankfully, or to the area of Salamis, where as many Greco-Roman ruins had been unearthed by the heavy jolt as had been toppled once more.

The most serious damage had been experienced in Varosha, where the commercial skyscrapers, apparently not constructed—in RayGo's rush to create a high-rise city—to take the possibility of quakes well enough into account, had collapsed. The ground-hugging dwellings toward the southeast cape of the island had fared better as even had the better-constructed coastal hotels—all built before the onslaught of RayGo. The RayGo Tower as well as the Ingrid Beach Tower were only so much rubble, and crews were still sifting through both in search of victims, with each passing day making the possibility of new survivors being found increasingly remote. The company's CEO, Ingrid Bittmann Isaksen, was surely among the victims, as she had been holed up in the RayGo Tower, resisting police apprehension. But her body had not yet been found.

The three discussed their separate experiences of the sins of Ingrid for a short period. She was someone Andre Piccard preferred to forget about, so he didn't have too much to say. Ginger was of a forgiving nature, and, although it had been revealed that Ingrid had done her a serious personal wrong, Ginger didn't seem interested in dwelling on the issue. For his part, Takis Koniotis, who had suffered derision and unfair exploitation at Ingrid's hands while they were both officials at the UN and who had reason to be bitter about the revelations of Ingrid's direct involvement in the international counterfeiting operation that had drawn Caitlyn into a deadly game, was actually relieved that the woman's death had obviated the need to bring her before the law. The honor of the UN could only have been besmirched by the revelations of Ingrid's activities while she was a high-level official there, and Ingrid was so slippery and influential that successful prosecution of her crimes would have been a messy, chancy affair—with all of it putting the UN and the island of Cyprus on Page One of the world's tabloids.

What was certain to Takis was that Ingrid had used her position in the UN to favor the terrorist elements in the Middle East peace negotiations. He didn't know how active a role she had had, as the conference chair, during what was supposed to have been the final peace settlement conference, held on Cyprus' Amathus coast over a decade previously, but he did know that, under her gavel, a conference that had very good prospects for success had broken down. And now it was revealed, through pages from her very own diary and verified by intense UNICIS computer research, that she had been favoring the Lebanese and terrorist forces within Lebanon since before that period. Takis almost shuddered to think that she might even have been implicated in the assassination death of her own husband, Eric Isaksen, at the Cyprus settlement ceremony, an assassination attempt that the world had been led to assume was directed at Ingrid herself.

And then there were her activities since leaving the United Nations. As CEO of RayGo, she not only was responsible for hiding the fact that Ginger's husband, John Patterson, had been murdered for his design of a compact solar energy collection and storage process and for using this process to bring RayGo into the forefront of the world's wealthiest businesses—his initials at the bottom of the invention documents proving they were his designs—but she also had become embroiled in Tehran's attempt to undermine the economies of the West by flooding their markets with counterfeit banknotes.

Ingrid hadn't been the most dastard villain in these activities. This "honor" went to her cohort, the Australian diplomat, William Stevens, but she most definitely had been a willing and enabling participant. Stevens had obviously been suborned by the terrorist organizations in Lebanon while he was serving there.

He had been in Beirut with John Patterson when Patterson died, and it was more likely that Patterson had been murdered by Stevens for his solar designs than that the scientist had died from natural causes. There were those in Lebanon who would have been happy to help Stevens cover that death up.

Stevens had been working in Cyprus as an agent of the Hizballah and, by extension, of Tehran. It had been he and Ingrid who had gone to Tehran recently from Beirut to consult on the use of Cyprus to help introduce counterfeit currency into the Western economies. As supposedly an official dedicated to fight the counterfeiting operation, he had been perfectly placed to help the counterfeiters circumvent these efforts. And, although Ingrid had not been directly responsible for the death of the RayGo computer official Christiana Tzavella, at Stevens's hands, she had revealed to him over the luncheon table that the young woman had been perusing RayGo's private files, files that could implicate both RayGo and Stevens in the counterfeit scheme. In that sense, Ingrid had signed the young woman's death warrant.

The conversation turned to the happier note of how Cyprus' own political situation had been strengthened despite the recent devastating earthquake—and, as a matter of fact, because of the quake. President Ioannou's ploy to move the integration of her people forward by publicly appearing in a Turkish area at the side of the Turkish vice president, Lala Hatan, had worked beyond her wildest dream., Although the effects of the quake had not resulted in anything more than a trembling of the earth at the Bogaz archaeological site the president and her World Bank guest were visiting, the quake—

and Vice President Hatan—had saved the president from assassination.

The reflection of the horror in Professor Visiliou's face of the effects of the quake on the Varosha area while he was lecturing the presidential group on the slope below the Bogaz exhibition hall had caused Hatan to turn around in time to see Bill Burch raise his gun. The trembling of the earth, coupled with his own nervousness, had put off both Burch's aim and his timing. Hatan's reactions had been faster than Burch's.

In a single act that brought the Greek Cypriot and Turkish Cypriot communities closer together than all of the negotiations of the previous half century had, Hatan had leaped between the gunman and President Ioannou and her World Bank guest and had knocked them to the ground, covering both with his massive body. And all four Cypriot television networks had gotten the event on tape. The tape was shown worldwide for the next two days along with footage of the earthquake, to the swelled pride of Greek and Turkish Cypriots alike. This one act by Hatan had set the stage for an unprecedented cooperation between the two communities in post-earthquake clean-up operations—which also was reflected in the world's media and which went a long way toward solidifying the common bonds of Cypriots as Cypriots, regardless of their ethnic origin.

For his part, Bill Burch had been a far poorer shot under the circumstances than had been the president's security guards.

Ahmad Jallud and Takis Koniotis reached the scene immediately following the assassination attempt and just before Burch expired. In his dying breath, he had admitted that he had acted at the direction of the Hizballah, which wanted President Ioannou dead because she had been too successful in unifying a country the Hizballah wanted to remain separated and at knife point.

Burch had not, however, identified Pierre Piccard as his immediate controller in his dying confession. Neither Jallud nor Koniotis felt it was necessary to publicly connect the Piccards to this action. Andre Piccard showed every sign of turning his family holdings fully toward legitimate enterprise, and Cyprus couldn't easily survive the simultaneous demise of both RayGo and the Piccard enterprises as its economy was trying to pull out of the effects of the massive earthquake.

As Burch lay dying, Takis reflected back on the information the UNICIS computers had given him on the American archaeologist. His previous work in an institute in France loomed larger now in importance than it had seemed at the time. Takis was sure that, by the time he got back to UNICIS headquarters, the computers would have zeroed in on a connection between the Piccards, the French institute Burch had worked for, and Burch's move to Cyprus.

At the point at which Ginger was carefully working into questions about what had really happened at the Salamis site when the earthquake hit, the three were disrupted by the noisy entrance of Ellen Larkin and Caitlyn Koniotis, who had been shopping down in Limassol and who had come up into the mountains to Omodhos separately from Takis and Andre.

"I'd let Caitlyn tell you herself," laughed Takis, "but she slept through most of the more interesting action."

Caitlyn took on a look of mock outrage, as Takis proceeded to tell those present, Ginger and Andre hearing this for the first time, that Ingrid Isaksen and William Stevens had not been the only ones who had been working with the international counterfeit operation. The American Secret Service agent, Wilhelm Jacobs, had been a double agent of the Iranians and had actually provided the genesis of the counterfeiting scheme.

"So," Ellen said with a bitter smile and flashing eyes, "The forces of good in the diplomatic community on the counterfeit counteroperation were more than a bit tainted. We always did feel we were working an uphill battle with Stevens and Jacobs on this issue. All of these bogus Bills—and I'm not talking about money."

Both Caitlyn and Takis noticed, with amusement, that Andre seemed to like the fire that had appeared in Ellen's eyes and was suddenly much more attentive toward the woman than he had been before.

"What do you mean, he provided the genesis?" Ginger pulled the group back into the conversation.

"It was something the UNICIS computer had found by the time we got back to Nicosia from the east coast much later that night," Takis picked up the thread again. "There had been a scandal in Washington when Jacobs last served there—but it had been so explosive that they had kept it a secret as much as possible. A series of high-denomination plates for the new U.S. currency went missing from the printing office. Some said there had just been a mistake in the paperwork on the number of separate plates that had been produced, and the engraver in question had died recently and couldn't verify positively how many she had made. The plates never showed up, and nothing incriminating was pinned on any of those who had had access to the plates. So, they were all just reassigned and the government fell back on wishful thinking that nothing had gone wrong.

"The Engraving Office also didn't order the redesign of a new set of plates, because these were the new plates, and a lot of publicity and preparation had been invested in them already," Takis sad. "They did, however, change the number system on the new bills slightly and had this section of the plates reengraved. Well, Jacobs was one of those who had handled the plates. He was reassigned to a mission to Iran, and a few years later, excellent counterfeits were flooding the European market. If the printing office had not taken the step to change the numbering system—and had released false information about the makeup of the paper the bills were printed on, there would have been no way at all to identify the counterfeits. The Iranians got their hands on some very good paper stock composed to the formula the U.S. government leaked as a red herring, and so they thought their counterfeits would pass all but the closest inspection. The little blue thread running through the fake paper did them in."

Takis went on to indicate that Isaksen and Stevens were aware of Jacobs's connections and he theirs, but the relations between the three had been a tenuous cooperation. Isaksen and Stevens had worked directly with the Hizballah with a certain amount of independence. Jacobs had become wholly controlled by Tehran.

It had been Jacobs who had taken the opportunity of the earthquake in Salamis to try to kill Caitlyn. Ever since she had run across him and Stevens at the Garden Café across from the Cyprus Museum in Nicosia while they were comparing notes and Stevens was messing around in the UNICIS computer with his own minicomputer, Jacobs had thought that Caitlyn was on to their activities and had been planning her demise.

Luckily for Caitlyn, Gladys "Billie" Holiday had also been a bogus Bill. She was really Ann Wynette, another American Secret Service officer, who had been sent to track Jacobs down and trip him up. The Secret Service had finally come to know of the scandal at the printing office and had been more persistent and smarter in collecting their evidence. They had become sure that Jacobs was their man, and Wynette had been sent to bring him down. She wasn't British and she wasn't an archaeologist; that had just been her cover. Where she had slipped was in telling Caitlyn that they had gone to the same Michigan university. They had, but Wynette had not been studying archaeology, and she wasn't registered there as Gladys Holiday. Wynette had seen that Caitlyn was suspicious of her and, more important, she had seen that Jacobs was suspicious of Caitlyn.

When Caitlyn encountered the young American in the Kakopetria handicraft center at the Old Mill, the Secret Service agent had been following Bill Burch. She had mistakenly suspected that he was involved with Wilhelm Jacobs and had later dropped her interest in him when she found out he was connected to Pierre Piccard instead. When Caitlyn had seen Burch that day, he had gone to Kakopetria to consult with Piccard in the apartment above the restaurant, which is why she hadn't seen him after he had taken the elevator from the parking apron. Wynette had made the mistake of not realizing that the coordinated Iranian and Hizballah activities in Cyprus were more complex than just the strand she was following that involved Jacobs.

It had been Wynette who had saved Caitlyn during the earthquake. When the fissure had opened up behind Caitlyn in the basilica while she was giving her lecture, Jacobs had seen his chance and had reached out to push Caitlyn into the abyss. Wynette had pushed him off center and it had been he, himself, who had fallen past her and into the opening in the ground, which had closed once again on its own accord a few seconds later. Wynette had then pushed Caitlyn down and out of harm's way while the quake was still in progress. Then Caitlyn had blacked out. Jacobs had evidently been crushed and was entombed beneath the altar area of the basilica.

"What was really ironic," Caitlyn took over the discourse, "was that I had been leery of Demetris Mattas, not either Jacobs or Holiday—I mean Wynette—at that point. It turns out that Demetris had been told to do something compromising or harmful to me by Ingrid Isaksen, who had called him after he had returned home from the Cassa Carioca the previous night and had threatened to publicly expose his previous gambling history if he didn't cooperate with her in keeping Takis and Maria from pursuing their investigation of his activities. Apparently part of Ingrid's plan was to keep Takis busy keeping me out of trouble and harm's way. But, although he was torn concerning what to do and thus followed me rather than the president's party when we split up, Demetris didn't carry through with any of her instructions. The masonry he'd nearly dislodged to bounce off my head was the accident he claimed it to be—his clumsiness caused by his consternation at not wanting to do what Ingrid had tasked him to do. He doesn't need to figure into any of this, Takis, does he?"

Takis indicated his agreement.

"But I would like to know about Irina Lukenov, the woman we knew here as Roulla Dahir," Ginger broke into the conversation. "I had grown very fond of that woman—in spite of her crying and secretive ways. Can't anyone tell me she is all right?"

"Well, she seemed to have had a very good reason to cry and to be secretive," Takis responded. "She was involved in very dangerous and illegal affairs. Her kidnapping experience, so closely following her experiences in war-torn Grozny, along with her hatred of her husband and what he stood for, not to mention having suddenly found herself in the same city with Sergey Stepanov, her old lover, must have made something snap in Irina. She joined with her captors, took on their lives and causes, and never tried to escape—at least not until recently when she had had enough and tried to retreat into obscurity here in Cyprus. She was directly involved in drug smuggling—at first engaged in weaving the baskets they hid the drugs in to transport them—and was supposed to have become a counterfeit currency smuggler for the Iranians. But something must have snapped inside her again, and she escaped here to hide as Roulla Dahir. Several different forces sought her here—her son Uri, the Iranians through Wilhelm Jacobs, and the Hizballah through

William Stevens. We can only hope that it was her son, Uri, who found her first. He disappeared at about the same time she did."

Takis looked expectantly at Andre Piccard, but the young Frenchman was being enigmatic.

"I'm afraid that might not be the case," whispered Ginger as she wiped a tear from her eye. "Irina had been very ugly one day when she saw me talking in the village square to two old friends and the young couple they had brought with them. From the newspaper photos, I know that one of those people was Wilhelm Jacobs, and I now know too that he was involved in this whole mess. I've been so afraid that he recognized Irina and that she fell into his hands."

Everyone was silent for a few moments as Ginger cried softly. Then, almost reluctantly, Andre reached over and put a comforting hand on the old woman's arm.

"I'm quite certain that didn't happen, Mrs. Patterson," the young man stammered. "I can't say any more, but I'm quite certain that both Irina and her son—both of her sons—are far away from here and are safe."

Takis gave an "I thought so" look and Ginger looked up at the young man with a dazzling smile of thanks. Then she turned and picked up the strongbox that had been laying on the coffee table.

"Well, I think it's time for the verification ceremony—the reason why you all came here today. Did you bring the photographs you were telling me about, Takis?"

He had and it didn't take more than a moment for everyone to clearly see that the formulas John Patterson and had given to her for safekeeping and that Ginger had locked up in the strongbox were the same, and written in the same hand—John Patterson's, as the documents Ingrid Isaksen had been keeping hidden away. And both sets had his initials in the bottom corner. There could be no question now who had been the real inventor of the solar energy storage process that had made RayGo so wealthy or any question to whom the process really belonged—and always had belonged.

"You can become the world's richest and most influential businesswoman now, Ginger," Ellen Larkin exclaimed.

"That's hardly a role I would accept at this point in my life," Ginger said dryly. "But then, of course, I'm sure I could put this to far better use to Cyprus and mankind than either RayGo or Ingrid Isaksen did," she added acidly.

"Well, something will have to be done with management of the process," pointed out Takis. "RayGo has collapsed, and it won't take long for everyone to learn that you control the formulas and to be pounding their way to Omodhos."

Ginger's face took on an initial look of horror and she almost dropped the papers as if they were burning hot. But then her face became more tranquil and she turned to Andre Piccard with a sly look. "As penance for all the naughtiness your family has been involved in here in Cyprus over the years, Mr. Piccard, would you be willing to take over the day-to-day management of these formulas and use them only for the good of the country? Of course," she went on to say with a twinkle in her eye, "I may have a few things I would want to say about the business as well, I'm sure. All secretly just to you, I hope. I trust there are mechanisms that can keep my involvement completely secret and I can continue living my quiet retirement right here."

Andre was moved. He was being given the chance to bring his family back from the underworld.

"Of course, that can be arranged, Mrs. Patterson. Perhaps with the help of the Cypriot government . . ." He was looking in the direction of Takis now.

"I'm sure the interior minister will be more than happy to help with this," Takis said, speaking for Maria Mattas, but knowing she would manage it brilliantly.

As the gathering broke up, the parties regrouped from the pairing that had brought them into Omodhos. Takis and Caitlyn took the short drive up to Platres, where they had booked into the grand old Forest Park Hotel to catch their breath and to decide where to go from here. They were both quite happy to see the pleasure with which both Andre Piccard and Ellen Larkin seemed to view their reassignment to the other vehicle for the trip over the mountain and back down onto the central plain. The Koniotises hoped that this could represent a new, more pleasant chapter in the lives of both Ellen and Andre. The two deserved far better than life had offered them up to this point.

As the Koniotis convertible entered the sweeping drive up to the Forest Park Hotel, Takis cleared his throat and spoke. "I talked to Andre as we drove to Omodhos. He is willing to give us a long lease on the flat above the Old Mill Restaurant."

But Caitlyn both surprised and pleased her husband. "Thank you for doing that Takis. I know the apartment has no attraction for you and you have done this only to please me. But I think this long chapter of our lives is over now. I think I was only attracted to that apartment because of my close connection with Eleni. It always seemed that her business was unfinished and that she was trying to influence events to some conclusion from beyond the grave—and through me."

Caitlyn stopped speaking then and laughed before she resumed. "You know me and my vivid imagination."

Takis did, of course, but he didn't hold Caitlyn's imagination up to ridicule. She and her imagination had solved many a puzzle.

Caitlyn shivered and grew serious again. "I think we've reached that conclusion. I think Andre turned out just as Eleni would have wanted him to turn out—as the one to bring honor back to the Piccard name and to Eleni's own rich Cypriot heritage. I feel Eleni is truly at peace now and will leave me at peace as well. I don't think I want her apartment now. I don't even think I want the Makedonitissa house she left me anymore, either. Let's move back into the Acropolis house your parents left you."

Takis couldn't hide his happiness, and, as he parked the car in the forecourt of the hotel, he pressed his luck. "I was also thinking, Caitlyn, that maybe we are too busy with our lives and our very demanding jobs in New York. Maybe we should move back to Cyprus permanently. I can always work with UNICIS or the Cypriot police department here and you now have your archaeological institute to set up."

"Maybe we should think of doing that," Caitlyn said sweetly, as she exited the vehicle. "I think we need to think hard about it, though, at least until the boys are out of college and we see where their lives are heading. But you just might have a good idea going for you there, Inspector."

A hotel official was standing in the hotel entry, a broad smile of Cypriot welcome on his face, as the two waltzed past the deer statue in the center of the courtyard and entered the hotel, embracing and giggling like newlyweds.

* * * *

The presses were whirring in the late night gloom of the basement of the Central Bank on Shohada Street in Tehran. The workers—actually more slaves than workers—were exhausted. General Ujay Khahalbi had been in a terrible mood for days, and he had been taking his ire out on the people spinning out his counterfeit euro and U.S. banknotes. The tension in the large room was palpable.

Khahalbi threw down the phone headset and backhanded the base of the telephone off the counter and onto the floor. He had been trying for days to reach any of his contacts in Cyprus—Jacobs, Stevens, Stepanov, Isaksen, or that so-called Turk—and none were responding. Surely the recent earthquake there couldn't be distracting them from their duty to him. And had they found that wayward Hizballah courier yet and disposed of her? Khahalbi didn't know what angered him most, their ineptitude or their failure to keep him informed.

However, others in Tehran had been kept better informed, and Khahalbi was not the only one in Iran to be totally unforgiving for ineptitude. The workers near the stairs to the upper floor heard the sounds of the marching boots first. But it was only seconds before everyone else in the room, including General Khahalbi, heard them as well. This was a sound in Tehran that couldn't be mistaken for anything else, and its purpose was well known. Yet another bureaucrat had upset the clerics, the clerics who had held onto power and influenced world events for decades longer than anyone thought they could.

Khahalbi edged toward the back stairs, the sound of the boots steadily increasing. The workers picked up spanners and steel machine levers—anything that came readily to hand—and edged toward the general. It was an interesting question what form of justice would reach General Ujay Khahalbi first.

Gina Drew

Gina Drew is a retired American foreign service officer who specialized in investigating and countering international crime and espionage and who still travels the world in both the imagination and in fact.

Years spent working on Cyprus have left her with a deep love of this divided island and its people.

www.cyberworldpublishing.com

www.ingramcontent.com/pod-product-compliance
Lightning Source LLC
Chambersburg PA
CBHW070404260626
47161CB00001B/268